ELLE GRAY | JAMES HOLT

THE
FLORIDA
GIRL

The Florida Girl
Copyright © 2023 by Elle Gray | James Holt

All rights reserved. Without limiting the rights under copyright reserved above, no part of this publication may be reproduced, stored in or intro-duced into retrieval system, or transmitted, in any form, or by any means (electronic, mechanical, photocopying, recording, or otherwise) without the prior written permission of both the copyright owner and the above publisher of this book.

This is a work of fiction. Names, characters, places, brands, media, and incidents are either the products of the author's imagination or are used fictitiously. The author acknowledges the trademarked status and trademark owners of various products referenced in this work of fiction, which have been used without permission. The publication/use of these trademarks is not authorized, associated with, or sponsored by the trademark owners.

CHAPTER ONE

DAY 1

10:30 AM. STAR ISLAND, MIAMI, FLORIDA

"**D**AMNED FLEA-INFESTED RAT!"
 The sound of the neighbor's dog destroyed the relative peace of this morning's first G & T, clutched in the ageing hands of one-time TV and commercial star Marjorie Collins.

Majorie Collins, star of such classics as *Love Tango!* and *EverBrill Lipstick*, had taken to a poolside recliner of her palatial

Miami Beach home mostly in the hopes to shake off the beginnings of a nasty hangover, but also partially to recover from this morning's even *earlier* intrusion of shouting voices from 'The Russian' next door, before his damn mutt had decided to bark its head off, that was.

"How many times!?" The seventy-three-year-old who was three times married, two times divorced, and one time widowed was not a force to be taken lightly as she rose from the recliner, her fragmentary attempt at peaceful inebriation shattered.

Moving with titanic majesty, Marjorie clutched her silk dressing gown about her person as she stalked past the giant palm trees to the edge of her property to see the usually calming blue waters of Biscayne Bay, attempting to peer past the giant Leylandii hedges to where 'The Russian' next door had clearly allowed his rabid nuisance of a floor rug to run rampant once again.

The Russian was a man named Aleksandr Bodrov, a new arrival to the mansion community of Star Island, a man-made island connected to the McArthur Causeway that joined Miami Beach to downtown Miami.

Marjorie heard the murmur of some bassy, thrumming music which did nothing to stop the incessant yapping.

"I bet the damn commie can't even hear his own dog! That's it."

This was going to be a complaint to the concierge service, at least.

But Marjorie had never been one to turn down an opportunity (hence why she had managed to amass a seven-figure income on product commercials).

"Hey! Hey, you over there? Can't you shut that thing up!?" she shouted over the hedge. She was sure that The Russian had his pool on the other side, certain because she had made sure to look at the architectural deeds of her neighbor, just in case he had been planning to build anything that would disturb the intoxicated serenity of her later years.

"Hey! I can get you thrown off and back to Mother Russia, you know! I know people in immigration!" she hollered.

The music, and the dog, continued.

Marjorie Wallace, her dyed blonde bouffant shaking, said some words that she would never have been allowed to be broadcast in the twenty-first century, let alone 1968.

"Fine. A complaint to the concierge and a letter to Judge Rudi, you have got it coming, Mister-!" Marjorie set off at pace to the black iron gate at the front of her property, turning to march across the sculpted lawns to the large, white security gates of her partner.

"Come on out of there! I've had enough of this!" she shouted, kicking the gate with a heavy clang before cursing at the pain that shot up her heel.

"*Ff!* And if I just broke something I swear to God I'm going to sue, goddammit!"

"*Der'mo!*" There were muttered voices and a mechanical rolling sound as the eight-foot, white security gate started to pull backwards, showing the annoyed faces of the two large security guards on the other side as they hurried out of the gate house – and releasing the sudden small orange blur and excited yapping of the offending canine.

"Peaches! *Blin!* Peaches, come back here!" the nearest of Aleksandr's security guards shouted, as Peaches shot past Marjorie Wallace's legs (she aimed a kick at it, but the thing was too fast).

"Out of my way! Is he in!? Of course he is. This has gone too far!" Marjorie took the opportunity to march past the guards in the confusion, as one of them scrambled after the chihuahua while the other looked uselessly at what they were to do about the ageing star.

"You touch me and I'll get you all deported!" Marjorie shouted as she marched down the gravel lane, past the vast mansion of the Russian oligarch and towards the pool.

"Mrs. Wallace, you cannot enter there! It is private!" the security guard, his accent thick to Marjorie's ears, flailed his arms a little helplessly, and chose to follow her as fast as he was able.

"Oh, don't you *Mrs.* Wallace me, young man! *Ms.* I haven't survived three useless men to be a *Mrs.* by the likes of you!" She continued to stalk, passing the white-painted walls and arches of

The Russian's house and under the avenue of palm trees to emerge at the back of the mansion.

"Now *Mr* Bodrov, if you don't get that mutt under control I promise I'll…" Marjorie was in mid flow when her brain caught up with what her eyes were registering.

There in front of her was the large, heated swimming pool that Aleksandr Bodrov had installed this October gone.

There was the floating inflatable pool lounger with its inbuilt drinks dispenser.

And there, inside their own rapidly expanding circle of red, was the body of Alexandr Bodrov himself.

CHAPTER TWO

11:45 AM. MIAMI INTERNATIONAL AIRPORT

F LORIDA SMELLED LIKE CITRUS SUNTAN LOTION AND THE crackle of fried hog. At least, that was the best that Agent Alexa Landers could describe it as she took her first step past the sliding doors of Miami International Airport.

"Hog roast, you say? Can't be all that bad, right?" said the voice of her younger brother Jed on the other end of the phone as the thirty-two-year-old Alexa blinked as she was assaulted by the fierce glare of Miami sun and car horns.

"I guess we'll see, right?" Alexa grumbled as she swapped out the sun for a pair of Oakley sunglasses. There was nothing she could do about the car horns, shouts, and the strains of electronic hip-hop coming from some of the new arrivals.

There were people everywhere, which wasn't an issue, but Alexa had just spent the last few years at the FBI Training Academy in Quantico, Virginia. Although she'd had holidays and time off, she wasn't immediately prepared for the chaos and bustle of Vice City.

"That's my big shot sister! Why smile when you can frown, hey? And here was me thinking that a stint in Miami would chill you out a bit," Jed quipped back as she heard him clunking around in the background.

"Oh yeah, I forgot you were such an expert," Alexa said, stepping back from the crowd to scan the bodies hurrying in and out of the airport.

"Where is he?" she muttered distractedly, knowing that the FBI Miami Division was supposed to be sending someone over to pick her up.

Or maybe they want me to show initiative? Find my own way to the secure HQ facility that doesn't appear on Google Maps? A tiny moment of anxiety bubbled through her.

"Easy, cool it," she whispered to herself. It was natural to have a few nerves on her first posting after graduation, wasn't it? But she had earned it. Top marks out of Quantico. Graduated top of her class. No faceless desk job for her until she found her feet, but straight into the field… She caught sight of herself in the window of the main airport lounge; a slim, athletic woman with mousy brown hair scraped back in a fairly severe ponytail, casual dark trousers and a light, form-fitting vest, as it was too hot to wear anything else. She looked good. Like a gym instructor maybe, or a low-pro athlete on holiday.

"Where's who – Dad? He's right here, racing to the phone like a beached fish," Jed laughed. He was like that, all jokes and quips and masking the fact that he'd come out of a really painful marriage eighteen odd months ago. Still, Alexa didn't reckon that gave him the right to be a dick.

THE **FLORIDA GIRL**

"Don't make me fly back there and kick your ass, *Jedward*," Alexa snipped at him as she surveyed the nearest parked vehicles. None of them were the large, tinted window SUVs that fairly announced governmental service, were they?

But then again, we're supposed to be able to operate undercover, aren't we? Alexa took a closer look at the parked Toyotas and Chevrolets.

"Here he is. But before I hand you over, you're still not even going to give me a hint of what you're up to down there? What is it...Cuban mafia? Mexican drug cartels?"

Alexa sighed. "You know I can't talk about it, Jed. I'm not about to start now."

"Spoil sport. Fine. Just try not to get shot, okay, *sistaah?!*" Jed shot back, as the phone was handed over to the sudden breathy voice of her father.

"Kiddo…"

Almost as soon as Alexa heard his voice, she felt like she was eleven or fourteen or sixteen or six years old again, and opening the door as her father would be returning from another tour with the Navy. Lt. Commander Greg Landers would be a vast, stocky giant who smelled of boot polish with a hint of stale cigarettes, and he would scoop her up in arms that were as strong as tree trunks and say that one word.

For a moment there was silence between them, as agent and retired commander drank in the words unsaid. He didn't tell her to be safe, or to take care, as he already knew that she would. That was one of the things that Alexa loved the most about him. She knew he was proud of her, and that he trusted her.

"You'll do a good job," he rasped. His breathing was getting worse by the year; Alexa winced.

"Despite it being Florida. Never had much good things to say about Florida," he added after a pause, which sent Alexa into a fit of giggles.

"Even despite it being Florida," Alexa agreed, and that was that. That was all that she needed to hear as she said her small goodbyes and clicked the phone off. Dad would be okay. Jed worked in the games industry, helping to author some wildly successful thing full of orcs and people hitting each other with swords, as far as Alexa could understand, which meant that he could work from anywhere there was a laptop, and would be with Dad for the next few weeks.

If Dad doesn't kill him, she thought as she once again tried to run through her investigative skills once again.

If I was an undercover FBI unit looking to goose a new recruit, what would I do? She narrowed her eyes, moving over the super-obvious parked lowrider cars that were pumping out the EDM tracks and not a small whiff of marijuana.

Too showy, she thought, *and the Toyotas would be a bad deal,* she also knew. The government got deals on transport and tech from US firms.

"So that leaves…" She scanned the nearest section of the parking lot, saw the Chevrolets (*good, but too showy*) and then settled for the line which held no less than three Ford F-series.

American-made. Patriotic, she thought as she started over towards them. The first two had their windows up, good for a/c, but the third in line had its windows open a crack. Even though she couldn't see who was inside thanks to the window tinting, she knew someone was in there. She got about three steps when the large, slate-grey Ford-F she'd picked out flashed its lights and wound down its window, for a man's face to poke out.

"Sheesh! They told me you were sharp, but I wasn't expecting Columbo," the man grinned, popping the door to hop out and extend a hand for her travel case.

He was tall, taller than her, Alexa saw, with wide shoulders and jet black hair that was only *slightly* longer than regulation. His eyes were a strong green, but with Asian inheritance.

"Kage Murphy," the man said with a smile, as Alexa paused for a moment.

"I'm afraid I'm going to have to see a badge, Kage Murphy," she said a little stiffly. It was procedure. It wouldn't do to jump into the blacked-out car of the first stranger she'd met in Miami, would it?

"Oh, right." Kage blinked, surprised, before a wide grin spread across his face. "Oh, the chief said you were the real thing."

What did that mean!? Alexa thought, as Kage half turned so that the open car door was shielding them from the airport, and he drew out his black leather fold-over. There was the golden shield badge of the FBI, and underneath it was the ID card that picked him out as Special Agent Murphy, Miami Division.

"And uh," Alexa began as she offered to do the same, but Kage waved her off, a gesture that instantly annoyed her.

Please don't tell me this is what Miami is like. Florida already had a reputation for sleaze and flakiness; she really didn't want to think that extended to the FBI as well down here…

"Come on, no time to lose. Field Chief Williams already has a message for us," Kage explained as he gestured to the large car. Alexa wasted no time in throwing her case in the boot and hurried to the passenger side.

"Us?" Alexa asked as soon as the doors closed. Immediately the noise and bustle of outside vanished as Alexa realized this was a soundproofed, and probably bulletproofed service vehicle.

"I thought you were supposed to relay me to the Field HQ, where I'll be briefed on my responsibilities and role?"

"Yeah, uh, change of plan," Murphy shrugged, turning to draw a black case from the passenger seats and hand it to her.

"Open it. The code is your FBI personnel number."

"Huh?" Alexa wondered if this was way beyond protocol or whether this was just how things ran in the field. She really didn't have anything to compare it to as she found there was an actual electronic keypad on the mouth of the case, where she tapped in the seven-digit number that identified her as a government worker for the FBI.

The case popped open, revealing foam security lining with a manilla envelope in the top side of the case, and in the bottom a thin slate-black smart phone, next to the heavy snarl of a Glock 9mm service pistol, and a spare magazine.

"I've got the jacket and holster in the back. I don't know if they couldn't fit in the case or Williams just wanted the drama," Kage said as he waited, looking at her expectantly.

"This, right," Landers nodded, taking out the manilla folder first to see that it contained a sheath of paper.

I, [SPECIAL AGENT ALEXA LANDERS] do hereby solemnly swear that I am of sound mind and not under coercion, duress, intoxication, financial or any other form of manipulation.

I [SPECIAL AGENT ALEXA LANDERS] have been reassigned to [MIAMI FBI HQ] by [FIELD CHIEF SUPERVISOR LEVITICUS WILLIAMS] as of….

Alexa skim-read it through with a small frown. It looked to be a statement, announcing her name, reassignment, and her receipt of her service firearm and phone, with spaces for her to sign at the bottom.

"I did all the paperwork before I left Quantico," she said as Kage offered her the pen.

"I know. This is extra. Don't sweat it, but the important stuff is in the last paragraph," Kage nodded for Alexa to look down and read out loud.

'I will undertake to perform my duty to the best of my capability, without fear or favor in pursuance of the law of the United States of America. I voluntarily withhold the right to free speech and am bound by the Patriot Act of the United States, and fully accept the hazardous, even fatal, nature of my profession. In the event of my harm, injury, or death, I agree that the Federal Bureau of Investigations may withhold information, knowledge, either partially or entirely, about my activities, location, accident or demise.'

"I particularly like the 'accident or demise' bit," Kage said with a grin. "It makes it sound kinda poetic. Like we might get lost at sea or something."

"I think it rather sounds like getting shot, and no one's going to tell our family about it," Alexa pointed out.

There was a moment of silence in the car, and Alexa saw Kage freeze for just a second. His body didn't tense, but the pause between his breaths was held.

"Is that a problem? You know signing that is a requisite to picking up that gun, right?"

Alexa thought of Lt. Commander Greg Landers and his bad lungs that probably wouldn't give him another five years. She thought of her stupid brother Jed*ward* and wondered if he was ever going to get his love life together.

But they knew who she was. They knew the path she had chosen.

"I know," she said, and signed the paper.

The tension breathed out of the special agent beside her in one smooth moment, as he strapped on his seatbelt and started the car.

"Usually this would be done with Field Chief Williams at HQ, you're right, but you, Agent Landers, are lucky enough to arrive in the middle of a shitstorm. I'm under orders to pick you up, get you signed on, and take you to your first case, a homicide out on one of the private islands near Miami Beach."

"My first case!? A homicide?" Alexa exclaimed as Kage kicked the accelerator a little more forcefully than was technically legal as they tore out of the airport.

"Yep. The request for a special taskforce just came through about a half hour ago. Bureau and local PD. We're going to be the first FBI on scene," the agent said grimly.

But the FBI doesn't deal in general homicides. That's a police job, Alexa mused as Kage took them out onto the main road, already turning for the McArthur Causeway, and Miami Beach beyond it.

We only deal with homicides when there's something REALLY bad going on.

CHAPTER THREE

12:32 PM. ALEKSANDR BODROV'S RESIDENCE, STAR ISLAND

"This place is a palace," Alexa said as she stepped down from the Ford to see the large white walls, colonnade entrance, and arching galleries of a house that looked almost as big as the White House.

(At least, from the one time that she had actually been in the White House, for her inauguration ceremony).

The palace had multiple levels, with stairs going up and down to a sunken carport. It was edged with giant palm trees and sculpted lawns, and surrounded by a high, eight-foot white metal security fence, complete with a small guard house at the front gate. Already, there were an ambulance and two police cruisers sitting in the wide gravel driveway, parked erratically around the fountain with what appeared to be a bear victoriously holding up a salmon to the skies.

"Welcome to Star Island," Kage said as he closed the car door with a grimace, adjusting his holster and throwing her a black bomber jacket with the large yellow letters F.B.I. emblazoned on the back.

"Every place here is a damn palace. The island was thrown up by the US Army Engineers back in the '50s I think, something like that, along with Hibiscus Island, Roccoco, created as gated communities for the super wealthy too rich even to live on Miami Beach."

Alexa whistled. She could see the long strip of colonized sandbank of Miami Beach from where they stood, over the blue glint of waters. She had seen the other islands on the way over, as they had crossed the long McArthur Causeway to get here, before arriving at the outer gate guard at the entrance to the island.

"How many residents?" she half turned, getting a measure of the place first.

Check your environment. Geography is opportunity, words of her Quantico trainers sprang into mind.

"Sixty-two private mansion plots. Impossible to tell as yet how many people were on the island." Kage gestured towards where the police were already waving them over.

"Never been on a case here, but I know we got singers and actors and ex-pharmaceutical bosses, tycoons."

"Right..." Alexa felt a small sense of vertigo. A few hours ago she had just been an anonymous woman on a plane, now she was about to be surrounded by some of the most important people in America. Maybe even arresting them.

"Our John?" she offered, as they arrived at the police gaggle for the largest and oldest of their number, a police detective in uniform black and blues, gold badge on his cap and red cheeks to wave papers at them and frown.

"Detective Dempsey, Miami PD, and I'll be damned if I know why the FBI wants in on this one," he said with a dark look at the other officers, waving them out of the way.

"We've been asked to put together a special taskforce with FBI and local PD, Detective, the paperwork should be with your office shortly," Kage said with a large, friendly grin.

"Yeah, I got the message," Detective Dempsey replied, clearly not impressed. "But I guess that doesn't change the scales on a fish, does it?"

"We're just here to help pool our resources, Detective. Bureau specialist investigation, PD on-the-ground knowledge..." Murphy was all smiles, but Alexa could see that the detective wasn't buying any of it. Dempsey shrugged and handed over the initial scene reports, still fresh with illegible writing.

"We kept everyone at the scene when your memo came through. That's one body, two security guards, and the neighbor. But we've already got someone going through the security footage, and that's ruling out the two security guards by the looks of it. They spent all morning in the guard hut playing poker. Your DOA is one Aleksandr Bodrov. Russian billionaire. Ran some sort of manufacturing company."

"A Russian billionaire," Alexa nodded, feeling even slightly more out of her depth. There hadn't been any training on *this* at the Academy.

We deal with federal cases that cross state lines, serious organized crimes, and crimes that incur a federal charge, she thought, frowning as the detective led them around the side of the house to where an avenue led to an open area at the back. Somewhere there was a dog barking.

This had to be a serious case. Maybe Jed had been right about that Cuban mafia thing...

"We're going to need a complete scene introduction, subject to federal protocols, by order of the Federal Bureau..." Alexa tried to remember the exact policy. She was sure that there was an order code she was supposed to announce.

"We're requesting any evidence bagged up and sent, with full chain of handling details, to the headquarters war room, along with statements of first responders…" Alexa said, thinking, *Have we even got a war room yet?* as she shot a look at Kage, who gave the smallest shrug in return.

"Yeah yeah, I got it, you're the big dog in the pound," Dempsey growled.

"Any previous charges on site?" Kage asked, and Dempsey shook his head.

"The neighbor had a DUI about thirty years ago, but the victim was squeaky clean, filed his taxes every year – although if anyone on Star pays their proper dues I'd be a baby before Christmas – not even a drunk and disorderly or nuisance complaint. He's got two sons, Dimitre and Vadim, and they all came over here from Mother Russia about ten years ago, looks like. At least that's what Google tells me."

"We got contacts for the sons?" Alexa asked as they arrived at the back of the house to find another small walkway leading out onto a wide, tiled area.

"Already sending a unit out to them. They live on the Beach, so it shouldn't take long, but maybe you boys in black can do that instead, huh?" Dempsey's voice fairly dripped with jealousy, and Alexa could guess why.

Any case about some Russian billionaire would probably make big news, and the detective who solved it would probably be given a promotion, right?

"And here we have it. Good luck solving this one!" Dempsey even managed a disgruntled laugh as he walked out onto the large patio to point at where there was a scalloped swimming pool with a checkerboard pattern around its edge, and instead of the water being a soothing blue, it was a dirty orange.

Blood, Alexa realized. *Watered-down blood.*

Beside the pool was a team of EMT around a medical stretcher, on top of which appeared to be a long, black PVC body bag.

"Our Mr. Bodrov was found floating in the pool, head down, with a bullet through his throat," Dempsey announced. "No witnesses. No one heard the shot because there was apparently a dog going haywire and the guards had their music up."

"Were the guards Star Island?" Alexa asked, thinking of the private security they had to pass to even get onto the island.

"No. Private security guards, armed. They claim they had no idea he was even dead until the neighbor came over to complain about the noise."

Okay... Alexa felt her jaws clench in annoyance. The numbers were piling up quick. One dead body. Two private security. One angry neighbor. Oh, and one dog.

And still no idea why the field chief wanted them to take over the case from local.

"Neighbor-?" Alexa started to say, to hear the sudden screech of a raised voice behind them from the mansion itself.

"*-do you KNOW who I have on my rolodex!?*" A woman sounded furious.

"That'll be the neighbor," Detective Dempsey grinned. "Ms. Marjorie Collins. You're going to have fun with this one."

"Are we?" Alexa said as she threw a glance at Kage, who raised his eyebrows.

"I hope you remember your witness engagement classes, Alexa," Kage said, as he pulled a thumb towards the body. "I got dibs on the body EMT report. You be my guest with the non-witnesses."

Gee thanks, Alexa thought, turning to the sound of haranguing and taking a breath. 'Top of her class' and 'Top marks' suddenly seemed like very vague terms when compared to actual people, and an actual case sitting right in front of her.

Wow, Alexa managed not to say out loud as she found herself in a large games room the size of a ballroom, with one ping pong table, another two pool tables, and leather sofas around the walls. Standing in front of two rather beleaguered Miami PD was a woman well north of her sixties, possible north of her seventies, with heavy purple eyeliner and acid-yellow hair piled up at the back of her head.

"Ms. Collins, I presume?" Alexa introduced herself. "Special Agent Landers, I'll be taking the details of the case."

"Oh! FBI, I see!" Collins said with a face that was scandalized but also overjoyed.

"I just knew that he was up to something, you see. What was it, drugs? Was he shipping Russian cocaine in to his dock?" she said with a nod, and Alexa realized that every residence here on Star Island had a dock. She half turned, seeing that the private small pier and mooring was located past the swimming pool, the pool house, and another line of palm trees. But she couldn't see any boat down there.

Something to ask later.

"I'm afraid we can't disclose any suspicions as yet, Ms. Collins, but I'd like to offer our sympathies at how traumatic this experience must be for you-"

"Traumatic!? Seeing my late husband's Amex statements was traumatic, I can tell you; this is a walk in the park. I knew nothing good would come from having The Russian next door. All those late-night parties, the noise; it's just not American, is it?"

Alexa attempted to suppress a frown. *Let the witness feel comfortable, let them speak,* she remembered from her training. Despite the dislike she was quickly generating already.

"Can we focus on the events of this morning? Would you mind walking me through them, Ms. Collins, and I will be asking you some questions after." Alexa attempted her best 'witness engagement' smile but thought it came off a bit more like a grimace. Either way, it appeared that Marjorie Collins was happy to talk.

"Well, it started with the damn dog-" She cast a scandalized eye at where the offending sound was still coming from somewhere in the depths of the mansion.

"There's always been noise here, ever since The Russian moved in," she said, the words sounding like it was a title, and

Alexa immediately got the perfect picture of where Marjorie came from: Heartland politics and 1950s' teeth commercials.

"I made complaints to the concierge service of course, all sorts of parties on the weekends, although I think that was mostly his sons. And the gold digger! She was clearly a menace!"

"The dog. The gold digger, right," Alexa tried to keep track. "Are you telling me that Mr. Bodrov was married?"

Marjorie almost choked on a snort of laughter. "Oh no! Not yet, anyway. Maybe the old Red saw it coming. But he brought over some young thing from the Urals, probably, barely twenty-five I can tell you, and she was always playing music, hosting parties here. I wouldn't be surprised if she was the one to bump him off for his money, let me tell you."

But they weren't married yet, Alexa frowned. It would have been a blindingly stupid move to shoot her fiancé before they were married, and this wife, or soon-to-be-wife anyway, would have a lengthy contest through the courts.

But it was something. Alexa made a note in her notebook.

Find the fiancée.

"Now, Ms. Collins, the events of the morning itself," she tried her best to direct the starlet, which appeared about as successful as directing a herd of stampeding buffaloes.

Let them talk, indeed…

But by the end of ten minutes of speculation over Aleksandr's source of money (*Russian cocaine!*) and his real reasons for being in the US (*The Red Scare wasn't made up, you know!*), she managed to get a general picture of the events of the morning, from the dog to the security guards to finding Bodrov floating face down in his pool. Marjorie, who appeared to keep quite a close eye on her neighbors, hadn't seen the soon-to-be-wife or the sons at the residence since yesterday.

Joint effort? Alexa scribbled. *Fiancée + Sons bump off Dad?*

"But of course, the whole reason I was awake at all was the shouting at some ungodly hour this morning. Sounded like the killer got to work early, let me tell you!" Marjorie said in a fierce whisper.

"Shouting? Here, before the dog?" Alexa's ears pricked up. "Do you have a time for that, Ms. Collins?"

"I can do better than that, I have CCTV footage! I was sleeping in the second guestroom because of my back, you know, and I always keep the window open where I sleep because it helps with the air. Anyway, I was awoken about nine to hear men arguing outside – my second guestroom overlooks the Bodrov's front lawn – and when I got up to take a look-"

Of course, Ms. Collins was the sort of neighbor who would get up to look.

"That's nine in the morning?" Alexa clarified.

"Nine am or thereabouts. I saw those two oafs hauling some other young man off the property, taking him out to the gate and throwing him out. His feet didn't touch the ground, I tell you! He seemed to be very angry, saying something wasn't fair at all, and that he wanted to talk to Bodrov immediately, but they wouldn't let him," she said, before her face suddenly fell.

"Do you think that was the killer? Did I see the killer!?"

Maybe, Alexa thought.

"Can you describe this other man? Would you be able to recognize him again?" Alexa made a note. *9:30 AM Male Suspect. Get Profile Artist.*

"I'd seen him around before. Crewcut, blonde sort of hair. Didn't like the look of him at all. I think he did landscaping or something for The Russian, but I wouldn't be surprised if he wasn't knocking knees with the gold digger behind the juniper bushes, if you catch my drift…"

"I get the picture, Ms. Collins," Alexa felt vaguely dirty.

9:00 AM. Male Suspect shouting. Security guards remove.
10:30 AM. Dog barking. M. Collins + guards find body.
2 x Sons + Fiancée not present.

"What about me? Do I get witness protection or something?" Marjorie asked, as all the glamor at being in the center of a high-profile case had suddenly turned to fear.

"Well, I'm not sure you actually witnessed anything yet, Ms. Collins," Alexa started to say, until she saw the screen star's face start to turn thunderous.

"But I will be asking a team to come over to do a proper witness interview, and take any CCTV footage you may have. I'll also ask Miami PD to swing by and do a safety check on your property," Alexa said, patting her pocket to realize that she didn't even have a card that she could hand over, not that Marjorie seemed to mind.

"Oh, I'll do my duty, Agent. Don't you worry. We have to keep our eye on our borders these days!" Marjorie said, as Alexa beckoned the police officer to walk Ms. Collins back to her residence.

"You don't think she shot Bodrov then?" said the voice of Kage behind her, arriving with the snap of elastic as he closed his notebook.

The starlet had already wobbled out of the room, but Alexa shot a despairing look at her back.

"How old do you think she is, seventy-three, four? I don't see her scaling those eight-foot security fences any time soon."

"You might be surprised. She seems tougher than you and me put together," Kage whispered, earning a small smile from Alexa, before she reminded herself not to get charmed by this man. He was too goofy, possibly even lax in her professional opinion.

"Speak for yourself, Murphy. I guess it's the guards next. They're the ones who had opportunity, but Dempsey said they were covered by the CCTV footage all morning. Ms. Collins did mention an altercation with an unnamed male at approximately nine-thirty this morning," Alexa filled her partner in before asking what Kage had found out from the EMTs.

"Well, they kept saying they weren't criminal pathologists," Kage said, nodding back through the glass doors of the games room that looked out toward the pool and the small marina pier beyond. Alexsandr Bodrov was once again secured in his black body bag, and they were starting to wheel the stretcher away.

"He'll go to the Miami coroner's office, where we'll arrange a proper pathologist's report. Might take a few days though," Kage said.

"On the whole, it's as you see it. A bullet wound through the neck, just below the right of his Adam's Apple, that fairly tore apart the back of his neck and upper trapezius muscle. Massive trauma and blood loss was the prime cause of death, with secondary drowning."

"Through and through?" Alexa asked, and Kage nodded.

"I had a preliminary search of the scene, but no obvious sign of the bullet. The problem is that because he was floating, it looks impossible to find the trajectory of the shot. It could be in the trees, the lawns, out to Biscayne Bay for all we know. The FBI Crime Scene Unit should be here shortly, and I'm guessing they'll want to drain the pool."

Alexa nodded with a small groan. This was going to be a mammoth task, if what she had learned at Quantico played out in the field. Every inch of the residence would have to be studied, and every item at the crime scene catalogued. That was even before they started looking at possible attack vectors, routes of entry, and avenues of opportunity for any suspected murderer…

Which, right now, was looking tricky, Alexa thought as she raised her head to cast another look through the pool.

The entire property was long and thin, with eight-foot security fences on three sides, the only opening being the gate at the front, and the marina at the back. Which led onto open water. The entire island only had one entrance and exit, a road connecting it to the MacArthur Causeway, and even *that* had gate guards.

Are we looking at a locked room case? Alexa groaned, remembering the FBI scenarios. The locked room case was where there was a murder scene with no obvious route of entrance or entry, but the solutions always boiled down to one of two things:

Either the killer was already in the room (or island)…

Or there was some fiendishly difficult process involving vanishing clues and bizarre solutions. Alexa really hoped that it wasn't the second one.

"Did they say how long the body was in the water?" Alexa wondered, but Kage shook his head.

"Like they said, they just save lives, but they reckoned it couldn't be more than a couple hours at most."

Alexa nodded. That put the murder right in the center of the time frame she was piecing together.

A thought suddenly struck Alexa. "We're looking at an incredibly tight window of opportunity. If this angry male suspect was here at half-past nine, then the question becomes whether the security guards informed Bodrov of the altercation, or when they saw him this morning before 10:30."

"If they didn't shoot him themselves?" Kage pointed out.

"Indeed. But they would have to find a way to doctor the CCTV footage of them." Alexa looked ahead of them towards the next room of the mansion, which appeared to be a hallway, leading off to one of the dining rooms where the two security guards were still being held by Miami PD.

But then why open the gate to Marjorie Collins at all? Why phone the police and wait around for us to arrive? Alexa thought, as she made another note on her pad.

Through-and-through. Find the bullet.

"Okay then, let's do this," Alexa said as she briefly thought back to her hours and hours of training videos, featuring murders being questioned. There was no way to tell whether the suspect actually committed the murder. There was no special clue, no special trait that gave a murderer away...

You have to find the evidence. Trust the chain of events, she thought.

"Officers, Detective Dempsey," she nodded to the group of Miami PD who surrounded the two seated security guards in the dining room. They were seated at a formal polished wooden table that stretched down the middle of the room for an easy fifteen or sixteen feet. The chairs that edged it had green velvet cushioning and were inlaid with gold paint. On the walls were giant oil paintings of pine forests and mountains under endless grey skies.

A touch of the Mother Country, Aleksandr? Alexa thought as she swept her attention to the two men. Both wore dark black uniforms of a sort, with the same puffy, stretched-fabric look of men who were used to bodybuilding. Dark hair, both shaved to within a whisker of their skulls.

Possible steroid use? Alexa wondered as Dempsey nodded her over.

THE **FLORIDA GIRL**

"Meet Artem and Fedor, from St. Petersburg, Russia. Been working for Aleksandr Bodrov for the last three years."

He said the last part heavily, and Alexa wondered if the entirety of Miami had a fear of the 'Red Scare.' Maybe it had something to do with communist Cuba being so close.

"I've taken their statements, and it seems to be corroborated by CCTV."

"Of course it is!" one of the men started to shout in a heavily accented voice, half-rising from his seat before the nearest officer made a restraining gesture. Alexa felt the tension shoot up in the room as the officer and the guard glared at each other, before the Russian snorted in disgust and sat back down.

They're combat ready, Alexa thought to herself. Something about the way the man fronted up so confidently. She would bet money that these two men were used to violence.

"Our guard hut *has* CCTV pointed inside as well as outside, so Mr. Bodrov can watch us sitting on our asses all day," the first security guard snapped. "All of this I have already told your Detective Dempsey."

"Well, now you are telling us," Alexa matched the guard's tone.

She saw the Russian guard do a double take as his eyes slid between Dempsey, Kage, and her. Maybe he couldn't believe that Alexa had the rank to speak to him, she thought.

Well, that was an illusion she was going to be happy to burst.

"And then there are these," Dempsey began, gesturing to the other side of the room, where another officer was in the business of writing evidence slips for two small, dark grey and black sidearms.

"Walther PDQ 9mms. We're checking licensing now, but they're a good make. Fresh," Dempsey said.

"Florida is an open carry state," Kage said under his breath, presumably for Alexa's benefit, she guessed.

As if I don't know that already!? Did Kage think she was a total idiot? Or was it just the fact that she was a woman?

"We have all the papers, cop! We are US citizens and we are allowed to carry them. We are also employed to protect probably the richest man on this island." It was the first guard once again, not standing this time, but still irate.

"Which you failed to do, clearly," Alexa said, and the security guard flushed a deeper shade of red. *Yeah, steroids, I'd bet on it.*

"I want to hear your security detail. What your rounds are. How many cameras. Did Mr. Bodrov have any reason to feel threatened?"

"Our rounds are all in the office upstairs. Every day, two shifts. 12 midday till 12 midday, rain or shine," the angry security guard said dismissively. "And have you seen this house, this island? Of course Bodrov had enemies. Anyone would want what he has!"

"Including the man you threw out this morning?" Alexa asked, as her eyes studied the guards intently. She saw the eyes widen from the angry guard, a gesture of surprise that she knew about it at all perhaps, but the reaction from the second guard was interesting. He smirked.

Like he enjoyed the memory of roughing the guy up?

"Ah. You think Max did this?" the angry guard said with a look of derision. "Probably would if he had the chance, too. Max Henderson. He worked for Mr. Bodrov but was fired yesterday."

"Fired for what?" Kage stepped forward.

The security guard shrugged. "I don't know, apart from the fact he was a toenail. Always late. Never respectful. Always thought the world owed him... It's a very *American* trait," the guard said sourly.

"What about you, got anything to say for yourself?" Kage turned on the silent guard, who looked startled for a second, looking at the first and then back at Kage.

"We've been here all night. Saw Mr. Bodrov when he got up this morning for his swim, about eight-thirty maybe? Then we're in the guard hut by the gate. Mr. Bodrov doesn't like to be disturbed, so when Max showed up, we showed him where to go."

12 AM Guard shift starts.
8:30 AM Guards see Bodrov for swim.
9:00 AM Max Henderson. Angry.
10:30 AM Dog barking. Body.

Alexa scribbled quickly, showing the notebook to Kage, who nodded.

"And there was no time that Henderson made contact with Mr. Bodrov on his own?" Alexa frowned.

"I said Mr. Bodrov doesn't like to be disturbed when he takes his swim," the second guard repeated a little more firmly. "It will all be on the tapes. I cannot believe this, you are questioning *us* who called you guys!"

You didn't call US; Lord alone knows why WE were called, Alexa thought as she stepped back from the pair and signalled Kage to follow her. She peered through the open door to see that there was another kind of reception room next door, this time with high, wall-to-floor ceilings, leather Chesterfield sofas, and a small fountain in the middle. She moved until they were on the far side of the fountain, so they wouldn't be overheard, but Kage was the first to speak.

"It'll take a couple of days for ballistics and the coroner's report," Kage said quickly.

"And it won't be easy to find the bullet," Alexa said, as she felt something nagging at her. Something about those guns...

"Damnit," Alexa nodded, looking back through the open doors to where the security guards were arguing with Detective Dempsey once more.

"I'm not seeing a motive, unless we can uncover conspiracy. Maybe they had an agreement with the sons, or the fiancée. Maybe this Max Henderson was involved in it too – but why wait around for the police?" she asked.

"Maybe the sons inherit the money, and they split it with the security guards; maybe this Max Henderson if he was involved?" Kage considered. "Although I am not seeing a lot of love between the guards and this Max guy right now."

"No, me neither." If she was to call it, Alexa would have to say that the scorn she had seen from the guards towards this Henderson character was real. But then again, there were plenty of people out there who could lie *really* well, she was sure. Especially if it involved a few billion dollars.

"I'm going to tell Dempsey to hold them," Kage said out loud. "We get seventy-two hours free. That should be enough time for the ballistics check-"

"Wait," Alexa jumped in, hit with a sudden thought. "We've got nothing tying them to the murder at all, apart from the guns. It would be circumstantial evidence at best until we tie a fired gun to a fingerprint."

"It's a pretty damn reasonable suspicion though, wouldn't you say!?" Kage pointed out.

But Alexa wasn't so sure. She knew they needed something stronger. "You saw the exit wound on Bodrov's body, didn't you? You said it was big. Very big."

Kage pulled a gross face and gestured with his hands, describing a shape in the air about the size of a small plate. "Like bolognese. Most of his neck was gone, and the top of his shoulder."

Well, that makes things a little clearer, Alexa thought, nodding to herself.

Because there was one thing that Alexa Landers was secretly proud of, and that had helped set her apart from her fellows at Quantico. She had been trained by her dad in firearms since she was old enough to hold a gun (and a good few years before that, truth be told). She had taken to marksmanship as naturally as her father had taken to water.

He always thought I should go into the army's infantry and become a marksman, Alexa recalled. She knew her guns.

"Then the bullet has to be a hollowpoint, or a larger gauge than a 9mm. And as you know-" Alexa started.

"Hollowpoints are illegal for US general carry," Kage went on, already turning to lead them back to the dining room, crossing to the wooden table and picking up the evidence bags. He slid both guns out as Dempsey turned around in shock.

"Hey-! That's chain of evidence!"

Alexa watched as Kage unlocked the magazine and let it slip out of the barrel, before checking the barrel.

"Clear in the hole. Clip all accounted for," he said, holding up the magazine of first one Walther and then the next, "and they're solid 9mm. Not hollow points." Kage looked at Alexa. "These weren't the guns used."

"Does that mean we are free to go!?" the first, angry security guard was on his feet again, as Alexa felt herself relax into her stance. If they got angry, tried to run, she would be ready.

"Well, Special Agents?" Detective Dempsey fixed them both with a hard stare that said, '*Do you have any idea what you are doing?*' Alexa could have punched him for it.

"*Sir?*" It was then that another, younger Miami PD officer arrived at the door, holding up in his blue-gloved hands a small data stick. Alexa guessed it contained the footage from the CCTV for this morning.

The young officer shook his head and Detective Dempsey sighed.

"Fine. You're free to go. But we'll be sending people over tomorrow to take a proper statement, won't we, Special Agents?" the red-faced detective glowered at Kage and Alexa, who nodded.

Artem and Fedor muttered angry Russian under their breath as they collected their coats and the police officers showed them out of the door, leaving Alexa and Kage behind with Dempsey.

"Well. This is looking as clear as mud, isn't it?" Dempsey said angrily. "I'm going to have it in writing that you just let our best two suspects go."

"Max Henderson," Alexa countered. "If he worked here, then Aleksandr should have his details on some sort of file. He's our best suspect over a seventy-year-old woman and two people sitting in front of a camera all morning."

"Yes, *boss!*" Kage said with a wry smile as Dempsey huffed angrily. "Let's check the mansion for Aleksandr's office, shall we?"

The Miami PD had already found Aleksandr's office on the third floor of the Star Island mansion, and Alexa found that it was a surprisingly subdued affair when she and Kage entered. Downstairs in the front driveway, the first of the larger black SUVs of the FBI Crime Scene units were arriving. Alexa didn't envy them their job.

"You can take the boy out of Russia, but you can't…" the tall Irish-American Murphy murmured as he nodded towards the wood-panelled walls of the small room, where paintings of woods and what appeared to be farms and rural, bucolic workers had been fixed.

The room was fairly small, with a large desk beside the bay windows, and metal filing cabinets along one wall. A laptop sat beside a pen tray and a variety of executive toys and smaller pictures in frames.

"Anyone found the-" Alexa started to ask, before there was a jangle as Kage pulled a set of keys from the hooks behind the door.

"We got a couple of car keys, what looks to be some Yale locks, and I guess that these are for the desks," he said, throwing the latter bunches on the table, as Alexa got to work sorting out what would open the filing cabinets, and what would open the desk drawers.

"Maybe he wasn't that worried about security after all?" Alexa mumbled, finding the right one for the filing cabinets and got to work opening them all up to find acres and acres of manilla envelopes.

Ugh. This was going to take ages. She pulled out one at random to find inside a series of invoices for COBOLT MANUFACTURING and a series of reseller invoices.

"Looks like he brought materials and sold them, brokered deals between manufacturers and clients." Alexa scanned the papers before putting them back and checking another random selection.

"Mergers and Acquisitions. Share reports. He was a busy man, our Aleksandr." She went through the drawers at random, realizing that they would probably need specialized legal advice if they wanted to understand it.

"And here we have personal memos, stationary…" Kage was at the desk drawers, suddenly exclaiming as he drew out a bottle.

"Black Label Vodka, of course, and, uh, some Cubans, and…" Another thump on the table as he set a smaller service pistol next to the bottle and the box of cigars.

"Twenty-two caliber. No round in the chamber. I think I'm seeing how Aleksandr liked to conduct his business meetings."

Alexa muttered her agreement as she instead looked at the desk pictures. There was one of his family, showing two baby boys and a much younger Aleksandr Bodrov, next to two more frames.

The first and largest was a picture of what was, quite clearly, a beautiful young woman on the arm of an older Aleksandr. She had long blonde hair and the sort of lips that Alexa had always thought looked 'sulky.' They were clearly at some kind of black tie event, with the younger bombshell wearing a shimmering and nearly sheer white-silver gown, split down the middle.

"Fiancée," Alexa offered.

Kage took a look and cleared his throat suddenly.

"She looks very comfortable in, uh, wealthy circles?" he offered.

"Why wasn't she at home in this circle? That's what I'm thinking," Alexa mumbled, holding up her FBI phone to take a picture of the woman.

The last frame held a grimy, ancient photograph of what appeared to be a man looking back at the camera, smiling and pointing at a treehouse that had been built in its middling branches.

"osobnyak v lesu, 1973." Alexa did her best to read out the words that were written on the back of the frame.

"That man looks too old to be Aleksandr back then, don't you think?" Alexa offered the picture to Kage, who was the last person to have seen Mr. Bodrov up close and in the cadaverous flesh.

"I think so. Father, maybe? Childhood photo?" Kage squinted, then shrugged as he turned to the next drawer, opened it with the keys to suddenly whistle.

"Well, Aleksandr was a believer in physical wealth," he said, pulling the drawer open a little wider to reveal that there was a metal tray inside, fit with foam, and indented across the foam were about a dozen small tokens of gold.

"Stamped. A certificate of authentication," Kage commented as he pulled out the tray and the paper. "If I had known that was sitting up here, I would have already booked my flight to the Bahamas!" Kage joked as he took one of the evidence bags and carefully wrote on it the amount of gold bars in the tray, before sliding the entire lot inside.

"This would certainly count as motive." Kage leaned over the desk. "If any attempt had been made to steal it, anyway."

Exactly, Alexa was thinking as she looked between the gold to the gun, to the picture of the fiancée and the boys. She was looking at three people with an awful lot to gain from the man's death. But still no – quite literally – smoking guns.

What was it Quantico said? The clues are always there. But sometimes you have to dig deeper to find them.

Dig Deep. Find the story of the victim's life. Their last few days.

Alexa reached over to grab the appointment book and the laptop, already flicking the appointment book to the last written page, and seeing the words **Mikhail Zholdin 3PM**, a phone number, and the entire entry encircled three times.

"He had an appointment today. And he didn't want to forget it," Alexa said, already flicking to the back to find a list of contacts. Zholdin was in there, alongside the word OGRE and an 800 number.

"It's a business," she said before there was a cough from the door and she looked up to see Detective Dempsey doing a double-take as he saw the evidence bag full of gold.

"Uh…"

"Detective?" Alexa prompted him.

"Right. The gate CCTV caught the license plate for the car Max Henderson left in, and we got his address. But that's not all. Max Henderson is a convicted felon on an assault and battery charge, and has been found in possession of an unlicensed firearm no less than two times previous."

"Sounds like a man with anger issues," Kage growled.

"Sounds like a man who can get his hands on firepower," Alexa said, already turning as she moved towards the door.

"We'll take point, with Miami PD back-up," she said, wondering if she would have to use her brand new sidearm on Day 1 of her first posting as she ran down the stairs beyond.

CHAPTER FOUR

2:15 PM. HENDERSON'S RESIDENCE, LITTLE HAITI

Little Haiti was a gridded residential area just a mile or so from the waters of the Biscayne Bay, and Alexa could see the change in income almost as soon as they entered.

The houses here were lower, smaller, and more compact, many of them with chain-link security fences around properties that would have fitted into Aleksandr Bodrov's swimming pool. Tinny Latin EDM music thumped out of cars idling on street corners, and somewhere there was a siren blaring past.

"You can see where all the money goes, huh?" Alexa murmured, as the tall spires of downtown stood behind them, and in the distance, the condos of Miami Beach reached towards blue skies like a disgustingly close but out of reach Never-Never land.

"Yeah, all the money skipped this side of the Bay," Kage said as he brought their Ford into park at the top of the block. They had already told Dempsey to hang back on the squad cars, not wanting any chance to alert Henderson yet.

"How do you want to play this, knock and chat?" Kage said as he threw on the light jacket over his athletic shirt and tactical pants combo. The jacket was tight, but with enough room to conceal the Glock snug under his arm.

"Well, Mr. Henderson is still only a potential suspect at the moment," Alexa pointed out, swapping out her FBI jacket for the one she had brought with her on the plane. A strange thing about this job, the thought flashed through her mind – was that the idea of the black-suited FBI agent was quite rare in the field.

"We just want to ask a few questions, that's all."

"Like did he return to the kill his boss?" Kage half-joked, but Alexa wasn't in the mood.

In all seriousness, Alexa was aware that could very well be the case. Aleksandr Bodrov had been shot through the neck; an intensely personal sort of violence, if she had ever seen one. There had been no attempt at a robbery of the premises or the guards.

All of which might suggest a murderer who had personal beef.

And Max Henderson, with two charges of assault and battery on his sheet, was certainly a guy who could nurse a grudge.

"By the book. You cover the front, I'll take the back. I'll be your backup if anything gets heavy," Alexa said, one hand moving slightly to the bulge of her gun against her side, and Kage nodded. They were both aware that the guy had firearms offences on file, so neither of them wanted to take any chances.

They slid out of the car and Alexa felt the heat of the Miami afternoon fall on her like a blanket. Someone somewhere was frying food.

"That's the one," Kage indicated the middle of three low, one-story houses with peaked tin roofs. There was a children's trampoline and a few thrown toys on the lawn of one, and large green shrubs grew over a thin wooden fence. The house in question had a small walk-up porch, but the front window appeared to be boarded over.

"I'll give you five, then I'm knocking on the front door," Kage said, and Alexa nodded and took off across the street, heading for the small alley that ran behind this stretch of three buildings and the next. The roads here were wide and far too open, while the houses were too close together. *Real* easy for a criminal to see you coming long before you saw them.

The sounds of Little Haiti were louder now, as Alexa walked quickly past the trampoline-house to the alley, hearing someone's television turned up way too loud. Something Spanish, with a lot of shouting and laughing.

Still, no one shouted at her when she turned the corner to the access alley that ran between the building, seeing that it was mostly filled with junk, old bedsprings, a beat-up washing machine and a few battered dustbins. More of the green shrubs had fought their way clear to overhang this space, turning it into a green tunnel, with a floor of escapee trash and dirt.

"Nice," she whispered with a disgusted pull of her mouth, before hopping over the washing machine and into the alley beyond. The sound of the TV grew louder and was met by the whine of someone doing home improvements on the other side over.

Damnit! Alexa realized that she wouldn't be able to hear if there was an altercation at the front door.

I'll hear a gunshot, for sure, she reckoned. But by then it might be too late.

She padded quickly down the alleyway past the trampoline house to see that the rear of the Henderson place was a chain-link fence and gate, not wooden slats. She paused, allowed her head to bob around the side to see that the gate was already propped open with a steel trash can, revealing a wild, trash heap of an overgrown backyard, and a few steps leading up to the one-story property itself.

Wait. Listen. She recalled her trainers.

First three seconds are gut response. Wait, if you can, for a count of ten.

Right now, Alexa's gut was telling her that this was dangerous. She would have to cross the fifteen feet or so to the back door and hope that it wasn't locked, right under the eye of the window. She had been hoping that she would be able to hear what was happening at the front door, or even better yet – get a glimpse inside before making the entrance.

'Sometimes you don't have any good options…' That was what her dad would have said, wouldn't it?

Dad. Thinking of him make Alexa's heart thump a little faster. If he could see her now, first day of the job, and already taking out her service pistol and checking it.

Good. Ready to go.

There was a shout, and a sudden crash of something from the Henderson residence, barely concealed by the television and DIY.

"Shit!" Alexa didn't wait for her three seconds, and instead threw herself around the corner and through the open gate, racing up the path of slightly less overgrown grass to the back door.

She covered the ground in seconds, her body locking into fluid motion that seven years of training had given her.

Final boot on the lawn. Next on the second porch step…

BANG!

The back door slammed open, and a figure burst out of it, clearly as surprised as Alexa was as he barrelled into her.

"Halt!" Alexa managed to shout as she hit the ground heavily, seeing a flash of dark trousers and a greenish top. Legs slammed into her gut as the escapee did more than just get back to his feet.

"*Son of a-!*" Alexa wheezed in pain as she doubled over, rolled to one side and scrabbled for breath as she raised her gun.

But the man (she was sure it was a man, he had broad shoulders and a small waist) was already spinning around the gate and disappearing.

Damnit. Damnit! She jumped to her feet and ran after him, not even at the end of the garden when she heard the thumping resonance as her accidental assailant hopped the fence to one of the rear set of gardens.

"HALT! FBI!" Alexa shouted all the same as she skidded into the alleyway between the houses – and then realized that she had no idea which garden the man had jumped into.

Fine. I didn't win Track for this! She took off down the alleyway, vaulting the washing machine at the end and skidding across the sidewalk as her side began to stitch. Alexa ignored it, spinning on her heel to run down the block to the front of the rear set of houses…

To see no sign of her guy. The street was quiet. Even the sound of the DIY had stopped.

"Oh, come on!" Alexa growled. She was sure that it was Henderson. Maybe he had seen them pull up. Whatever his reason for running was, fleeing a scene was a damn good admission of guilt in her book. Maybe Henderson had thought he had gotten away with it. Maybe he had only been packing a bag to flee the city entirely…

"Hey, Miss, are you alright?" There was a voice from one of the gardens beside her as she walked the block, trying to listen for the sound of running footsteps. It looked to be DIY guy, a not-very tall but large man with his power drill still in his hands.

Not my guy, Alexa saw immediately.

"Special Agent Landers, FBI. You seen a tall guy in dark clothes running through here just a minute ago?" She slowed down.

"Nah, lady. You really FBI?" The man looked vaguely terrified and impressed, and Alexa thanked him and cursed as she turned back towards the house. If that was Henderson, then he was gone, but maybe Dempsey could put out an APB for him…

She got back to the alleyway to hear yet more shouting coming from the Henderson place, and with a brief muttered curse she was once again vaulting the washing machine, angling past the discarded trash cans and rounding into the Henderson backyard to see the back door wide open, with the sounds of shouts coming from inside.

"*Get off me, man! This is harassment!*"

Alexa ran up the steps to see that there was a short hallway that opened out into a grimy kitchen on one side with dishes overflowing the sink, and the main living room ahead, where Kage currently had his knee in the back of a man on the floor, restraining one arm in order to cuff him. The rest of the living room was a state around them, with a smashed table, two ripped couches, and plenty of foil wraps and old beer cans littered everywhere.

"What took you so long, pard'ner?" Kage grunted a little heavily as he snapped the handcuffs on the man, before hauling him with no gentility onto his back.

"*What the hell, bro!? This is home invasion!*" the man was shouting.

"Alexa? Meet Max Henderson," Murphy sighed, taking a few steps back and breathing heavily.

"What?" Alexa stared down in disbelief at the enraged man.

"Looks like Henderson was running a nice little racket back here," Murphy said under the sound of police sirens as another squad car parked up in front, ready to take Henderson into custody.

"Yeah. We got him on multiple drug offences, and there's an unregistered Remington in the bedroom that I'm sure you're glad he didn't have in his hands when you busted open the door," Detective Dempsey opined as he surveyed the edge of a room, where crime scene officers were already starting to catalogue the drug paraphernalia, making notes and taking photos.

"I heard a shout. Some sort of fight going on, so I knocked *loudly*," Kage said with a wry grin. Alexa realized just how athletic her Japanese-Irish-American agent partner actually was. He was built big, but also tall, like a semi-pro football player. He must have taken out that front door in seconds.

"And I guess I got the other end of that fight," Alexa said sourly. The man who had knocked her over and kneed her in the stomach.

"What do you think, drug deal gone bad?"

"He was robbing me, *goddammit!*" There was a shout from behind them as Henderson was struggling with the officers holding him.

"I just got back and there this *pendejo* was, standing in my own house, going through my things! But you're not going to investigate *that*, are you? Nah, you just want to mess up my day like always..." Henderson ranted as Alexa felt a sinking feeling.

"You just got back? Where from, Mr. Henderson?" she said as she strode towards him.

"Why the hell should I tell you?" he spat back.

"Absolute charmer, isn't he?" Murphy whispered.

"Special Agent Landers and Special Agent Murphy, with the Federal Bureau of Investigation," she introduced, and flipping her card for him, she saw his eyes widen.

"FBI? What-?" Henderson looked in confusion between the police around him, the spilled drugs on the floor, and the two FBI agents in front of him.

"Where were you between the hours of 9:00 AM and my friend Agent Murphy here doing home improvements on your front door, Mr. Henderson?" Alexa said in a steely voice.

Follow the eyes. See if he looks away.

Henderson didn't look away, but he did blink several times. "Is this about the drugs? Because I tell you, all I do is recreational..."

Well, that looked to be a lie, Alexa thought from the amount of wraps and ties they found in this room alone. But whatever. She wasn't about to argue with him.

"It's about Mr. Bodrov, and where you have been for the last five hours," Alexa said heavily.

"*Bodrov!?*" Henderson burst out. "This is about that old goat? I should have known he'd stitch me up. He's a nasty piece of crap, is what he is!"

"It would be fair to say you didn't like him, then?" Kage took a step to loom over Henderson. "Because Mr. Bodrov was found dead this morning, and there's a couple of guys who are saying you were pretty angry with him."

"*What?* Bodrov's dead! Like, dead-dead?" Henderson spluttered for a moment, his eyes searching. He gazed up at Murphy and Landers for a moment, and then burst out laughing.

"Ha! Should have known it was coming to him eventually, one way or another. He's as crooked as they come, right? Has to be. And a terrible boss. I worked for him for three years straight, no problems, then this morning he just ups and fires me by text!"

"Can we see the text, Mr. Henderson?" Alexa said, as Max gestured to where his phone had been placed on the table by one of the CSI, but then suddenly paled.

"But don't you need a warrant or something before you go through my phone? I don't consent!" he said quickly.

He's scared of what we might find on his phone, but not scared enough, Alexa considered.

"Fine. We *will* get that warrant, Mr. Henderson, and a special order allowing us to seize and investigate any digital systems you have. But if you don't want to help us in our investigations, then I have to assume you have something to hide."

"Hide? What are you talking about? I was getting robbed and now you think *I* killed Bodrov!? Well I didn't, but I would have if his guards hadn't pulled me clear, though!" Henderson swore, spitting on the floor.

Declaration of motive, not the brightest, either. Alexa was starting to get a bad feeling about this suspect.

"Anyway. After I was thrown out of that commie's place I was at the VIV Lounge *all day;* go check with Perelli if you don't believe me!"

"*VIV Lounge?*" Alexa turned to Kage.

"Adult Entertainment Lounge, downtown Miami. It's known in the area," he muttered in monotone.

"You bet it is. Opens at nine, I was there before ten. I bet you wouldn't dare go breaking down doors on Perelli's place, would ya?" Henderson snarled.

"*What does he mean?*" Alexa whispered, and Kage shook his head quickly and firmly.

"You got proof of any of that?" Kage said.

"I got receipts, and Perelli has cameras on all his girls, so you'll be able to tell I kinda had my hands full between nine-thirty and now!" Henderson snapped.

Thank you, no thanks for that image, Alexa thought, as Kage dutifully went through Henderson's jacket pockets to find the receipts.

VIV Adult Lounge Miami
downtown Miami 453-821
10:12 AM

1 x Cobra XTRA STR
1 x Jamesons Whiskey
1 x Performance (adult services)
1 x Performance (adult services)

VAT: 10%

Alexa leafed through three small squares of printed receipts and felt even grubbier after reading them than when she had been sneaking through the trash alley out back. None of the receipts covered between nine-thirty and ten, but then how long did it take to drive between Star Island and wherever the VIV was? There was also no certain proof that these receipts were even Henderson's.

"Don't worry, Mr. Henderson, we will certainly be checking with the VIV Lounge," Alexa said with an exasperated nod to the police officers.

"Thanks, you can take him away, officers."

"I'm going to sue, you know! I'll sue you for my door and for false accusation!" Henderson was still caterwauling as they dragged him out the door.

"You do that, Mr. Henderson, you go ahead and do that," Alexa said wearily. Her side still hurt from where she had been kneed by some junkie athlete earlier.

"I'll hold him in custody for as long as I can, but the drug and gun charges alone should put him in jail, I reckon," Detective Dempsey said. "Henderson won't be going anywhere, all you got to do is get your evidence on him."

The detective clapped his hands together and cackled. "Phew! Who knew working with the FBI would be so easy!? Thank you so much for all your specialist experience!" the detective laughed as he sauntered back through the hallway to oversee the suspect transport.

Yeah, Alexa had to agree just a little. Maybe Bureau cases weren't always fiendishly difficult.

Or maybe they totally had the wrong man.

"Okay, that's Chief Williams," Kage was just sliding his phone back into his pocket. "He wants us back at HQ to brief on the case – and to meet you."

Wonderful, Alexa thought grimly, as right now she didn't think that she had anything much at all to show for her first day at work.

CHAPTER FIVE

6:25 PM. FBI MIAMI HQ [UNDISCLOSED LOCATION]

THE MIAMI FIELD OFFICE LOOKED TOTALLY NONDESCRIPT from the outside, and Alexa thought you could easily mistake it for a small investment bank or legal firm in the heart of the city. It even had a plaque over the door and a key card machine to allow entry. Alexa didn't have one of those yet, so she had to wait for Kage to let her in, revealing a short hallway to a large service elevator on the far side.

Instead of going up, they descended downwards with a sudden judder. It was a short journey, and within a few moments the doors were opening again to reveal a wide hallway with a guard booth right in front of them.

"Agent Murphy!" called out the guard on duty, a large man in anonymous black tactical clothes.

"Elijah, meet Alexa Landers, straight from the Academy." Kage gave the man a high five (which Alexa was sure *wasn't* procedure at all) before he signed in their guns, which Elijah stacked away in sets of metal cabinet boxes behind them.

"Agent Landers," Elijah said, and Alexa was surprised to see such a broad and warm smile. Quantico hadn't been like that. She appreciated it, but not for the first time she wondered if the Miami office was a little 'different' to the other FBI field offices that were secretly dotted up and down the country.

"Pleasure to have you on the team, but I have to warn you, the chief is already looking stressed and decaffeinated." Elijah pulled a warning look down the long hallway, where there were several glass doors and more corridors leading off of both sides.

"Conference Room 3. He specifically asked for you to go straight through," Elijah said, which didn't exactly fill Alexa with confidence.

But this is why I'm here. This is my job, Alexa thought to herself as she let Kage show her to where Conference Room 3 was, finding that it was down the main hallway and through a large set of sound-proofed glass doors to what appeared to be a busy office room. Alexa saw a large workspace made up of multiple office desks in the center with whiteboards all around the walls as well as full, three-foot screens. Computers and laptops sat on smaller desks around the edges of the room.

"Agent Landers," snapped the tall African American man in white shirt and almost midnight blue trousers standing in the front of the screens at the end of the room.

"I'm Field Chief Supervisor Williams, been running the Miami Field Office for a long time now, and we're glad to have you," the man said perfunctorily, as there was a brief round of smiles from the two other suited man and woman already in the room. Neither of the smiles were very warm, though.

"However, I have to say that you have arrived in the middle of what could be the most important case in the Miami office's history, which means that I *really* hope that your Quantico assessors were right about your ability."

"Thank you, sir-" Alexa started to say, before she was cut off by the chief.

"As you know, we operate in an autonomous way here, each investigation and taskforce is fully expected and empowered to perform its duties to the best as it is able, but this case is different, as you will see. I will require updates and reports every day."

"On your right is Cecil Pinkerton, our Chief Scientific Officer and CSI guy, then we have Dee Hopkins, Chief Digital Supervisor, and on the screen behind me here we have Officer Voorn," the field chief paused and stepped away from the screen to reveal a middle-aged woman with a small frame and a short, stylish bob of blonde hair. She was sitting at a nondescript office deck, with a blue drape backdrop behind her.

The only identifying thing about her was that, on the drape, there was a round design.

Oh, Alexa blinked in surprise because the design was the eagle's head and shield of the Central Intelligence Agency.

"Officer Voorn, please continue your briefing," Chief Williams said, and so she did.

"Good evening, everyone," Officer Voorn said without the briefest shadow of a smile.

"I am here to brief you on Mr. Aleksandr Bodrov, and explain a little as to why the FBI was flagged immediately when his death was reported to Miami Police."

"Mr. Bodrov was considered an agent to our Agency, which in our parlance means an intelligence asset. He had a history of providing the Agency with sensitive information regarding Russian manufacturing processes, in particular, Russian military manufacturers."

Holy crap. Alexa felt that same moment of vertigo. This changed things.

"I cannot go into operational details of course, but suffice to say that there are reasons to believe that his involvement with the American government, and the tensions that caused with his country of origin might have bearing on the case. We believe that the Bodrov family have been on active SVR Watch List for the past ten years, since their emigration to the US-"

"SVR?" Alexa asked, earning a small look of annoyance to flash across Voorn's features.

"There are a number of intelligence services in Russia broadly analogous to our own. The SVR, *Sluzhba Vneshney Razvedki,* or Foreign Intelligence Service conducts intelligence operations for the Russian Federation overseas. There is also the FSB, their internal intelligence service, and perhaps of interest to this case, the GRU, which is the military intelligence service."

"What are you trying to tell us, Officer Voorn – that we're looking at an inter-state assassination?" Chief Williams said heavily.

On the screen, Voorn's eyes flickered and she pursed her lips a little before speaking.

"At the Agency we avoid jumping to conclusions, Field Chief Williams. I am merely presenting facts that might be pertinent to your case. The Agency is hoping that the Bureau will be able to discover whether this is an internal or international crime."

"It's all on us then," Alexa heard Kage murmur as the CIA officer continued.

"Mr. Bodrov's family was relocated to Miami with the help of our office, but apart from general monitoring, his role with us ceased to be of value."

"Until he ended up shot," Alexa said. She couldn't quite believe how blasé the woman was being. Maybe she saw this kind of thing too much.

"Indeed. We can, however, provide two pertinent details for you that our analysts have uncovered. One, that his fiancée, the Ukrainian-born Alena Grinin has been recorded boarding a flight from Miami to Paris as of 12 this afternoon, and two, that Aleksandr Bodrov was due to meet with one Mikhail Zholdin, another Russian ex-national living in Florida, who runs the OGRE social media platform."

"We know that already," Alexa said a little testily. "But what do you know of this Zholdin?"

Again, another flash of annoyance from the officer before she spoke. "Like I said, the Agency cannot comment on operational issues, apart from saying that any Russian businessman with such wealth and ties to their home state is of interest to us."

"You thought he was spying for Russia?" Alexa pressed, but Voorn held a steely gaze at the camera and said nothing.

"Well, the Bureau thanks you for your co-operation, Officer Voorn," Williams heaved a sigh. "We'll be sure to forward our investigative notes to the Agency should it be relevant."

"As soon as anything seems relevant, Chief Williams," Voorn said before reaching to click off the connection abruptly, leaving the people in the room looking at nothing but a black screen.

"There you have it, people. Aleksandr Bodrov was wanted by the Russians, but did they want him enough to kill him? Thoughts and reports?" the chief looked at them all with a frown.

"My unit is going through the CCTV cameras for the Bodrov estate, and so far they are showing everything exactly as described by the initial witness statements," the only other woman in the room spoke up. She had pointed, flaring glasses and a bob with dark hair with a tiny bat pin pushing it away from her ear.

"Dee Hopkins, Chief Digital Supervisor for the Miami branch," she introduced herself again.

"We've received the files Landers and Murphy sent over from his house, Aleksandr's company, Bodrov Manufacturing was a multi-million-dollar company, still small in terms of American manufacturing, but was starting to take on more substantial contracts. Originally he seemed interested in hard infrastructure, cement, oil drilling and so forth, but appeared to be looking into electronics. However, it's going to take a while to run that paper trail."

"Did you get his laptop, the one at the residence?" Alexa asked.

Dee grimaced. "Yes, but, uh…it's proving tricky to get into. We've got it on code-cracking software at the moment, but Mr. Bodrov seemed to like to keep his affairs very well protected."

"I would too if I had been selling Russian state secrets," Kage pointed out, as Dee shrugged in a *maybe not, maybe so* gesture. Alexa liked her. She didn't commit to speculation, not yet.

"We don't know what he was doing that got him killed," Alexa said, earning an agreeing grunt from Chief Williams. The field chief was looking at her intently over his hand as he stroked his goatee.

Now's the time to show off all that expensive training, Alexa took a breath.

"We've got one suspect in custody, one Max Henderson, for an unrelated offence. Lots of priors, and clear motive. But his window of opportunity is very tight indeed, only about twenty minutes to return to the residence and commit the murder before he arrives at his stated alibi, that we still need to check. The two security guards at the scene were on camera all day."

Next it was the chief scientific officer's turn to speak up. He was an older man with greying hair and it turned out that he didn't have much to say at all.

"Body has been received by the Miami Dade coroner, but the local pathologist says that their case-load is heavy at the moment. It might take as long as forty-eight hours to get a full autopsy and report done on the cadaver. All initial observations are deemed correct, death by massive bodily trauma, shot through and through to the neck."

"Hollow point?" Alexa added, with the CSO Cecil Pinkerton giving that same non-committal shrug that his digital opposite had done a second earlier.

"It certainly made a mess of the body, but the forensic pathologist and ballistic study will tell us more. The problem is where he was found, if I may...?" Cecil leaned forward to pick up one of the controllers in the middle of the desk and flick a button, prompting one of the other screens in the room to light up, showing a broad, very rough three-dimensional mock-up of a pool, and a stick man floating in the center.

"We usually determine trajectory of attack based on wound, body location, and blood spatter," the man said, clicking through a few buttons to show dotted attack lines lancing out across the pool, striking the stick figure.

"However, blood spatter was effectively reduced to zero because of the surrounding water, and we guess that the body had at least some time to spin," Cecil said as the image of the stickman continued to spin in the center of the pool, and different attack lines created a spin in one direction, and then in the other.

Another click, and the image of the pool shrunk, now showing the broad lines of the house and walls around it.

"Therefore, at present we have no way of ascertaining whether the shot came from the house or wall side, but my best CSI team is working on site as we speak," Cecil said.

Great. Just wonderful. Alexa pinched the bridge of her nose. She remembered earlier what she had thought about locked room cases. This was going to be one of those fiendishly complicated ones, wasn't it?

"Okay people, priorities of investigation. If we can't find immediate conclusive evidence at the scene, what do we move to?" The chief looked around the room, then nodded when Kage raised a hand briefly.

"Victim's routine, and victim's life story," he announced what was clearly a textbook answer.

"Go on," Williams urged him.

"Well, we're getting some of his life story right now in the fact that he was a wanted intelligence asset. That opens up a whole can of suspects-"

Kage very certainly didn't say *hired killers* or *assassins* or *Russian Intelligence operatives,* but then again he didn't have to either. Everyone in the room was thinking it.

"And we have his fiancée, Alena Grinin, fleeing the scene for Paris," Murphy stated.

"She wasn't home the day previous. We don't know why she left for Paris," Alexa pointed out. "Do we have operational links with Paris law enforcement?"

Chief Williams groaned loudly, massaging his temples. "We don't, but I'm sure we can. I'll put in a request to the section chief, see if we have a contact overseas. Either way, bringing an international case will be a headache, as we'd have to put in an extradition request to our people, to give it to their people… We'd need a watertight case against her. Why would Alena kill Bodrov?"

Alexa cleared her throat. "The fiancée suspicion only works if the sons were in on it, too; they would inherit the business and Aleksandr's wealth and would have to split it with her. But we did have the first witness, Marjorie Collins, saying she suspected that Max Henderson and the fiancée were intimate."

"Any evidence for that?" the field chief asked.

Alexa held up her hands. "None that I have been given."

"Sweet suffering heavens, people!" Chief Williams went from conversational to thundering in less than a few seconds. "This case is a mess. No clear suspects. No clear motives. If we're going to rely on speculation and hearsay, we need it backed up by hard evidence. Remember that all of this will eventually have to stand before a court of law!"

"Sir," Alexa nodded, feeling like she had just been slapped. *Welcome to Day 1 indeed.*

"I can perform a timeline analysis of the fiancée's social media," Dee Hopkins said as she twirled a pen in her fingers. "That might show connections between various people, or when she was available."

"Do it," the chief said. "Get the alibi checked out for this Henderson character, but concentrate on the routine and life story, too. I want to know why he was seeing Zholdin, and whether Zholdin has ties to Russian intelligence."

How are we supposed to do that!? Alexa thought. It wasn't exactly like it was something that someone just offered up in casual conversation.

CHAPTER SIX

8:50 PM. FBI SAFE HOUSE, MIAMI NORTH

"Dee's working on the CCTV footage from Aleksandr's estate. Miami PD is working on the evidence at Henderson's place, looking for a tie to Bodrov, and we're still waiting for ballistics to tie it all together," Kage Murphy said conclusively as he once again tried to remind Alexa that she had done enough today.

The pair sat in Kage's Ford as he took them down North Avenue, turning off into the northwestern suburbs.

"Our top suspect is behind bars. It's time to get food and some rest, and come back fresh tomorrow morning," Murphy said with one of his trademark grins. Alexa still thought it made him seem unprofessional. Like being warm wasn't a desirable trait for an FBI Agent.

But maybe he was right, she had to admit, as she felt an electric sort of tiredness behind her eyes. It was a familiar feeling. Not tiredness per-se, but a wired and chemical-like jitter that she knew would mean that she would either stay awake until morning or fall asleep as soon as she found the first bed.

Outside, the Miami night had well and truly fallen, with the skies a deep black, and the skyline lit with streetlights and the glow of distant attractions. If anything, Miami seemed to get even busier at night than it did in the day, with the roads filling up and groups of people heading towards downtown on various missions of hedonism.

"I'm not tired," Alexa pointed out, as the revellers reminded her of the waiting VIV Lounge where she still needed to check this alibi.

"Perelli," she suddenly remembered. That was what Henderson had said, wasn't it? He had said the name like it meant something to everyone in the room, and when Alexa had looked at Murphy, she saw that it had.

"Rest," Murphy insisted instead, pulling off the main road to lead them into a smaller neighbourhood where the houses looked quieter, cleaner, and fairly nondescript. He kept on driving until he reached the end, where an entire block was given to some sort of smart, wide motel.

"This is the place we've got you billeted in, at least until we can arrange a more permanent safe house for you," Murphy said somewhat apologetically as he parked.

"The owners used to work with the Bureau, so they keep a few rooms spare at all times for us. They allowed us to install a few extras too, metal-lined doors, security windows, that kind of thing," Murphy pulled into park and Alexa looked ahead at the *Lucky Bird Inn.*

It was doing a really good job at looking like a seedy one-nighter motel, Alexa grimaced.

I'm glad my dad can't see me now.

Anyway. "Perelli. Why aren't we heading over there right now?" Alexa was starting to feel stubborn. Maybe it was the way that the chief had exploded back in the war room. Or maybe she really was just tired, she wasn't sure.

"He'll still be there tomorrow, and without any evidence tying Henderson to the scene we'll just be fishing anyway," Murphy said, but Alexa could see that he was stalling.

"Spill it. Who is this Perelli guy?" she pushed, still not budging from her seat.

"Ah. Well, we're going to have to approach him right because he won't give up his tapes without a warrant," Murphy said.

"You're sure? Not even to help in our inquiries?" Alexa asked.

Kage suppressed a snort of amusement. "Definitely not to help with our inquiries. We're pretty certain that Perelli is the local mafia *capo* for Miami Beach and has been for the last twenty years or so."

"Why didn't anyone tell me this before!?" Alexa burst out in frustration. *This* was important information for the case.

"Our top suspect has mafia contacts? Maybe Henderson was involved in a mob hit on Bodrov!"

Now it was Murphy's turn to call for evidence. "Landers, easy, I get this is your first case, but you have to understand something about Miami…"

Did you really just talk down to me? Alexa thought with a flash of annoyance.

"…There are a LOT of interesting characters here. From mafia to gangbangers, Haitian cartels, Cuban sympathizers, and now we've got Russians, too, apparently. Miami wasn't called Vice City for no reason back in the '80s. If we go after Perelli, even to corroborate an alibi, then we need to have all our ducks in a row."

Alexa nodded that she understood.

"It's a sea of different alliances and feuds, some going back decades. That's what makes this case so complicated. Was Aleksandr killed in a drug feud? Did he have any ties to the drug industry at all? Did he just annoy the wrong local kingpin or another and earn a bullet for it? Or was this just your regular, run-of-the-mill murder?"

"It certainly wasn't that," Alexa responded. "The thing about the way that Aleksandr was killed, was that it was *horrible* and that it was *close.*" Alexa shuddered.

The crime tells you as much about the murderer as the scene does, she remembered from her training. Any wound to the neck was generally a crime of passion, or punishment; a deeply personal act.

"So your money is still on Henderson then?" Murphy said after a moment.

No, that didn't feel right either, Alexa thought, but instantly pushed the assumption aside. She hadn't been trained to deal in assumptions, only facts.

"I don't know. But he would have had to get thrown out, and then find a gun from somewhere, scale the fence, shoot Bodrov without the guards noticing, climb back and get out and drive to this VIV Lounge, all without showing up on any CCTV footage," Alexa grumbled. Okay, maybe she was tired. She was letting this case get to her.

"I don't know," she repeated. "Maybe you're right. Fresh eyes tomorrow."

"Yeah, good idea. I'll arrange a meeting with Zholdin in the morning. Pick you up about nine?" Murphy said, his previous seriousness apparently disappearing into good humor just as quickly.

"I picked up these," Murphy said, offering her a trench of flyers from the glove box. All of which were for takeout.

"Takeout. The Bureau's best friend," he said with another grin, and Alexa groaned and said her goodbyes to experience her first night at the *Lucky Bird.*

As it turned out, the takeout was a lot better than she would have guessed, and the *Lucky Bird* was marginally more comfortable than how it appeared from the outside. Alexa phoned her dad to find that Jeb had gone out for the evening to 'catch up with the old crew' which she assumed was a euphemism for getting outrageously drunk in the local watering hole. Alexa remembered a few evenings in there herself, but she remembered pulling her brother out of there far more often.

"I'm guessing it's your case that's made the news, kiddo," her father rasped on the other end of the line.

"It has?" Alexa was surprised that she hadn't even stopped to check the news since she had arrived. She felt like today hadn't given her a moment to breathe, and her side still hurt from where the athletic junkie had kicked her.

"Yep. FBI called to the residence of murdered Russian oligarch, Aleksandr Bodrov," her father said.

Marjorie Collins. I bet it was Marjorie who leaked it to the press. Alexa could have screamed.

"You know I can't talk about any case I'm involved in, Dad," Alexa said.

"Of course, kiddo," her father's tone was breathy and coming in fits and starts. She could have murdered Jeb, too, for leaving him.

But then her father said something that she wasn't expecting at all.

"All I'm going to say is this, *be careful*. I've had my run-ins with the Russians during service. No live fire, of course, but plenty of times when it was nearly so. They're crazy, kiddo. They'll throw themselves at you just to prove a point. Don't wake the Russian Bear, that's what we were always told. Just be careful."

When had her dad ever told her to be careful before? Alexa wondered.

"You know I will, Dad, I always am," Alexa said before they said their goodbyes and the phone clicked off.

Or didn't completely click off. Alexa heard a series of odd clicks and whirrs on her phone before it finally cut to the empty dial tone.

Odd, she thought as she looked at the phone for a moment longer, before hurriedly putting it back in its cradle. She sat for a moment longer, but then crossed to make sure that the door was locked before going to bed.

CHAPTER SEVEN

DAY 2.

9:15 AM, OGRE HEADQUARTERS, HOLLYWOOD, FLORIDA

Mikhail Zholdin didn't base his company in Miami it turned out, but in the neighboring Miami-Dade city of Hollywood, Florida, which for Alexa and Kage meant just a half-hour trip straight up the I95 through the urban developments and into a land of large, blocky white buildings.

"Dee phoned this morning. She said OGRE is some kind of data service for social media. I don't think they handle platforms and emojis and what have you – but the user data for them instead." Kage shook his head a little as he led them away from the interstate, and down wide roads edged with trees, clearly heading for some of the private industrial parks on the western edge of the sister city.

"Oh great. Russian involvement in data servers. This is sounding just the sort of thing I wanted to wake up to," Alexa muttered as she looked out past the perfect white buildings to deep blue skies and vivid green ornamental trees. Everything in Florida was so *bright*, as if all dust and moisture had been sucked out of the very air. She felt exposed and open.

"Well, Bodrov was a manufacturer. There's nothing in his portfolio that has any connection to data services, but I guess we'll see. Zholdin would have been the man he had met that day," Kage commented as he pulled in front of a very modern looking two-story building with a sloping, curved roof, more like a skate ramp than a roof. A lot of the frontage was made of darkened windows, presumably so that the people inside wouldn't boil to death, Alexa thought.

And the CIA is interested in OGRE and Zholdin. Was Zholdin working with the Russians? Alexa ran through various scenarios in her head as they got out of the car and were immediately hit by the wave of oppressive heat.

But if Zholdin himself was a Russian agent of some kind, why would he kill the man before he had met him?

Maybe to throw suspicion off his tracks?

Alexa wondered how she was going to get this guy to admit to any of this, if it were true. Evidence. *Try to find the evidence*, she repeated over and over in her head.

The entrance door was guarded by a bored-looking security officer who checked their badges, but seemed to know they were coming, as he ushered them personally through the wide entrance lobby, past rooms full of people typing at computers and upstairs to a set of glass-fronted offices on the first floor.

"Mr. Zholdin? I have your nine o'clock here," the security guard said as he stuck his head through the door, which Alexa saw had a key card access, and was similarly blacked-out from the outside.

"Send them in, don't leave them waiting!" a clear, high voice with a thick Russian accent said and Alexa and Kage were walking into a modest office room with glass on the inner and outer walls, showing the skyline of Hollywood, Florida, and the crystal-blue seas beyond.

Mikhail Zholdin wasn't like Aleksandr Bodrov, Alexa saw at once. He didn't announce his Russian pride but instead had an office that looked much more in keeping with something out of Silicon Valley. There was a desk and a computer chair, but other than that there was a low couch and three plush sink-in cushion chairs around a bright lime green rug. Over his desk was a wildly impressionistic painting, but apart from a laptop and a small filing cabinet, that was about it.

"Special Agents Murphy and Landers, I take it? Greetings! Welcome. How can I assist the good people of the FBI today?" Zholdin said, and Alexa was surprised to see that he was a man of Bodrov's middle-to-later years, but he spoke and acted like a much younger man. He had a shock of blonde, gelled hair combed over to one side of his head, with the bare side shaved almost completely bald. He wore casual slacks and a light shirt, too, although a pastel blue sports jacket was thrown around the back of his computer chair.

"Tea? Coffee? The Americans love their coffee, don't they?" Zholdin said, his eyes a bright blue as he smiled and gestured for them to take seats, which Alexa realized he meant either the giant plush cushion seats or the low sofa. She perched on the end of the sofa and felt entirely too old.

"Nothing thanks, Mr. Zholdin, line of duty and all that," Murphy said with a grin.

"What, are you afraid that I will poison you? Ha!" Zholdin clapped his hands at the joke as he took a seat beside them, and his smile fell.

"Now really, why would the FBI come to my premises, unless this has something to do with Aleksandr?"

Alexa was stunned a little at his forthrightness. It was a tactic, she realized (*these Russians will throw everything at you*) as she took a breath and found his bright blue eyes peering intently at her. He was way more intelligent than he appeared, she thought.

"I presume you mean Aleksandr Bodrov, the man found murdered yesterday," Alexa said. "Why would you think we are here about that?"

Zholdin laughed just once, a bark of a laugh. "Oh, when you are a Russian with my sort of power in your country, you come to expect a few questions now and then. But more so, I heard about the sad death of my friend just yesterday, and I knew I had a meeting with him. When you called, I naturally assumed you want to ask what that meeting was about?"

Alexa blinked. She had expected at least a little cat-and-mouse before they got down to it.

"Precisely, Mr. Zholdin," Murphy jumped in. "I am sorry to have to ask these questions at what must be a very emotional time for you…" her partner placed the words with heavy certainty, with the clear message saying *you don't look bothered at all that your friend was just murdered.*

Zholdin squinted his eyes for a moment, as if waiting for the right words to come. When they did, they were a hiss.

"Agent…Landers? Yes, Landers. I have been friends with Aleksandr for a long, long time. I have utter contempt for this act, and no, I did not kill my friend and comrade. The fact I am not shouting about it and tearing out my hair is because what good will it do? Your police and your agencies will take one look at me, a Russian ex-national, and you will assume that I am somehow to blame. That somehow this is all some BIG conspiracy, and where will that leave me? My company blacklisted and dropped by shareholders? How is there anything I can do that could possibly help?"

He fairly spat the last words at the end.

There we are, that's the emotion I wanted to see, Alexa thought. Zholdin was putting on a breezy front, but that didn't mean he was telling the truth.

"You can help us, Mr. Zholdin, by describing your last dealing with him, giving us a picture of his life, and telling us what he was scheduled to meet with you about. You never know what piece of information might help us with the case," Alexa said as she leaned forward...

Just as the door opened, and there was another of the security guards, a different one this time, standing in the doorway.

"You have everything you need, Mr. Zholdin? Coffee? Water?" the guard said.

Zholdin's eyes flickered for a moment, and then he shook his head. "We are absolutely fine, thank you, Peter," he dismissed him, and Alexa noticed Zholdin wait for the guard to close the door and for it to mechanically buzz behind him before Zholdin let out a sigh.

Like he doesn't want to speak in front of his guard, Alexa thought with a nudge to Murphy's foot.

"Aleksandr was hoping to expand his portfolio, and he came to me for advice. He wanted to get into electronics, computing, and data services such as mine. Naturally, I was keen to have him throw as much of those billions he made in cement and oil into OGRE. We were due to discuss what his options were," Zholdin's voice was clipped and exact, and Alexa wasn't sure she believed him for a second.

"What about the last time you saw him? Can you remember him talking about any troubles he might be having?" Alexa asked as she scribbled notes.

Data services. Investments. Zholdin hiding something.

"Well, I saw him on Zoom just a few days before he died. He was Aleksandr, always moaning about his sons going off and spending all of his money, moaning about how his wife always wanted more and more of his money to jet off here and there to some fashion show or another," Zholdin said and threw his hands in the air. "What can I say? He was Russian. We like to moan!"

But you just said there was no point in moaning and complaining, Alexa thought. Even though it was a small lie, it was one that stuck in her mind.

THE **FLORIDA GIRL**

"He knew that Alena was just a trophy, but he didn't care, and why would he? Thirty-two years younger than he was and with much better skin!" Zholdin managed to crack another grin, which sent a shiver down Alexa's spine.

Dear God, save me from pervy older men, she thought.

"He always had enemies, but no one he particularly pointed out to me. It seemed that he was more concerned with getting peacefully drunk and making lots and lots of money, so no, I have absolutely no idea who might have killed him..." Zholdin shrugged.

Murphy cleared his throat, leaning over to show a message on his phone to Alexa.

Ch. WILLIAMS. Warrant on VIV Lounge has come through. Ready to pick up at HQ.

Alexa nodded that she got it, shaking her head a little to stay on track.

"Did Mr. Bodrov ever mention the name to Max to you, or Henderson?" she asked.

Zholdin seemed to draw a complete blank. "No, not that I am aware of."

This wasn't going anywhere, Alexa thought with an internal growl. She was pretty sure that the VIV security tapes were going to corroborate Henderson's story, as well. A surge of frustration rushed through her. If Zholdin was behind the murder, then there would be almost no way of proving it through questions alone.

Screw it, she thought.

"Mr. Zholdin, where were you between the hours of eight and eleven o'clock, the morning of Monday the 14th of June?"

Zholdin blinked, but then gave a slow leer of a smile. "There we have it. I knew you would get around to asking me that eventually. You think I killed him. You think I killed my friend!"

Alexa gave him a steely glare (*throw everything you have at them first*). "Do I have to repeat my question, Mr. Zholdin?"

"I was here," Zholdin slapped his hands together. "I, unlike much of my American co-workers, take my duties very seriously indeed. I arrive at my office around seven-thirty, and then I work right through. I believe that starting about nine I was in a conference call with some people from Google. You can check our security cameras if you don't believe me!"

"The Bureau will be putting in a request for them," Murphy nodded before slapping his notebook shut, clearly thinking that the interview was blown.

Not yet, Alexa thought. *I've only just got him angry, and angry people make mistakes.*

"Mr. Zholdin, one last question, if I may. You said that you and Aleksandr go a long way back, I presume you meant you knew each other in Russia?"

Zholdin nodded. "Of course. A simple Google search will confirm this. We grew up in the same village, East Urals Mountains. Aleksandr stayed in Russia and built his empire, and I fled to America at the first opportunity. When he came over, I told him he should come to Florida, where the sun is always shining and it is nothing like the snows of home."

"Oh!" Alexa was surprised. Same village. Same friends. Same enemies?

"So you were *very* close then?"

"We were comrades, Agent Landers." Zholdin said smartly. "Now, if you are done, then I must ask you-"

"If you knew him so well, I will ask you again. Did Aleksandr have enemies *in Russia*?" she asked pointedly.

Zholdin's body suddenly went very, very still. His eyes flickered to the door, and for a moment Alexa was certain that the man was scared that someone was going to come in again.

"Agent Landers. You must be very, *very* serious if you wish to talk of enemies. It is easy in Russia to make enemies. Many people have them, and many people do not survive them."

Yes, Aleksandr did have enemies in Russia, Alexa thought, and those enemies were probably the state. Was Zholdin telling her that the Russian government knew that Aleksandr was one of our assets? That he was killed for betraying the motherland?

But then Zholdin was suddenly leaning forward over his knees, his hands clasped together and he was staring almost feverishly into Alexa's eyes. When he spoke his accent was thicker, truer, like the memories of home had summoned the boy he had once been.

"But let me tell you something about Aleksandr. He would build those ridiculous treehouses in the woods and he would always ask me to come admire them. He said to me, 'One day, Mikhail, I will build a real palace!' and he did. Aleksandr was a very dedicated man, and he did. He built his palace here, in America, and he was free of his enemies….at least for a long, long while."

Mr. Zholdin stood up suddenly as the door opened once more, and this time it was the first security guard, bringing round a tray of bottled water.

"For your guests, sir," the security guard bumbled, and Zholdin laughed suddenly and nervously.

"They are just about to leave, aren't you, Agents? I am sure I have taken up enough of your valuable time already this morning."

"Indeed, Mr. Zholdin," Murphy replied with a brief, perfunctory smile as he and Alexa stood up, nodded at the security guard and then left.

∽

"Did you see his reaction?" Murphy said as soon as they had folded themselves back into the car. Alexa thought that he had the air of an excited puppy when presented with something to dig at.

"Definitely something going on, but what, that is the question…" He quickly pulled them out of park, and took them out of the parking lot and onto the industrial access road.

"He was lying about something," Alexa agreed. "But he didn't at first seem surprised at Aleksandr's death, despite their claimed long friendship…" Alexa drummed her fingers on the windowsill of the car. There was something here, she could feel it.

"He was nervous about the security guards, no?" Murphy pointed out.

"You got that, too? Especially when I started pressing him on Russia," Alexa nodded. "Like maybe he didn't want his guards to overhear him. Do you think…"

She didn't say it, but Kage did.

"That Zholdin is scared that people in his office are Russian agents and the CIA were right? This is a Russian hit, and if so, did Zholdin know about it?" Kage asked about a hundred questions, all of which added an entirely new dimension to their case.

"Okay, three lines of inquiry now," Alexa tried to pull it in. "Henderson/Perelli and any possible drug connection. Alena/Fiancée and the money. Zholdin/Russians and an assassination. Wow. That feels like a lot."

"No better time than to start eliminating suspects then," Kage took the turn out of the industrial park and then pulled over to the side of the road under a stand of large trees. To Alexa's surprise, he took the keys out of the ignition and tossed them to her.

"What?"

"We split up. The warrant has come in on the VIV Lounge, so I suggest that one of us stays to scope out Zholdin, see what moves he makes after we've rattled his cage a bit, and the other goes to the VIV Lounge and checks Henderson's alibi," Murphy said. "And I call dibs on the Zholdin stakeout first."

There was a moment of tense silence in the car for a moment.

"Ugh!" Alexa grumbled. "I was going to call that! I thought you said that you didn't want me charging into Perelli's on my own last night?"

"That was last night, and today we have a warrant." Kage gave one of his winning grins once again.

No, I am not going to get charmed by you, Kage Murphy, Alexa thought.

"Is this some 'I want to be the big shot agent who takes down a Russian spy ring' type deal?'" Alexa said in disgust. She was already pretty much sure that Henderson's alibi was going to clear him anyway, and to her it seemed as though Kage was trying to play the knight in shining armor and 'save the little woman from danger.'

"Mostly," Kage nodded amiably. "Call it job superiority, and I just love stakeouts. But also I don't want to be the agent who got his partner shot on the second day of work. Don't worry, I'll phone HQ to drop me off a spare car..."

I knew it, Alexa thought.

Alexa looked hard at Kage, trying to work out if this was going to turn into a problem, but her big, handsome partner, for all of his apparent affability, wasn't budging.

"Fine." She leaned over and swiped the keys from him as he hopped out the car door.

CHAPTER EIGHT

12:00 NOON. VIV ADULT LOUNGE, MIAMI BEACH

THE VIV ADULT LOUNGE WAS SITUATED ON THE BEACH itself, and it looked to be just about as seedy a place as Alexa had feared.

The FBI agent pulled into the cramped parking lot of a tall purple and white building with a glitzy, mirrored signage that Alexa thought could probably shoot actual laser beams when the Beach was lit up at night. In the front there were palm trees and a fountain, and where they had parked faced a small outdoor smoking area, where a few patrons looked up in alarm at the large black Ford and Detective Dempsey's squad car that had pulled in beside it.

"First warrant," Alexa half cautioned, half congratulated herself as she slid out of the car, fully aware that the management inside had probably already seen them, as two very large security men in tight black tuxedos stuck their head out of the door and hovered nervously.

"You want me to tell them to clear off?" the detective prompted, slamming the door of his car and pulling at the waistband of his jeans as his fellow officer joined him.

"Nah, I got it," Alexa said, feeling a slow burn of anger at all of these men around her who, even in the security services, clearly saw her as another 'little' woman.

If she were to put her finger on it, it would have been Kage smoothly boondoggling her on the Zholdin stakeout, like he was trying to protect her from the dangerous Russians. It hurt, she was happy to admit.

It also made her annoyed.

"FBI, don't even bother," she snapped at the VIV door guards as she flashed her badge towards them. There must have been something thunderous about her tone, as the guards took one look at the small blonde woman coming marching straight for them and stepped out of the way.

"Perelli doesn't pay you enough, huh?" Detective Dempsey laughed as he and the other officer followed the agent in.

Alexa found herself on a sloping upward walkway, leading to a large, darkened room that smelled vaguely of something chemical and scented, like cheap potpourri and spice. The ramp led up to an upper raised area with tables and discrete booths, curving around a lower area with more general tables clustered before a round performance stage, and at least one bar on from that. Already, the place was busy but not crowded, and there was a duo of dancers on the poles of the main stage, and several more scantily clad women speaking in small voices to gentlemen in the booths.

All of this did nothing to help Alexa's mood, especially when she saw the nearest single customer look her over in a bleary, already drunk fashion, doing a double take when he saw Dempsey and the officer behind her.

There was movement at the bar opposite, and Alexa saw one of the bar staff turning and almost running across to where a set of stairs led up to a small balcony above the stage.

Going to warn your boss, huh? Alexa thought as she led the way straight across the raised area to cut a beeline in front of the stage itself to get to the bar.

"Is this costumes night!?" another patron, a white guy with long hair and a Motorhead tee catcalled as he tried to hold his arms out to Alexa, and she spun around and prodded him hard in the chest.

"Back up and sit down before I put you down!" she hissed, stepping forward to get into his face for a moment that made him blink and stagger a few steps back. She saw his eyes take on Dempsey and the officer behind, and realize that *no*, Detective Dempsey was certainly not a part of a dance troupe.

"Oh," the drunk slid down to his seat.

"What's this? What are you doing upsetting my patrons!?" a voice shouted, as a small man in a very expensive steel grey suit pants and white shirt emerged from the office overlooking the stage. The man was completely bald, and his fattened fingers were encrusted with gold rings.

"Mr. Eduardo Perelli, owner of the VIV Adult Lounge?" Alexa looked up. "I have here a warrant for the seizure of your security tapes, covering the period between midday Saturday June 12th and midday Monday June 14th."

The man didn't even splutter, but his face flushed a deeper shade of pink (if such a thing was possible). She saw his eyes squint, flicker towards Dempsey, and then direct his attention at *him*.

"She new, Dempsey?" Perelli asked with a sneer.

"I am the federal agent who is presenting the warrant, if that is what you are asking," Alexa said with a grim smile as she flipped open her badge ID with her free hand.

Perelli scowled for a moment before shrugging as if it were no big deal.

"Sure. Come on out back, and I'll get the files for you. Although they're all on the computer which I need for my business, so…"

"Oh, the FBI budget has already stretched to data sticks," Alexa patted her pockets as Perelli shot Dempsey another heavy scowl before turning to lead them into the back room.

"Maybe Detective Dempsey didn't tell you, Agent, that VIV is a very reputable business. We don't have problems here," Perelli stated as he clomped up the stairs to the small office secreted at the back. Alexa noted how large it was inside, with large black leather sofas in one corner and a small desk crowded with papers. The window down to the performance area was reflective glass, so he could leer to his heart's content; Alexa pulled a disgusted face.

"We've had many influential clients here, too. Mayors, judges, aides, even a senator or two!" Perelli grinned at her the way a cat might do at a mouse.

"And I am sure that you gave them a very warm welcome," Alexa countered, refusing to be goaded. Was he trying to threaten her? Let her know that their client list was so powerful that he could do anything he wanted in this town and get away with it?

Well that's not going to work, Alexa thought as she sat down at the computer desk to find that it was an ancient desktop, and asked Perelli to log in.

"You know that VIV Management will of course be putting in a complaint," Perelli said lightly as he leaned over Alexa's shoulder and put in the necessary password, opening the windows that showed the array of security camera files, each one in neat yellow file folders.

"I'm sure you will," Alexa said. She didn't bother to hide her disgust at what she saw around her. It wasn't just the objectification of women that she objected to in principle – she knew full well that many of the women below probably made good money out of their work – it was all the other risks and dangers that came alongside it. What happened if a woman got groped? Or if they tried to complain? How many 'special favors' were they asked to perform by clients with far too much money?

"What is this all about, anyway? If you have suspicions of something that happened in these walls, you need to say it, I know the law!" Perelli grumbled, for Alexa to select the files and copy them over to the data stick. She wasn't going to say anything, but to her surprise, Dempsey spoke up behind her.

"We're looking for someone. Max Henderson. He claims he was here Monday morning, and we need to know if that checks out," the detective stated matter-of-factly.

Shut the hell up, Dempsey! Alexa spun around in her chair to stare at him, but the detective had his back to her.

"Oh, Henderson! I see what's going on here. He's the guard for the Bodrov father, isn't he?" Perelli gave a large chuckle, the sort you might hear when someone *else* falls on their face.

"You know him?" Alexa interjected.

Perelli shot her a quick glance and then continued talking to the detective as if she wasn't even there.

"Everyone on the Beach knows Henderson. He's been causing trouble and mouthing off for years. And everyone knows that he was working for the Bodrovs, mostly because Dimitre and Vadim are usually in here with him!" Perelli laughed.

"Was Mr. Henderson here on Monday 14th, around 9:30 am, Mr. Perelli?" Alexa tried to work out what this meant. It wasn't just Henderson who was connected to Perelli, it was Aleksandr's two sons, as well.

"Yeah, he was here, early, too. I remember because there's only a few diehards that ever come in first thing, and Henderson looked desperate to burn some money before lunchtime." Perelli gave another mountain-sized shrug like it was no big deal.

Damnit, Alexa thought. Henderson had just had his alibi confirmed, and she was sure that when they checked the tapes that it would only prove it, too. *That leaves Mikhail Zholdin, and the wife.* She slipped the data stick into her pocket and stood up.

"Off so early? Keep an eye on your mail, you'll be getting a complaint, no doubt about it," Perelli said with his shark-like grin as Alexa made to leave.

"Thank you so much for all your cooperation, Mr. Perelli," she growled at him as she marched out.

CHAPTER NINE

1:30 PM. OGRE HEADQUARTERS

THE WORST THING ABOUT DOING A STAKEOUT IN MIAMI was the heat, Kage thought as he once again sipped at his water bottle and regular grey cap that he had been supplied with, along with the spare FBI car.

The problem with this particular stakeout, however, was the fact that there weren't really any suitable places to hide out and watch the building; and he couldn't even get a good eye on the building from this range, either. Kage cursed under his breath.

The OGRE Headquarters was sited in an industrial park of similar business units, so Kage had chosen a neighboring unit across the street to park in before settling back in his seat and watching the doors. He had a camera with a telephoto lens which he kept trained on the doors and windows, and it was powerful enough to even see Mikhail Zholdin's office.

"But so far, all that it looks like you've been up to is pushing paper," Kage sighed, tightening the focus on the camera so that he could see inside the window of Zholdin's desk, for the man to be leaning over his laptop and apparently working.

Ugh. It was kind of boring, Kage had to admit, and, in that way that it did, his thoughts wondered to his new partner, Alexa Landers.

I hope she's alright down there, he grimaced to himself for a moment. Perelli was a tricky customer, not the least because there was heavy evidence that he was family, a mafia capo, but also because there were rumors that he had politicians and judges and cops on the payroll. It wouldn't be the first time that people were paid off to turn a blind eye, Kage thought.

But then he considered what he had seen of Alexa so far, and he had to stifle a sudden laugh.

"Good luck trying to intimidate her!" he whispered to the empty air of his car.

Alexa reminded him of someone, didn't she? Someone he once knew... Kage realized as he stared at his reflection in the driver's mirror. That was what was so appealing and inspiring about her. That was why he had warmed to the new agent from Quantico as soon as he had met her. Alexa had the same sort of stubborn spirit, the same infallible belief that she could do anything.

"Damnit!" Kage hissed, as he felt the heat build up behind his eyes, wanting to turn into tears, but he wouldn't let it. Mel had been his fiancée, and she was three years dead now. Truck accident. Died instantly.

Kage snapped at himself, irritated that his emotions could be so close to the surface after all this time.

Brap-Brap-Brap!

Kage jumped as there was a sudden rap on his window on the other side of him; he startled and looked around to see that there was a female security guard from the building he had chosen to park at, leaning down to peer into the window at him, but clearly couldn't see much thanks to the fact that the windows were darkened.

"Hey, who's in there!? You can't park here, you know!" Kage heard her voice as a muffled reply, but in fact he knew that she had to be shouting it.

Damnit! Kage stashed the camera in the glove box and slid over to the window side of the seat to lower the window.

"Who do you think you are? This isn't somewhere you can just park! If you've got an appointment with Maria's Veterinary Supplies then you need to come to the front desk!!" the woman was demanding, scowling at Kage as he considered whether or not to try and bluff his way through, and thought better of it.

"It's okay, it's official business. I need you to go away," he said in a perfectly calm manner, holding up his FBI badge.

"FBI!? What's happened?" the security guard asked in alarm as Kage inwardly raged.

Just go away! Get the hint and go away!

"I'm on official Bureau business, ma'am. I *really* need you to go away now thank you," he stated once again, a little clearer, and shook his ID.

"Oh, I see. It's a stakeout-" the security guard responded, just as he heard a roar of a car engine behind him.

No-no-no-no!

With a sick premonition, he knew what was about to happen even before he got eyes on the large metallic blue Chevrolet that was pulling out of the OGRE parking lot.

"Is there anything I can help you with-?" she asked as Kage tried to peer at the license plate.

Florida 44C-

It was a match to the car that Mikhail Zholdin had registered with the DMV. Apparently this 'workaholic XCEO' was taking the afternoon off early, just as Kage had feared would happen after their interview.

"Are you watching the OGRE building?" the security guard asked as Kage swore again, and again as he stashed his badge, seeing

Zholdin's Chevy turn down the street back towards Hollywood and turn the corner at the entrance to the industrial park.

"I gotta go. It's been a pain in the ass-" Kage said as he started the ignition, and with barely a wave to clear the guard out of the way, he was pulling out of park and turning to follow.

Where you going, Zholdin? You got something to hide? Kage thought as he turned the corner to the main industrial park throughway to see it clear. Zholdin had turned left at the end, not down towards Miami, but up the coast.

Maybe he was just heading home after a long day. Maybe he wasn't.

Kage allowed his car to speed up to the corner and take it moderately fast, and was immediately thankful for the long, straight roads that were common to Florida. He could still see Zholdin's metallic blue Chevy up ahead.

He wasn't the only car on the road, which was good. Less easy for Zholdin to spot him right behind him, although Kage knew from experience that drivers rarely made a note of the exact cars following them.

Most people only pay attention when they have to make a decision, or have to react, Kage thought. Like if someone was chasing their bumper or threatening them. It was a strange quirk of human nature that Kage had never really understood, although he remembered the way that Mel had always told him, "Most people are too busy thinking about their own lives! They can't be on alert all the time!"

But Kage never thought about what he did as being on alert. He was curious, that's all. Intensely curious about life and the people around him and their lives. That was at least part of the reason why he had become an FBI agent in the first place.

Zholdin's Chevy stayed on the 95 for the next twenty minutes or so, until they passed out of the reach of Hollywood and then he was turning abruptly left, along one of the roads that stretched out to…

The Everglades. Kage suddenly got a whole lot more interested. Out here the houses were cheaper and it was mostly workers in the local resorts and factories. The further west you went, and you would be seeing people who worked in fishing, who had lived out here for generations.

Zholdin kept driving, taking the smaller side roads until the houses were getting sparser and further apart, and the land on either side of the road started to look watery. The road itself rose a good few feet from the surrounds, and Kage allowed Zholdin to pull way ahead until he was little more than a golf ball in the distance. There was nowhere to go out here. Nowhere unless you really liked fishing or bird life.

The thing about Florida was that half of it was swamp and the other half of it was a playground of wealth and vice. There was a good reason it had been known as Vice City during the '80s because it was easy to move large shipments of cocaine through the endless shifting swamps and tributaries of the Everglades and very rarely get caught at all.

The horizon all around was a green haze, and the water had disappeared for the road to be densely surrounded by large overgrown swamp bushes and spindly, twisting trees. Overhead there passed a flight of some large white birds with wingspans so wide that Kage reckoned they would have been even wider than he was tall.

Zholdin was slowing down ahead of him and turning off where there was a causeway-type road leading to the left. The track wasn't even freeway anymore, but layers of ageing tarmac poured over itself every spring by the Florida Highways state people.

Nowhere to go to, Zholdin, Kage thought as he allowed his own car to slow as it followed to the turn off, reaching a crawl as he didn't want to suddenly turn to face the parked car sitting right there in front of him.

There were homesteads and old porch houses dotted around out here, of course, people who had bought up partials of the old swamp land back when the state was selling it for a mere hundreds of dollars per acre. The state had wanted anyone they could find to do something with it, Kage thought. Back then they had deemed the Everglades an unmanageable green hell and hadn't seen the advantages for wildlife and tourism that it did now.

"But I really don't think that you own any of these places out here, do you, Mikhail?" Kage murmured to himself as he edged around the corner and parked under a wide overhanging spray of green.

The metallic blue Chevy was a good three hundred yards ahead, where the road branched off to meet one of the old observation towers. It was parked at the bottom, next to another car.

"Oh sheee-!" Kage froze for a moment, wondering if the two cars had registered him, but they hadn't. Very, very slowly, he reversed his car back up to the corner as if he had just taken a wrong turning, and instead parked where he couldn't be seen.

Now came the fun part.

Moving quickly, Kage got his camera and hopped out of his vehicle to jog to the turn in the road, hunkering down by the side of the road and aiming his telescopic lens at the base of the tower.

"One metallic blue Chevy, registered to Mikhail Zholdin," he whispered for the aide of his phone's recorder. He felt the tremor of excitement as he focussed on the next car.

"Smaller cream sedan. Florida plates." The range on his camera was just good enough to be able to get a clear shot of the second license plate, and then there was the muffled slam of a door as Mikhail was getting out, and another slam as another man did, too.

Snap. Snap-snap.

Kage started to taking photos of the second guy, but he could already see that there was something very suspicious going on here. The second figure was shorter than Zholdin, dressed in an orange sleeveless button-up shirt with a large-brimmed panama hat on. Kage thought he might have short dark hair, but he couldn't tell for sure from this distance.

The man in the panama hat was gesticulating at Zholdin, using his hands expressively as the Russian appeared to hold their ground, nod, and then interject with their own exhortations.

Kage wished that he had better listening devices, or any at all. But that would require quite a serious court order, and right now in their investigation, without any solid evidence or motives leading straight to Zholdin, Kage wasn't sure that they would get it.

"What does Zholdin look to gain from Aleksandr's death?" Kage once again murmured for the purposes of his phone's voice notes. As far as he could see, that was precisely nothing.

Oh, of course there was the idea that maybe Zholdin was in on the assassination of Bodrov along with the soon-to-be-wife and the sons, maybe they would split the money four ways…

"Nah," Kage muttered. That sounded too complicated, didn't it?

"Maybe a better question to ask is how could Zholdin have aided or supported the killing?" he whispered, as the argument was clearly a heated one ahead, and the man in the panama hat appeared to be telling Bodrov off.

"Some sort of hold over Zholdin? A superior?" Kage whispered, taking as many snaps of the car and the mysterious man as he could before the argument abruptly concluded, and the man in the white panama began striding back to the driver's side of the car.

Kage swore, scrabbling backwards from the corner and racing back to his car. He was sure that he heard the distant roar of an engine as he threw open his own door and jumped in.

I have to get out of here. Kage turned the key and hit the accelerator. Whatever business it was that Zholdin had been undertaking out here, Kage didn't know what it was.

But who drove way out into the Everglades just to have an argument with someone?

CHAPTER TEN

10:30 PM. OUTSIDE MIAMI HEIGHTS, MIAMI BEACH

IT WAS NIGHTTIME, BUT THE MAN IN THE DARK TRACKSUIT and hoody knew that wouldn't slow down his targets.

That was the thing about rich playboys, they never had the sense to stop, the man considered as he waited on the strip below the expensive, luxurious apartment complex known as Miami Heights.

The building itself wasn't one of the tallest ones on the beach, but it was probably one of the most expensive, the man considered. For one thing, each level had a wide balcony that ran around each level, with the glint of windows behind. At the top was a pool, he already knew, and it had a full twenty-four-hour concierge service.

The man narrowed his eyes a little as his hands tightened inside the pockets of his hoody. There was a glimmer of anger there, but he pushed it down, always down. Let the anger concentrate and harden, becoming carbon, becoming dynamite…

The Beach was busy as it always was, the man saw. He sat on one of the ornate benches by a giant palm tree as lowriders bumped and shook their way up the Beach road, blaring out bass-heavy tunes and hoots of laughter. There were parties going on on the Beach behind him, just as there always was.

In short, this night was very much like every other night at the Beach.

The man smiled a small, thin-lip smile. Perfect. It was almost too easy in this town, not that he wanted things any different…but for a moment he wondered if all of those years of Miami being one of the most degraded, decadent cities in all of America had somehow made murder a fact of the air, and the climate. It was the hot weather, it sent people crazy. It was also a town that was used to accommodating predators, like the alligators and crocs out in the swamps, or the Blue Whites out in the seas.

Maybe people here were more eager to turn a blind eye to the predators in their midst. Maybe the Floridians had learned to keep their eyes down and not say anything…

But that was enough philosophizing; the man noticed the two small, black, people carriers pull up that was the change of shift for the staff inside Miami Heights.

Perfect timing. In his hand he clutched at the small square of black plastic that didn't belong to him. If he brought it out and held it to the light, he wouldn't see his name (not that anyone used the stranger's real name anymore, he had made sure of that) but he would see Max Henderson, GUEST PASS, Miami Beach.

He waited for the two vans to pull into the staff parking lot at the back of the complex, and then followed them in.

"Henderson!? Is that you?" said the tinny, scratchy voice of Vadim Bodrov on the other side of the apartment intercom.

Ridiculous, the man could have laughed at the state of the security. *Why didn't they have an actual screen viewer?* Another problem of these super rich apartment blocks, they think that their wealth protects them. They get sloppy, just like Alexandr Bodrov had.

Instead, they had this ridiculous intercom system inside the apartment, thinking that the only people inside the building would already be the ones with the special pass cards.

(Which was technically true, the man considered).

His injection into the site was considerably easier than he had thought as well, and the guest pass that the Bodrov brothers had given to Henderson was all he needed to get through the public area doors. It didn't let him into the actual room of course, but that wouldn't matter in a few moments.

"It's not Henderson. He couldn't make it, but I've got a package from him," the man said in a gruff, restrained voice.

"What?" There was a snarl of glitchy sound from the intercom, and then the voice came back. "We didn't order anything, but-"

The sound of splintering glass behind him.

"*Dimitre*, shut it!" the man shouted, before his voice returned to the intercom.

"You'd better come in. God knows I'll be glad for something right now…"

I bet you will, the man thought. He didn't smile at this. It wasn't close enough to the kill for him to get any pleasure yet. He flickered his eyes towards the small corridor camera mounted at the end of the hall and saw that the light was still off. *Good. The jammer had worked.* Again, he briefly considered how stupid wealthy people were.

There was a small chime of a buzz, and the door opened to reveal the pale, mortified face of Vadim Bodrov. He had been a thin, pale fish of a man to begin with it seemed, and despite the short, oiled hair and the very expensive clothes, there was a *weak* quality to him that the stranger took an instant dislike to.

By the deep shadows around his red-rimmed eyes, and the way that he was clutching onto the door frame, it was clear that the man was terrified. And drunk. Or intoxicated. Probably both.

Death does strange things to people, the stranger knew only too well. Some people became catatonic with grief. Others descended into hedonism from which they never returned, and it appeared that the two Bodrov brothers, already well known on the Miami Beach elite party-scene, had taken the latter route.

"Well? Where is it! Only Henderson usually comes up here!" Dimitre said, sniffing several times loudly as there was a groan from down the wide hall, somewhere in the palatial apartment.

"I got it, it's a bit delicate, y'know?" the man said gruffly, shrugging a shoulder down the hall towards where the camera was.

"Oh, this building doesn't give a crap about what we do, or who we do it with!" Vadim nearly shouted as he staggered back down the hall, waving the stranger in behind him.

"And I should think so, the amount of money that we give to them for the apartment!"

Vadim, with the air of those who had been born with vast amounts of wealth, blithely accepted the fact that the delivery man would follow him in as told. Aleksandr's eldest son led the way down the hallway past doors leading onto at least two bathrooms (both were bigger than many people had the square-feet to rent as an apartment) and another curving corridor that must have led to the bedrooms.

The center piece of the entire luxury apartment, however, was the living room. It occupied almost the entire length of the apartment itself, with glass-fronted windows and doors leading onto the spacious balcony beyond.

The room was split into three levels, with the lowest level holding giant floor cushions and low sofas, and steps that led to a middle 'dining' area with a full banqueting table underneath suspended chandeliers. The stranger wasn't surprised to see that the final area past the dining space *wasn't* a kitchen, as presumably the people who could afford to live here didn't have to worry about getting fresh food delivered, but instead it was wood panelled, and looked more like a large study.

It was in this final space where Dimitre, the younger Bodrov brother was currently sprawled on green leather armchair, barely able to open his eyes.

"Well, come on, where is it? I'm not here playing host, buddy!" Vadim snapped at the stranger. The man never had a problem with his job at all, but that small moment of insolence and arrogance was enough to make sure that he enjoyed it.

The strange pulled out the package from where it had been snug against his ribs.

It certainly wasn't drugs; it was a gun, and now the stranger was calmly screwing in the silencer-suppressor in full view of Aleksander Bodrov's eldest son.

The stranger didn't look down. He kept his eyes focussed on Vadim's because he wanted to see the moment when he realized what was about to happen. He wanted to see the shock, the surprise, and the sudden acceptance of how wrong he had been.

The stranger didn't have to wait long.

CHAPTER ELEVEN

DAY 3.

9:00. AM FBI HEADQUARTERS

"Murphy, we have it! Pinkerton is saying he has the attack vector!" Alexa said excitedly as soon as her partner walked into the war room, still with a steaming cup of coffee in hand.

"Huh?" Kage blinked a little blearily, and Alexa saw him taking in the fact that the war room was a mess, and that there were folders, diagrams, and papers everywhere.

And the rolled up sleeping bag that she'd used last night on one of the chairs.

"Did you sleep here last night, Landers?" Kage groaned as he cleared a space amidst all the papers and sat down, nursing his coffee.

Has he got a hangover!? Alexa almost kicked him. Her partner looked terrible, like he was ill.

"Yes, I did. It's easier for me to think when I'm nearer the information," Alexa said, throwing her empty carton of coffee, with all the practise of a long night shift, into the wastepaper basket before forcing herself to slow down.

"This won't do. Not everyone can go as fast as you do, kiddo," echoed something her dad had told her, and not just once. Back then it probably had been something about Jeb, and how Alexa always resented waiting for him to catch up. But it wasn't just that, and that wasn't just what her father had been talking about.

Sometimes I can't stop. Alexa shook away the decades' old argument. It was a thing that others might have called perfectionism, or obsessiveness, but it had secured her the top graduating marks from Quantico, after all.

But still, her dad had been right. Sometimes it was worth slowing down for the others in the room, wasn't it? Especially when you were a team.

She looked at Kage.

"Are you okay? You look awful."

"Ha, thanks for the compliment," Kage laughed before he wiped his face with one of those big hands of his and took a long draught of coffee.

"I just didn't catch much sleep myself last night. No biggie," he commented and shrugged it off, and there, once again was his bright and engaging smile. "Did you get my lead about the car, and the man that Mikail Zholdin met yesterday? I think we're definitely onto something there…"

Hm, Alexa looked at her partner for a moment longer, and this time she wasn't fooled by his breezy and what she had considered to be insubstantial nature. *You have some hidden depths to you,*

Special Agent Kage Murphy, don't you? she thought before turning back to the case at hand.

"Right. Yes, thank you, I got your messages, and I've already put in a request to the DMV for the vehicle owner. That shouldn't take long. Zholdin sent over the time logs and CCTV footage of where he was on Monday 14th – he must have done that before leaving work early yesterday – and they show him entering the office, at his desk and in web meetings during the time of the murder, so we know that it wasn't him who pulled the trigger, but it's clear that Zholdin is up to something that he doesn't want anyone else to know about. Suggestions?"

She watched him as he pulled a face, then spread a hand open in the air.

"At this time? Could be anything, but what are our facts?" He held up a finger for each point.

"Aleksandr Bodrov arranged a meeting with Zholdin, his old friend, for later that day to discuss business deals."

"Zholdin wasn't the murderer."

"Henderson wasn't the murderer."

"We know that Zholdin was pretty damn jumpy. Especially when it came to talk of the GRU or SVG."

"Then, after our questioning him, he arranges a meet with – somebody – that he goes so far out into the Everglades that it's obvious he doesn't want anyone to know about it."

"Us, or the Russians?" Alexa asked, standing up to start working the whiteboard. In the center, she put ALEKSANDR BODROV in large capital letters, around which she wrote MIKHAIL ZHOLDIN and MAX HENDERSON. After a thought, she also added PERELLI VIV, ALENA GRIGIN (fiancée) and then the two sons, DIMITRE and VADIM.

Alexa looked at the chart, already full of names, and crossed a line across ZHOLDIN and HENDERSON's names.

"Working hypothesis," Kage called out. "We know that Aleksandr was an American asset. He was involved in American business with Zholdin. What if the Russians decided to take him out for betraying the motherland or something. Zholdin knows that his OGRE is as leaky as hell, and he tries to warn Aleksandr."

Alexa hummed and moved to the nearest whiteboard, writing RUSSIAN STATE. "That is entirely plausible, given how the CIA warned us just yesterday, but we need some concrete evidence. Also, who would Zholdin be driving out the Everglades to meet? How does that connect with Aleksandr?"

She stepped back and looked at the board for a second. "Of course, it could just as easily be the other way around. Zholdin is in fact coerced or in league with the Russian intelligence services, arranges the hit and the meeting – uses the no-show business meeting as cover – then, when we push him, he meets his Russian handler or whatever to say the heat is on him?"

She stepped forward and wrote /ZHOLDIN ALLY next to RUSSIAN STATE, and then underneath it wrote RUSSIAN STATE /ZHOLDIN COMPLICIT, and next drew a line from both of them across to the adjacent board and the name of MIKHAL ZHOLDIN.

Kage grumbled that it could be the case. "We'll need evidence of conspiracy to commit murder to hold that up in court. Even if we get a positive ID on the man that Zholdin met, without a record of what they said it is all conjecture."

Alexa sighed. Kage was right; it felt like that they had a bunch of the pieces in front of them, but there was no way to fit them together. Not yet, anyway.

This is one big puzzle. It has a solution, we just have to see how the pieces turn and fit... Alexa thought before a fragment of something her father had said long ago resurfaced.

It was when she had been struggling at the Academy. It was her second year after graduating cum laude from her criminology degree, and she had thrown herself into Quantico with all the speed and obsession that was her nature.

And she broke. She was happy to admit it now, the FBI Academy had asked more of her than anything else every had done in her life, and she gave it more still. Her workload had been punishing, ten-hour days at the academy and then another six to eight in physical training and study. She had come home on one of the breaks uptight and emotional – and that was when her father had given her the best piece of advice yet.

'It's all about perspective, kiddo. You might be looking at this situation from where you are now, but turn it around, step out of it, look at it from the other side and you might see that there's something else entirely going on…'

"Perspective," Alexa said, as an idea struck her and she grabbed her phone.

"What is it?" Kage asked.

"We need more information. More perspective. I'm sending an email to that Officer Voorn woman from the CIA to see if they are willing to forward us any potential Russian operatives they might have tracked in the area. I want a list of anyone who might have got off a plane at Miami airport in the last month."

"Can they give us that information?" Kage asked out loud.

Alexa grimaced. "If they want to solve a murder on home soil, they'd better!"

She fired the email and then turned back to the board, placing a question mark in front of the two RUSSIAN STATE hypotheses.

"Can you put a request into Chief Williams for surveillance on Zholdin? I'm sure the CIA already do that, but that might be a step too far, and it wouldn't be admissible in court-"

"Right on it, but I gotta say it's unlikely," Kage said, moving over to one of the drawers to pull out a form from a stack of various departmental requests.

"The chief will have to okay this, and then it will go the legal team, and finally before a judge. They can be pretty twitchy about surveillance given the current climate, but the issue for us is that Zholdin already has a cast iron alibi. The courts like to see clear and pressing need to invade a citizen's security."

Alexa nodded. That was fair, she guessed. Annoying, but fair. "Tell them it could be a case of national security, which if we discover a GRU/SVG ring here in Miami, it certainly would be."

Alexa paused as she realized what she had just said. Was she really about to bust a secret ring of spies and murderers? How much stink would this cause, both politically and nationally?

Whatever, she growled to herself. At the end of the day, an American citizen was killed on American soil in what appeared to be a cold and calculated attack. That couldn't be allowed to happen, no matter who had fired the bullet.

Next, she moved back to the hypothesis board and, underneath RUSSIAN STATE, she wrote PERELLI / DRUGS? She knew that she was going way out on a limb with this one, as the evidence was even less for this than there was for the Russian operatives.

"Henderson is in the clear, but he has connections to a reputed mafia capo, aka Perelli. That isn't something that we can ignore lightly. Working hypothesis: Aleksandr somehow pissed off the mob, I guess with his business dealings, and they took him out. Thoughts?"

"Well, no evidence now that Henderson is in the clear," Kage pointed out.

"Henderson turning up to have a fight with the guards pretty much around the time Aleksandr was murdered?" Alexa countered. "Sounds like a pretty good distraction if you ask me."

Kage made an agreeing noise. "Of course, we know the mafia have the resources, the skills, and the contacts to get this done. But their hits are usually much more showy, aren't they? They whack people to make a public statement, a warning to everyone else."

Whack? Who says whack anymore? Alexa thought. "Okay, '90s," she smirked, but still drew a dotted line from the theory back to Perelli's name, and then another leading to the two sons, DIMITRE and VADIM.

"Perelli told us that Henderson was usually at the VIV Lounge in the company of Bodrov's sons, whom we still haven't heard from yet!" Alexa scowled at her phone.

Dempsey said he was going to get a car sent over to bring them in for questioning. Why hasn't he done that yet!?

Of course, there were always many reasons why suspects couldn't be questioned when you wanted them to be. They could be at work, away, in hiding. But the idea that they hadn't seen the news of their own father's death was ridiculous.

Unbidden, her mind flew to her last exchange with Detective Dempsey. How Perelli had known him, talked over her, and asked whether 'she was new.'

Was there something there I need to look into? she thought. She even flickered an eye at Kage, but he was busy writing his surveillance request form.

We'll cross that bridge when we come to it. The very notion of police bribery and corruption was odious to her, and perhaps just as alarming as the idea that there could be foreign agents running around assassinating people under her watch.

BRRP!

It was at that point that one of the laptops made a sound.

Incoming Call: Pinkerton CSO.

"Oh great! That's the ballistics report!" Alexa moved to tap the laptop screen before casting it to the big wall screen in the room.

"Good morning, Officer, I hope you have some good news for us!" Alexa said, already moving to the board to start writing down extra notes as needed.

The face of the older man creased a little, reminding Alexa of the way that clothes crumple.

"I would hardly say that any news is good about a murder, Special Agent; however, I can share with you some findings from my team."

Okay. Remember to slow down. Be human, Alexa thought.

For a second the face the Cecil leaned in as he squinted at his own keyboard, and then he was typing something on the keys for the screen to suddenly show a stub of bronze, compacted like a squashed-out cigarette.

"Our CSI team drained the pool at the Bodrov residence, and we found this, the remains of the bullet that presumably killed the victim-"

There was a click and then a hi-res picture of the emptied pool (still with a faint pinkish sheen from the blood-dyed water). The pool was tiled, with a checkerboard pattern running around the lip of the pool before being replaced by white tiles. In the center of the picture there was a large, smashed tile just under the checkerboard pattern, radiating cracks.

The next image showed a close-up of it, where the tile had been completely fractured in a spider web pattern with a hole punching through to the cement mortar in the middle.

"This was below the water line, and as you can see, the bullet did considerable damage when it hit."

"That's no hollow point," Alexa said immediately. She had handled plenty of guns in her life, and one thing she knew was that a hollow point did obscene amounts of damage to the target thanks to its fragile nose rupturing upon impact, but it would very rarely have the energy to do something as fierce as the damage she was seeing *after* passing through a body as well.

Unless there were two bullets? she considered.

"*You are correct, Special Agent Landers.*" The slide moved back to the original brass circular stub.

"*This is indeed the bullet that passed through the victim, as it has traces of his DNA in the form of microscopic blood on it. It is also no 9mm or hollow point, but a 7.62 rifle bullet-*"

"Oh crap," Alexa said, as she felt the blood drain from her face. She knew what that meant.

"What!? What's up?" Kage asked, who clearly couldn't see the implications that Alexa could, just from that one bullet.

"Bodrov was shot at distance. That's the only reason to use a rifle," Alexa replied. A rifle was also a marksman's tool. It gave precision and lethal killing power thanks to its larger shells.

"*I will leave the analysis up to you, but yes, I believe the same thing,*" Pinkerton commented, as the presentation images once again changed, this time to the previous simulation of the pool and the spinning stick man inside of it.

"*Working with the pathology team, I believe that I have even managed to ascertain the attack vector,*" the chief scientific officer stated, as the image magnified to show the stick man in much closer detail, with a dotted red line reaching towards the throat, and then out again.

"*When the bullet struck the victim, there was damage to the spine in the neck. This resulting in the bullet altering its course by a fraction of fifteen degrees or so, if its exit is placed in the center of the wound on the victim's shoulder and neck...*"

There were attending images from the autopsy, too, and they were grisly. Aleksandr Bodrov no longer looked like a human anymore, but a doll, a puppet made of meat.

"*In ballistics, we then draw the fastest line from the point of impact, which in our case is the swimming pool tile. As the tile was at the rear right of the pool, and we know that the bullet performed a fifteen-degree ricochet when it struck the harder bones of the victim's neck, we can orientate the body to the correct position when they were shot."*

The next slide zoomed out, showing the stick man with the entire schematic of the pool around him. He was facing out towards the end of the estate's garden…

"The private marina," Alexa said. "Bodrov was shot by either someone on the marina, or someone on a boat. But what was the force of impact? Have you got a calculation?"

On the other end of the screen the CSO blinked. *"I hadn't expected you to know so much about ballistics, Special Agent."*

"I know more about guns, Officer," Alexa admitted.

Pinkerton nodded and explained that the Bureau had acres of data on force tests from projectiles of varying calibres at different ranges, and what sorts of changes occur when they hit slabs of pig flesh, brick walls, and so on.

"The 7.62 is a very powerful shell, especially in the right rifle. From the size of the exit wound and the amount of damage done to the tile, then we estimate that the shot could have been fired from anything between approximately 400-to-500 yards away. The bullet still had enough force to cause that much damage to the tiles, but the damage to the cadaver would have been much worse had the shot been closer," Pinkerton said dourly.

"Worse? It tore his neck apart?" Kage said with a faintly queasy expression.

"Exactly," Alexa said. She'd seen that impact data before, and it could have been worse, so much worse.

"Four-to-five-hundred yards away…" She didn't have to find the schematics for the entire Bodrov residence. From the pool to the very end of the marina could only be twenty yards at most.

"The shot came from the water?" Kage said.

"More than just that," Alexa pointed out, as her hands scrambled through the papers to find a large map of Star Island, the McArther Causeway, and the adjacent Miami Beach beyond that.

"How far is it from Star Island to the Beach? It's not a mile, is it?"

Kage shook his head. "No way. A couple of miles at least, looking at it on this."

Realization hit Alexa hard. "The killer must have been military trained."

"What!?" Kage asked.

"That's technically a long-range shot, anything over that distance is considered long range. While there are civilians who can perform at that level, we are talking dedication to the level of professionalism. Even game hunters and sport shooters don't generally have those kinds of skills…"

But the military does. Quantico does.

"Are you sure?" Kage asked.

Alexa nodded with certainty. "I would bet on it. The impact damage isn't enough to place the shot from the Beach itself, but as Pinkerton says, from the water. And that means that the shooter had to be on a boat. Which, because it's on the water, is always moving, right?" Alexa thought quickly, her mind racing as all the bits of information rotated and fit together in her mind.

"Shooting a moving target, that is, Aleksandr bobbing about in his pool."

"Shooting *from* a moving target because they had to be on a boat."

"And on top of all of that, shooting at distance, with enough precision to score a kill to the neck." Alexa unfolded her evidence in rapid, staccato burst style before leaning back.

"We're looking at a military sniper, I'd bet on it."

She looked up to find Kage regarding her heavily.

"Okay, I'm buying it, and to be honest it's made this whole investigation look even more terrifying. Because now we have to ask what military trained the killer – and I'm guessing Russian!"

It was at that point that Alexa's phone rang once more, and this time it was Detective Dempsey.

"Special Agent Landers? You might want to get your asses over to Miami Heights, on the Beach right now. I'm standing on the seventh floor of the apartment building, looking down at the two dead bodies of Dimitre and Vadim Bodrov."

CHAPTER TWELVE

10:45 AM. MCARTHUR CAUSEWAY – MIAMI BEACH

"We need to find out what boats were on the water at the time that Aleksandr was shot," Alexa said as they raced through traffic to the MacArthur Causeway. It wouldn't be a long ride, but for Alexa it couldn't be fast enough. It felt like everything was coming at them at a hundred miles per hour.

Did I get that perspective, Dad? Alexa thought.

Military trained sniper. Russian connections to both Aleksandr and Zholdin. A part of her didn't expect the case to be adding up this way. It felt too huge, too large for an agent straight out of the Academy to deal with.

"Let's say we *have* got a Russian assassin, probably working for the GRU, the military intelligence inside Russia, they'll probably be long gone by now!" Alexa said in exasperation as the traffic slowed to a crawl, and a warning light came on Kage's dashboard.

"Damnit. You didn't fill the car up when you brought it back from Perelli's last night?" Kage said, and for the first time there was a twinge of annoyance in his voice.

"Oh snap, sorry, I didn't even realize…" Alexa said, but her heart wasn't in the apology. Couldn't Kage see that this murder case was about to go international?

We're going to need flight manifests of all Russians or Russian-adjacent citizens travelling probably not just in the last week, maybe the last month. They might not even have alighted at Florida International Airport, but up in Tampa, or Orlando, and travelled down by rental.

And *then* there was the nightmare of trying to figure out who it was, and getting in touch with the State Department.

"I mean, Russia will never openly admit it was them that killed Bodrov anyway, will they? And it'll be some miracle if we could ever get any kind of extradition order agreed on…" she said as they pulled into the gas station, with Kage muttering his apology for the delay, before stating that "Well, the Bodrov sons won't be any less dead by the time we get there…"

Alexa supposed that the small detour would perhaps give the CSI people time to conduct their preliminaries.

With nothing better to do, she got out of the car as Kage filled up the truck to go pay at the station and pick up bottles of water. She had already drunk a lot of bottled water before coming to Florida, but this omnipresent heat made her feel like she was constantly in danger of turning into a dried-out husk.

"Ninety-eight eighty, please, ma'am," the till operator said as Alexa gave him a quick, unemotional smile and flashed the service card that Kage had given her, which put all FBI expenses on a singular account, and when the man saw the card, his face blanched, then nodded abruptly as he took payment.

That done, she turned back down the aisle to the forecourt, and was just leaving the door when a man bumped into her.

"Ah, sorry-" she said as she stumbled out of the way, for the man, a tall, slender middle-aged man to scowl at her and pick up the paper he had dropped, and march into the station behind her.

Fine. Some people are just uptight, she thought briefly and disregarded the experience until she had gotten back into the car and they were once again moving, joining the stream of traffic on the McArthur Causeway, heading straight across to Miami Beach.

Kage was already busy on the phone with FBI HQ.

"Switchboard – is that Nolene? Hi, Nolene, I need you to put me through to Miami Coast Guard. Direct line, please," Kage instructed as they exited the Causeway and instantly bogged down once again in traffic as they started up the main Beach Avenue.

A few moments later, and they were connected.

"Miami Coast Guard, this is Officer Henshaw speaking..."

"FBI. Special Agent Kage Murphy, operating out of the Miami Division," Kage said quickly, pointing ahead of them to where the tall apartment blocks sat further ahead. Alexa could see where the traffic was slowing down, a collection of police cruisers, an ambulance, and a criminal science van had cordoned off the area.

"Thank you for the time, Officer Henshaw. How would I go about getting a list of the boats on the water around Miami Beach for a particular time and day?" Kage asked as they slid behind the other cars, eking their way forward.

There was a pause on the other end, and then an embarrassed cough.

"Well, that's almost impossible, son. We can get you the larger hauling craft, the trade and the cruise liners and what not, but there's an awful lotta personal craft on the waters, too..."

"You don't keep records of that?" Alexa butted in. "Special Agent Alexa Andrews, sir."

"Ma'am, it would be impossible to keep records of that. It also infringes certain privacy laws, too," Henshaw said huffily. *"But for the commercial stuff, they have to file routes and ports of call here with us. I can forward those over to you. What time are you looking for, Agents?"*

Kage gave them the hours in the morning before asking, "How would I go about finding the details of the smaller vessels though, Officer?"

"Whoo-wee! That is a toughie! A whole heap of people have pleasure craft on the waters, and just so long as they got a license they're pretty free and clear to sail 'em as they want," Henshaw said. "The best bet is to ask at the home marinas, they might have logs on what's going on, but it's not a legal requirement…"

Kage mouthed a very bad swearword, and Alexa could only agree. If the shooter used a private boat (which they would be crazy not to) then there might be no way of finding out who, or where, they were.

They flashed the police cordon for Kage to lean out and show his badge to the officer waiting at the line, who waved them on. Above them towered the Miami Heights, a vast condo complex with balconies at every level.

"But every boat has to have a registration?" Alexa asked the man on the end of the speaker line.

"Yep. You need a boat license to take a craft on the open waters, and you have to also title register it with Highway Safety and Motor, like the DMV, which is a registration on the boat itself. Like a car registration."

"License and vehicle reg, got it," Alexa stated as Kage pulled them into park. Outside, the parking lot was busy with police forensic teams moving back and forth from their van to the open doors of the block.

They thanked Officer Henshaw, but before he went he also offered one thing that Alexa found interesting.

"Of course, none of this means pie if you can't prove where it was when. Some vehicles are fitted with internal GPS systems, but that's generally only for those that go out onto the open water, about a mile off the coast…"

They promised that they would bear that in mind and be in touch with any further questions before Alexa turned to Kage.

"Looks like we're going to have to do a lot of footwork, if we need to ask every marina where any possible boat was seen.

Luckily, the attack vector might give us a tighter frame of search, but..."

Kage groaned. "I know. But the Beach is full of CCTV. Somebody must have caught something, don't you think?"

"Yeah," Alexa sighed. But first they had to deal with the fact that there were two dead bodies above them of Aleksandr's sons. Perhaps the clues here would be less maddening than the scattered few around their father's demise...

Alexa was holstering her pistol when a scrap of paper fell from her jacket pocket. At first she thought it was a receipt from the gas station, but it turned out to be a folded piece of lined paper. Kage had already got suited with his FBI bomber jacket by the time she opened it to read the words.

Agent Landers. You need to be very careful. Very careful indeed.

She stared at the note for a full five seconds, wondering if this was a joke or not. The note was in her personal jacket, and not the FBI one. Had Kage put the note in there...? Only it didn't look like his handwriting at all; she knew because she had to countersign the surveillance request on Zholdin.

When was the last time I wore this? she internally questioned herself before realizing that the answer to that was all yesterday, and this morning.

Was it Perelli, at the VIV?

But then she thought of that man at the gas station, the way he had bumped into her, and Alexa's thoughts ran cold.

'Be careful around the Russians, kiddo. They're crazy. They chuck everything at you...' her thoughts paraphrased what her dad had told her.

Nope. Probably just a practical joke, Alexa told herself. Rag on the new girl at the Bureau office.

Surely.

But as Alexa got out of the car and got ready to look at some more corpses, she couldn't shake the feeling that she was being watched.

CHAPTER THIRTEEN

11:15 PM. MIAMI HEIGHTS, MIAMI BEACH

"**T**WO DEAD MALES, SIGNS OF A BRAWL – AND LOTS OF partying," Detective Dempsey read out the scene particulars once more as Alexa and Kage stood in the main living room of Apartment 7, Miami Heights.

It was indeed palatial, Alexa thought as she tried to see this place without the filter of the two dead bodies on medical stretchers in the middle of the room, or the white-suited forensic experts carefully moving around everything, once again taking photos and cataloguing everything they could.

There were chandeliers hanging from the ceilings. There were actual marble pillars acting as wall corners.

But still, it was still a six-room, two-man apartment, Alexa thought to herself.

"Both brothers shared this space," she said out loud to hear an agreeing 'yup' from Detective Dempsey.

"Didn't they have enough money to rent their own apartments out? Their father was one of the richest people on Star Island…" she considered, wondering at this. Not that it mattered, dead was still dead. If anything, it clearly made the killer's job easier.

"Well, neither of them appeared to have any actual employment," Dempsey pointed out. "Unless you count being an 'influencer' – whatever the heck that means these days."

"What, not even at their father's firms?" Kage asked, surprised.

"Nope. Maybe daddy didn't figure them for the managerial type," Dempsey said, nodding to where there were still small packets (mostly empty) of mysterious powder scattered over the grand table, as well as bottles of wine that probably cost as much as a month of Alexa's wages.

Difficult relationship with father. The brothers knew Henderson and Perelli. Brothers end up dead, Alexa scribbled in her notebook, before turning her attention to the actual facts of the scene itself.

"Have we got a time of death yet?" Alexa asked.

Dempsey harrumphed loudly and peeled through the layers of his own notebook.

"Best guess is last night. They were found this morning by the building clerk approximately 9:30 am, and the docs say they couldn't have been dead more than twelve-to-fourteen hours, given the state of rigor mortis."

"Twelve to fourteen? That puts the killing from eightish to ten-thirty last night," Kage said, as the agents took another sweeping look around them. From the evidence of all the bottles, glasses, and various implements, the party was already in full swing by the time of the killing.

"Okay, let's run through it," Alexa said, pointing at the nearest body.

Vadim Bodrov was currently on a medical trolley, his skin and flesh pale as milk, with a faint sheen that Alexa associated with the dead. He had a rattish, greasy sort of appearance and featured a small bullet hole just above his right eye that looked little more than a serious puncture wound – from the large dark red stain on the hallway entrance, however, the back of his head must have looked a whole lot worse.

"Small entrance wound," Alexa stated. She didn't want the medical team to turn him over.

"It can't be the same bullet grade as used on Aleksandr, right?" Kage hazarded a guess, earning a perfunctory nod from Alexa.

"No, this looks even smaller than a 9mm, a .45 or even a .22 maybe," Alexa said. "It's also some pretty fancy shooting, if it was a hip shot."

"Hip shot? I don't remember them teaching that in Quantico?" Kage said, already moving to the taped-out outline of where Vadim had been lying when he had been found.

"Turn of phrase, 'shoot from the hip.' Old cowboy thing who doesn't have any time to point and aim," Alexa said distractedly as she next moved over to Dimitre, on another medical trolley at the back of the gargantuan apartment room.

"Two shots to the heart. Very effective, but the mess is extensive…" she said, seeing how Dimitre had managed to make even more of a mess than Vadim had, with a wide circle of dark black extending over the floor.

"Signs of spatter," she remarked, noticing the nearest leather armchair covered in a fine gauze of red, as was the table and the side lamp. "I'd say brother was getting up when he was shot. Probably heading towards the killer." Alexa looked back behind her. Vadim was by the hallway to the front door, and Dimitre had been found in the cut-away entrance to another lounge area at the back of the main living room.

"The killer took out Vadim at the entrance way, then moved and," she said then mimed walking a few confident steps and plugging two shots into the lounge. Easy kills. The brothers must have been completely surprised by the attack.

"Vadim fell back, hit the wall and slid down," Kage agreed. "Pretty instantaneous. It looks like the killer's attack vector must have come in from the hallway – which means they must be on the CCTV cameras outside. There's one for every floor, and every floor covers just one apartment. I'll go check with the building manager."

"Thanks, Murphy," Alexa said, looking down at the bodies and feeling suddenly at a loss. What else was there to say? The killing had been so immediate and quick that it didn't look as though the killer had bothered to spend any more time in here than needed to get the job done.

Of course, from the mess that the two brothers lived in, it was almost impossible to tell whether anything was taken or not, but all of the crystal ornaments and paintings on the walls, the Rolexes on the brothers' wrists were still intact.

Then there was the double-tap on the second brother. That was what trained killers were taught to do, Alexa knew. Assassins. Military.

But we have to at least entertain the possibility that this murder is not connected to the father, she thought as she struggled to see any signs that the alternative could be true. It was too exact, too precise.

Just like Aleksandr.

"But the bullets don't match, obviously," she said out loud as Dempsey turned to look at her, one eyebrow raised.

"This was a small side arm, I'm pretty sure about it. The exit wounds are too small, and the idea of a killer lugging a rifle up here in broad daylight would be insane..."

"Although, looks like the brothers had plenty on their hands, I don't think they would notice!" Dempsey said. At first, Alexa thought he was talking about their father's murder, but then the round detective nodded back to the hallway.

"Take a look at the bedrooms."

Do I have to? Alexa thought, dreading what she would find already, but she turned and looked to find a crime scene investigator in each one, cataloguing the disarray.

Both brothers' bedrooms were larger than the entire motel apartment that Alexa was staying in, with giant king-size beds as well as sofas and chairs and, in one, a dancing pole on a marble floor. Both bedrooms were also in a scene of upheaval, with clothes spread around the floor, and a variety of bottles and glasses on one of the side tables.

"Drowning their grief, I take it?" Alexa murmured, as one of the CSI gestured to one of the evidence markers, where a black lacy slip had been dropped.

"Ah," Alexa said. Obviously, there was no way of telling how long it had been there, but it fitted with the overall story that the brothers had spent a lot of time being otherwise occupied in this place.

But no other bodies? Alexa reasoned. *The killer must have patiently timed it well…*

"Alexa!" It was Kage, appearing at the door and out of breath. "I've just been chatting to Clements, the building clerk on yesterday, and I think you'll want to hear this…" he said, beckoning her to follow him as they jogged out of the apartment and to the hallway beyond, where a thin, middle-aged man in a smart, blue zoot suit and with a pencil moustache was waiting for them.

"Mr. Clements, if you would be so good as to tell my partner Special Agent Landers, what you just told me," he said.

The man blinked and licked his lips. He was clearly terrified of what had happened here, Alexa could see, but he was holding onto his scraps of professional dignity with all the look of a drowning man.

"I was on duty last night, ma'am…"

It's actually sir, Agent, or Officer, Alexa thought. *But never mind…*

"I was the one to find the bodies this morning, when the maids couldn't get access to their rooms. I tried phoning the apartments several times, but as the brothers had always said they want maid service, I came up here about nine-thirty this morning, well… It's my job to answer questions, fulfil the needs of our residents, ordering food or booking cars, that sort of thing…"

I bet, Alexa thought.

"I also field anyone coming into the complex. We get reporters sometimes looking for guests. Not many get past security, but it happens," the man continued, licking his lips nervously. Alexa wondered if he was fearful of losing his job over the murder.

"So it's my job to know who comes in and what have you... But yesterday the only people who came up here were the two girls."

"Two girls?" Alexa suddenly asked.

Clements nodded. "Yes, they've both been here before. One was blonde, the other African American..." he paused for a moment, and Alexa saw him calculating something, before his next words came out in a rush.

"Well, I don't suppose it matters now they are dead? The girls, well, they had the appearance about them of *professional* entertainers, if I may say so-"

How can you say that!? Alexa narrowed her eyes in annoyance. She didn't doubt that the Bodrov brothers were the sorts of men who regularly hired the affections of 'professional entertainers,' but it didn't automatically make sense that just because a woman wore clothing that was fun, or expressive, that she was automatically a 'professional.'

"Do you have any evidence for that, Mr. Clements – the professional entertainers part?" she asked carefully.

"Well, I'd seen them before in the company of the Bodrov brothers. And I know that they returned with them on previous occasions on the nights that I booked a car to take the brothers to the VIV Adult Lounge, if you know it...?"

"We know it," Alexa sighed. She didn't like it when first impressions were right.

"Mr. Clements, can you remember what time those two girls came over? Did they return with the Bodrov brothers?" Kage said.

Clements shook his head, then nodded, then shook it again.

"Oh, the brothers haven't been out of their room for about two or three days, so no, it wasn't with them. The girls arrived about seven-thirty, I believe. I remember because they don't have any of the guest passes reserved for trusted visitors, and I had to phone up the brothers to allow them access to the floor."

"Guest passes?" Alexa frowned. "What do you mean?"

"The Miami Heights has multiple levels of security, or it did have. It was *supposed* to have. There's the guards at the door, and then past that we use a system of passes. If you are a resident your door key obviously works everywhere, but given the sorts of lives of our residents, we also use a system of guest passes that the residents control. They give them to their family, special friends and what have you, and those guests can come and go through all the public areas of the building. Just not into any actual apartments," Clements explained before ending emphatically, "so it should be completely impossible for any stranger to even get through the lobby door to the stairs or open the elevator door without a pass. Nothing will work for them."

"Looks like someone managed it," Alexa said as she turned to look at the door. No signs of forced entry. The killer must have been invited in. In fact, the killer must have made it up here past every automatically locked door and lift and window – who were they, Houdini!?

"But you have cameras on every floor," Kage commented, turning to look at the small round eye that sat overlooking the entire hallway between elevators and apartment doors.

"Yes, we do," Clements nodded vigorously. "You would like to take a look at them?"

"Yes, that would be excellent, thank you, Mr. Clements," Alexa nodded. At least there was no need for a warrant this time around…

They followed Clements down the elevator, Alexa watching as he used his own staff pass card to open the doors at both ends before crossing the marble lobby downstairs and through another security door. The level of opulence shot down dramatically as soon as they were inside the staffing areas, Alexa saw, but Clements still had to use his staff access card to get into the secure office, a small room filled with filing cabinets and one top of the range computer.

"Please excuse the clutter, this will only take a moment…" Clements said as he navigated through the system to the surveillance app, *MySpy*, to open up the windows for all of the

THE **FLORIDA GIRL**

various cameras on every floor, showing small, black and white footage of the corridors, with only the Bodrovs' currently busy with police and CSI.

"We also have cameras out front and back," the clerk said as he toggled the view from over the front slide doors and the rear, overlooking the parking lot.

"Can you rewind? Find the recordings for last night from when the women arrived?" Kage asked.

"Not in this. This is the live feed, but everything is downloaded and held for a month…" The man clicked out of the windows to open up different areas of the *MySpy* dashboard, eventually navigating to a series of windows with a long list of numbers, which made Alexa think of the footage from the VIV Lounge.

"Each one is timestamped, and they run for two hours at a time," Clements said, moving down to the 7-9 pm recording for apartment 7, and double clicked.

At first, a whole lot of nothing happened, even when Clements forwarded it 2x, then 4x, and finally 8x speed; that was, until a sudden duo of girls sped through the frame, giggling at the door to the Bodrov apartment.

"Freeze!" Alexa said quickly. "Can you go back?"

The controls were clunky, but Clements managed to move the frames back until a clear shot of both girls who entered the apartment the night before were clear. Even in the grainy footage, Alexa could see that one was stick thin, wearing not much more than a slip dress herself and with a bob of hair and heavy eye makeup. The other was a larger lady with long braids, wearing not a whole lot more than her friend.

"They've been here before in the company of the uh, the deceased," Clements reiterated.

"Can you send this footage to this address?" Alexa said, scribbling down the discreet email for the Miami HQ.

"We'll get those pictures enhanced and blown up," she murmured to Kage, who nodded.

"Now can you fast forward through until about 11 pm?" she asked.

Clements explained that would go into the next recording, but he resumed play and sped it back up to x8, as before...

The women vanished into the apartment, and once again they were treated to the exciting world of a whole lot of carpet design and nothing else for what felt like a long time, until the first recording ended at 9 pm, and Clements opened the next. For a third time, they were treated to the joys of hallways until, that was-

With a snarl of static, the image suddenly dissolved into white noise.

"What!?" Clements coughed, looked at his computer, then tried clicking through the controls once again.

Every time that he forwarded to precisely 10:54:17 pm, the exact same thing happened.

"Keep going. Get to the end of the tape!" Alexa said.

"Technically it's a file, not a tape-" Kage managed to whisper.

"Shut up!" Alexa hissed back.

But the tape before them continued its static snowstorm right up until it finished at 11 pm, and the next, the *third* recording started with the snowstorm and lasted until 11:22:40.

"I'm sorry, I have no idea what's happened, it's never done that before," Clements said as Alexa looked at Kage in surprise. Her partner pulled a face and a shrug, which, even without using any words in front of the building clerk, appeared to say it all.

Could be a coincidence, but I doubt it.

"Those two women, do we have them leaving the building?" she asked desperately.

The clerk returned to the footage and hit fast forward. They didn't have to wait long into the small hours of the night, around one-thirty, when first one, then another of the girls left the apartment. Alexa studied their walk.

They were trying to play it cool; she saw how the braided one tried to move faster to the elevator, but the one with the bob of hair, holding onto her arm, pulled her back tighter.

"Follow them. Elevator cameras?" she said.

Clements shook his head. "The next we have is the lobby..."

The next footage, coming up to two in the morning showed the two women walking through the lobby clutching at each other quite casually. They even nodded at the security guard who spared a word before they left, and then they had vanished.

"We need to find out who those two are," Alexa stated as she looked at the last image of them. Was she looking at the killers? Had she been wrong all this time, imagining some big and burly Russian superman?

Working as a dancer would be a great cover for a killer, too, Alexa considered.

She also thought that she knew exactly who might know their names, too.

CHAPTER FOURTEEN

2:35 PM. VIV ADULT LOUNGE

"Well, color me surprised, if it isn't Special Agent Landers again!" Vincenti Perelli, the large and clearly exasperated owner of the VIV Adult Lounge shouted as soon as he saw who was menacing the bodyguards at his door.

"Now, why oh why did I think that I would see you again?" he snapped, as he stood at the top of the ramp that led down to the stairs, effectively blocking it for Alexa and Kage.

They had failed to convince Dempsey to bring a squad car to back them up this time, as there had been a shooting out in Little

Haiti, and all of a sudden it was all hands on the radios for the Floridian police.

At least, this is what Dempsey had told them, but he had also mumbled something about 'not having a warrant' – which was a fact that Alexa knew Perelli would jump upon.

"I don't know, Perelli, why *did* you think you would see us again? Anything you wish to unburden yourself of?" Kage shot back quickly with a smile, as the large nightclub owner just glared at him.

"You got the files from the other night. What more do you want? I can't have the FBI or the police showing up at my door every night; it's bad for business and I am sure will only add to my harassment case!"

"I'll be pleased to respond to that when it happens," Alexa said as smoothly as she dared. She held her ground and refused to go back down the ramp to the outside.

"We're here just following up, that is all. Got a few questions. We can be out of your hair in a minute," she said a little pointedly, for the entirely bald Perelli to glower even hotter, if such a thing was possible.

"Who's got time for questions? I don't see any bit of paper with you, lady, so-"

"That's *Agent* Landers, Mr. Perelli," Kage said hotly, taking a step forward so that, even though she was on a ramp and technically beneath the owner of the club, she was still the same height as the man.

"You are totally in your rights to choose not to cooperate with our questions, as you know-"

"-good!" Perelli turned to go.

"However, as we are pursuant of witnesses to a murder scene, it will seriously *not* look good on you, or them, when this becomes public knowledge. Think of the papers. Are you sure that you want a murder case associated with your club? Does your 'management' want that?" Kage growled the words at him.

Perelli slowed his stride and then turned around.

"You both already tried to question me about a murder case, kid," he said.

"Well now we're back here with another one. Another two. And when it comes out that the victims were regulars right here at your club, then I am guessing that there will suddenly be a *lot* of police interest in your dealings," Kage snarled once again.

Perelli held his gaze for a long moment. "What you talking about? That Bodrov guy?" he muttered.

Kage glanced at Alexa, silently checking if he was heading in the right direction.

Let him have it, she thought. She wanted to see the man shake in his skin a little.

"The sons," Kage said heavily. "Vadim and Dimitre. Both regulars here with you, right? In fact, when *was* the last time you saw them, Mr. Perelli? Can you account for your actions between when my partner spoke to you and now?"

"*Gah!* Enough! Come in, goddamn it!" Perelli barked at them, turning to wave them in behind him.

Well done, partner! Alexa thought at Kage as she found herself once again walking across the smooth and shiny floor of the adult lounge, where there was a scattering of patrons already receiving dances or laughter from the working women of the club. Once again, Alexa was aware of the many eyes that settled on her as she walked (she had made sure that they both wore their FBI bomber jackets this time, just to prove a point).

But the one thing she wasn't sure about was how Kage was going to handle this questioning. As of this morning, they were strongly thinking that they were looking at a Russian hitman or another, but now there could just as easily be a strong link to Perelli, couldn't there?

We can't go easy on him, or reveal too much of our case, Alexa thought. She was sure that Kage knew that.

They went up the stairs to the same office that Perelli had taken her and Dempsey last time, and this time it appeared that Perelli was more comfortable complying with Kage's directions.

Ugh, Alexa thought, trying to suppress her anger. Was this just Perelli or was it Florida? Home to 1950s, man!?

"Go on. Tell me what's happened," Perelli said as he sat on the large, broad leather chair at the back of the room, and picked out a thin cigar. Alexa wondered if it would be a contraband one from Cuba. Probably.

Don't let him control the interview! Alexa thought at Kage, who hesitated, just for a second, before he plunged in.

"This morning, the bodies of Vadim and Dimitre Bodrov were found dead. You have told us yourself that they were regulars at your club here. Would you care to elaborate on that?"

Perelli rolled his head and creaked his neck, like he was getting ready for a fight.

"Do I need a lawyer? I can get the best Miami lawyer here in ten."

"Have we stated this is voluntary, Mr. Perelli?" Kage frowned. "This is just helping us with our inquiries, although, I am required to inform you that anything you will say will be recorded."

Alexa held up her notebook.

Perelli flickered his eyes over Alexa, and then back to Kage before he nodded, just once. "Fine. I'll play. I got nothing to hide. But if I hear any suspicion or probing question, I'll slap you with a lawsuit as quick as you can say it."

Kage just smiled as he gestured to a seat. "May I?"

It was then that Alexa started to see the strength in Kage's approach. He came across as an affable, likeable character. Friendly. Perelli must think he was a pushover, until Kage proved that he wasn't.

"Of course, of course, Mr. Perelli. I've got to say, though, at the moment we have one guy, Henderson, connected to this establishment and a murder, and now we have two other clientele of yours wound up dead in the same week. It's not looking good, is it?" Kage smiled unemotionally.

"Spit it out, Agent," the club owner growled.

"Just tell us about your involvement with the Bodrov sons, Vadim and Dimitre."

Alexa watched the man closely, scribbling as many quick notes as she could. He pulled a face and then groaned.

"You want the truth, Agent? The truth is they were in here more nights than most, and they seemed very keen to blow daddy's money – and you know what? I was only too happy to help them do that. Why should I care if some Russian playboys want to give me all their money, huh!?"

He was angry, Alexa saw. But then again, he was angry last time she'd seen him.

"They spent a lot of money here. Then they must have felt very welcome. Is that how they knew Henderson? Did Henderson introduce them to this place?" Kage asked, and Alexa wondered if he might well have asked, *Did you get Henderson to introduce them to this place?*

Perelli shrugged. "How am I supposed to know that? The VIV is a well-known, quality establishment."

"Did the Bodrov boys have a tab with you? An account? I understand that many adult venues offer such services," Kage said, and this time Alexa saw it. Perelli flushed a little darker. *He must know that if we need to, we can get a warrant for their books, and who knows what sorts of things they don't want an FBI Financial Forensics team to find there...*

"Yeah, yes they did," Perelli stated.

"How much did they owe?" Kage pushed, and Alexa saw Perelli start to resist, but battle with his own judgement.

"Mr. Perelli?" Alexa leapt in. "Just so you are aware, if you do choose to call in a lawyer, we'll have to take this to the next level, a full-scale interrogation. The Bureau will have to consider your involvement with *closer* scrutiny…"

We'll get a warrant for everything you have in here, and we'll go through all of your books with a fine-toothed comb, she could have said.

"Those goddamn Ruskies owed me a bit, okay!?" Perelli burst out. "To the tune of nine or ten thousand. Which might sound a lot to you government employees, but believe me, to an entrepreneur like me it's chicken feed. We can clear that in a week!"

"I'm sure you can, Mr. Perelli. The VIV is clearly where everyone wants to hang out. Perhaps it is the quality of your staff," Kage said, as Alexa drew forth two high quality print outs of the two girls seen in the Miami Heights footage. They'd had to return to the FBI Headquarters to get them cleaned up, but Alexa thought it was worth it.

"Have these women ever worked for you, Mr. Perelli? And be aware, that we can subpoena all your business records and accounts," Alexa stated.

Perelli held up the sheets for what appeared to be a long time before he grunted.

"Yeah. That's Trixi, that's Leela. I can't remember their last names, not that it matters because the strippers are always changing their names and using fake ones all the time anyway."

"But you must have employee information. Payment details, home address, that sort of thing that we can confirm?" Kage pressed.

Once again, Perelli looked as though he might clam up, but he scoffed and turned towards the comparatively tiny computer next to the chair. "I'll get what I have for you, but I can't guarantee it's accurate. The girls can say anything they want on their forms, and many of them only want cash-in-hand work, which is all above board and I give receipts and their W-4s as well as my cut before you ask!"

"Are they working for you now? When did you last see them?" Alexa said severely.

Perelli waved one large hand once again.

"It's on the work schedule. Shifts and hours. I can't be expected to keep an eye on everyone!" he said, cursing and muttering as he grumbled to his feet and retrieved a handful of printouts from an ageing, spasmodic printer in the corner.

"Here. Just tell 'em that if they're in trouble, then they needn't come back to work for me, huh? Is it over? Are you done!?" Perelli growled. Alexa perused the paper, noting shift times for Trixi Kiss and Leela La Blue, along with an address. The same address, as it appeared that the two girls lived together.

Kage looked over at Alexa, who nodded.

We're going to need a warrant and an interrogation if we want more, Alexa's eyes said, and Kage nodded as if he had understood everything perfectly.

"Your cooperation will be noted, thank you, Mr. Perelli," Kage said with that strong, affable smile once more and stuck his hand out for the night club owner to shake.

"*Eat crap, Agent!*" Perelli hissed as he refused to shake the man's hand.

Kage opened the door with an even broader smile, and he and Alexa walked out.

"Keep walking before you laugh-" Kage managed to murmur, and to Alexa's surprise, they got all the way to the front door and out before they burst out.

"He's scared. He knows that we can turn his place over, brick by brick, and he doesn't want that," Alexa said enthusiastically once they had gotten back into their car, and Kage was taking them out of the VIV parking lot.

"You know what I think?" Kage offered. "I think it's a classic mafia sting operation. They've been doing it for years in Las Vegas. They run a casino, get people into debt, then pile on the interest. That's the scam that the family likes to run best. Perelli employs Henderson as the point-man, Henderson pulls Vadim and Dimitre in, then they owe Perelli money."

"And if you don't pay up, then they start taking a cut off your profits, or one of your fingers," Alexa said. "But killing the father and two sons for ten grand…?"

"Yeah, okay, admittedly that seems pretty harsh," Kage offered. "But what do I know? Maybe Perelli is sending a message?"

"Hm," Alexa agreed. Perelli was now much more of an active suspect than they had thought before.

"We need something tying him directly to the father, other than through Henderson. If there was bad blood between the two, then the rest starts to fall into place… Which is why those two

THE FLORIDA GIRL

girls are even more important to our investigation," she thought out loud.

"Whatever the truth is, those girls were in that room at the exact time that the murder happened. Either they were in on it, or they're key eyewitnesses. Either way they'll know more of what was going on between Dimitre, Vadim, Henderson and Perelli..." Alexa said.

"But we still have to check out the marina cameras, too," Kage pointed out. "If we get footage of the boats on the water, at the right time, in the right place, we can run the DMV registrations. *That* might be the link between Aleksandr and Perelli for all we know."

Alexa agreed it was vital, and Kage permitted himself a mischievous grin. "Second time lucky?"

"Huh?" Alexa shot him a questioning look.

"You stake out the club this time. See if we rattled any cages, just like I did with Zholdin... I'll check the marinas," he offered.

"Do you really think that trick will work a second time?" she asked, but he shrugged all the same.

"Worth a shot. And I could do with the legwork. The marinas are only a walk away from here," Agent Murphy said cheerily, "and if you haven't sat for mind-numbing hours in a car looking at a locked door, then you aren't even in the FBI, that's what I say."

"Gee thanks," Alexa groaned.

CHAPTER FIFTEEN

4:25 PM. MIAMI BEACH SOUTH MARINA

"Wow. Screw my life," Kage muttered as he paused at the end of 14th Street with the super high-rise condominiums shouldering all around him, and the small Biscayne Bay Path running ahead of him.

The Path itself was a part of a marina access route that ran all the way around Miami Beach, but in places it was blocked off by the private condos with their own water frontage. In some places it widened out to allow car traffic, but the stretch that was before Kage Murphy was a pedestrian stroll, with palm trees on one side, and the open fences that led to one of the latest developments.

THE **FLORIDA GIRL**

Kage had lived in Florida all his life, but he still felt that shiver of being a stranger in a strange land when he was here, neck deep in the holiday party glamor of Miami Beach.

He sauntered over to the railing at the water's edge to look down and see that the tide was out – as out as it ever got when the entire island (and much of Florida) was little more than a peninsula of shifting sandbanks and swamps.

Even this late in the day, there was a whole *heap* of boats on the water here, Kage considered as he turned his head to look south. There was the crowded Bay of Biscayne, and just to the south of his position sat Star Island. He tried to figure out whether he could even see the Bodrov place, but all he could make out was the green of the palm trees and bushes that most of the super-wealthy chose to screen their getaway mansions.

"Oka-aaay," he sighed, looking at the number of boats that were already out there, anchored in the deeper slip of water between Flamingo Point, Miami Beach, and up to Belle Isle – itself another small, man-made residential island that was mostly home to the Venetian Way causeway that ran north of Star Island.

There were many problems with this picture, Kage thought.

One, even on a general 'normal' day, there had to be at least thirty or so boats anchored out there. It would take forever and some Coast Guard assistance to go around and chat to each and every one (*'excuse me, are you a Russian super assassin/expert mafia hitman? Can I see your collection of sniper rifles, please?'*). And two, there wasn't even a big enough marina up this end of Flamingo Point to accommodate for all of those boats. When Kage turned his head south, he saw that there were other, larger marinas heading towards the McArthur Causeway at the bottom of the island of Miami Beach, and then there was the super-giant, public Miami Beach Marina, which was like a boating factory. Some 400 'slips' Kage had found out on the way over here (*thank you, no thank you, Google*) that anyone with a boat license could book a reservation at.

Yeah, Kage had kinda been hoping not to have to start hassling the massive Miami Beach Marina, although he figured that if he was a *Russian super spy/mafia hitman* then he might just want to get 'lost' in the immense amount of traffic down there.

But the main Miami Beach Marina was a fair ways to the bottom of the Beach, and any potential boat would have to travel up, under the McArthur Causeway and then would be adjacent to Star Island, to take their shot…

"I've got a hunch you might not want your boat recorded on every security camera between there and the bottom of Miami Beach, would ya?" Kage whispered to himself, following the line of the Island's coast up to see his next and final problem.

Three, there were indeed other marinas between the massive public one and Flamingo point, but most of them were in areas where the Biscayne Bay Path was blocked off by private security gates. In other words, these much smaller launches that belonged to the super-large condominiums, where they provided sight-seeing visits to their guests.

And THAT seems kinds unlikely, doesn't it? Kage was thinking to himself. The killer would have to be a guest at one of these condos, book a trip out, and then what – excuse himself while he just sets up a very rifle-shaped bird telescope?

Kage grimaced as he kicked the railing. He didn't like any of his options.

"Hey, friend, is there a problem over here?" said a voice behind him, and Kage turned to see that there was an older man dressed in what Kage thought of as 'the Miami tee' – really a short-sleeved Hawaiian shirt, and a short-brimmed white panama hat. He had with him some sturdy fishing shorts, the sort of pair with pockets every which way you could need them, and quite a few places where you didn't.

"Sorry to bother you, sir, no problem," Kage replied, but the man looked interested enough. He had a Floridian tang, and Kage guessed that he was talking to an actual resident of Miami, rather than a visitor.

"Well, sure thing, son. But you be careful by the water now, plenty go over the side, especially in the hot months!" the man said, offering Kage a sympathetic look.

THE **FLORIDA GIRL**

He probably thinks I'm drunk or down on my luck, Kage thought. He was about to go when he thought, *Hey, why not? Worth a shot.*

"Actually, sir, there is something you could help me with," he said, pointing out to the anchored boats out there in the deep between Flamingo and Belle.

"How would I go about getting a boat moored up there. Is that private condo waters?" he asked.

The man looked at him aghast for a moment, and then laughed out loud, a big, booming bark of a laugh.

"Heavens no, and I'm thankful for it, too! The condos are eating up all the available moorings, more every year, leaving us Floridians trying to fish in waters thick with Adderall packets and worse!"

Kage had guessed right; the man was a native Floridian.

"What you're looking at there is one of the last stretches of pure and simple pleasure water – that's the technical name for it, son, it comes from pleasure cruising – left around the Beach. Anyone can use it, but only residents or rentals can stay overnight."

"Rentals?" Kage asked, looking hopeful.

"Uh-huh," the man grunted, giving Kage a 'I know it, I know it' look, as though he had clocked Kage as yet another tourist in *his* zone.

"Well, there's the Miami Yacht Rental down the way, right up from the Bentley, you see? It's one of the few places where people can rent their own boats, but you have to have a license before you go out on the water, all your safety certificates in order. If not, they do a very good job at matching you with a professional touring company…"

"No need, sir, thank you, thank you!" Kage responded, turning around to trace where the man had pointed. There was indeed a much smaller marina down there at the back of a large building, but he would have to cut back into the Island, along 13th Street and down again to get to it.

Our guy walks in, hires his own boat, gets the job done… Kage thought it through as he hurried through the streets, aware that the work day was already nearing its end.

It was busier on the streets around the super-massive condos than Kage had expected, as there were always arrivals and departures streaming back and forth from the megaplex buildings. Each of these megaplexes had also brought quite a substantial amount of waterside estate, with no easy route back to the Biscayne Bay Path, so unless Kage wanted to flash his badge and hop fences (he didn't) he had to detour the long way around.

"Ah, *nuts!*" he gasped as he turned the final corner, under the strains of electro-salsa music coming from behind him on the avenue to find that Miami Yacht Rentals was indeed closed. He jogged down the open path that led to the waterside road at the back of the building, back to the Biscayne Bay Path, to find that the security link fence was also locked around the small Yacht Rental marina.

Kage counted, seeing that there were only spaces for about twenty at most yachts, half of which were out (which he guessed meant that they were moored out in the 'last public pleasure waters' that the guy had been talking about).

The special agent looked beyond the marina to see that there, right there, was Star Island.

"About six or seven hundred yards away, I'd say," he murmured to himself.

It was one of these boats, it has to be, Kage thought, turning slowly around to see the large Miami Yacht Rental building, so large in fact, that it had several smaller businesses renting out its lower street-level frontages.

One of them, a taco and Delhi place near the marina was still open, but only barely as Kage saw a woman with dark hair and a bright shirt knotted in front of her chest starting to take signs indoors.

It's worth a shot, right? he thought, "Hey, Miss? Miss? Can I have a word?"

"We're closing. No tacos left. I can do you a salad and takeout," she said over her shoulder as Kage followed her to the door, for her to turn around with an annoyed look on her face before she saw the open FBI badge he held in hand.

"Sorry for the intrusion, Miss, but I see you have security cameras over the door. Do they look out over the yacht marina and the Biscayne?"

The woman gestured for him to walk closer as she leaned over to stare hard at his ID, and then, seemingly satisfied, she nodded.

"Sure. First one covers the tables and the marina mostly, second I angled out to get a view of the Path, too. We got burgled a couple years ago, and the cops think they hopped the Path fence," the woman said, before extending her hand.

"Maria Scalla, this is my place. You still want that salad?"

A little while later, Kage was reviewing the footage to see that there were an awful *lot* of boats out on the water on the morning of July 14th, between 8 and 10 am. Even that early, and the first of the pleasure cruisers were already on the waters.

None of the boats and yachts that went past Star Island that day paused in the straight between here and the Island. No one stopped.

And none of the Yacht Rental boats had been taken out.

Damnit! Kage tried to contain his disappointment. He had been hoping to find a fairly easy link between a rental and the killer's boat, but once again the easy answers had eluded him.

"You looking for a particular boat?" Maria said, leaning on the door frame as she peered over his shoulder. Kage sat in the small back room of Scalla's Cuban Cuisine and his obvious disappointment said everything.

"You know what type? What colour, size?" Maria asked him.

"Unfortunately, no... All I know is that there was a boat on the water between eight and about ten-thirty that the Bureau has an interest in," Kage groaned.

"I bet it was that pink one," Maria laughed, before turning back to the kitchen beyond.

"What!?"

"I'm only kidding. But there was a salmon pink and a white boat that was being a real pain in my ass all morning that day. I have this little restaurant boat, you see, my sister takes over the shop and I go up and down the marinas, selling street food. You can see it out on the Yacht Rental marina, the *Cuban Lady*, see?"

Kage looked, and indeed there was a fairly small yacht out there with wreaths of plastic flowers along their boughs and sides.

"Wait. Do you rent the *Cuban Lady*?" Kage asked. "I thought that marina was only for yacht rentals."

"It is. I'm renting the *Lady* and she's costing me my first and second born every year!" Maria scoffed.

"Anyway, I was getting ready to haul off, but there was this pink and white yacht in the way. Battered old thing. Wouldn't go anywhere, no matter how many times I hailed it. I gave up, came back in to get more done here, and by the time I went back out, must have been around eleven, it was gone. I took the *Lady* out, that was that. I bet it was that one you're looking for, or at least, it would really please me if it was."

Kage turned back to the footage on Scalla's CCTV to slow it down, frame by frame. Instead of looking at boats that motored past Star Island, he concentrated on the ones that *didn't*.

"What an idiot!" he growled to himself, moving rapidly to slide the timer to before eight, and then after ten, to see a battered pink and white yacht turn up, stop just on the open side of the Yacht Rentals place and then just...sit there. He saw Maria Scalla go out and shout at it a few times, for there to be absolutely no movement or sign of life from the boat at all.

Of course the shooter would want have to stop to take the shot, but instead of drawing attention to themselves, he pretended to be moored at the Yacht Rental!

Then, just after ten-thirty, the boat suddenly powered off, heading south. Kage froze the image, but the resolution was too fuzzy to make out the name, but he thought he could read a few of the registration numbers.

Gotcha! Kage was thinking as he asked Maria if he could take a copy of these files.

"Sure, go for your life, agent-man," she said with a wave of her hand, and Kage sent the image to Dee and the Bureau digital team to see if she could get any more sense out of it.

You're mine, Kage thought, as he stared at the image of the pink and white boat, which he was sure contained their shooter.

CHAPTER SIXTEEN

4:25 PM. VIV ADULT LOUNGE

About the same time as Kage was feeling very pleased with himself about boats on the Yacht Rental marina, Alexa was feeling very far from enthused.

Just as Kage had suggested that she would, she had spent a long time seated in their car parked across the street watching the doors to the nightclub, only they clearly weren't locked.

Patrons and would-be patrons came and went, with the security guards turning away a few who were already too inebriated to clearly walk straight. Alexa had done her stints at observation training and demoing stakeouts during the Academy, but she had to admit that nothing had prepared her for the apparently ceaseless boredom that was pretty relentless, from either way you looked at it.

Still, she kept her eyes on the door, and she paid attention every time someone came and went.

Her mind wondered over the case, however, and in particular, to the note that she had found in her jacket pocket.

Agent Landers. You need to be very careful indeed…

It was clearly a prank being played on her by the others at the Bureau, wasn't it? Alexa scowled a little as she looked at the paper once more, and then back to the door. It wasn't in Kage's writing, but then again there was a whole lot of people who worked at the Bureau, and she was New Girl™.

"It probably was you Kage, you dufus," she muttered when her phone rang. It was a message from Dee from the digital team.

DMV has returned your results on the car that Zholdin met with. It's on the system as a rental for Florida Speedies, Miami Beach 212.

Results back on Aleksandr Bodrov's laptop. He's running state of the art security equipment. Military grade. Impossible for my office to break.

"What!?" Alexa looked at the message, and then re-read it once again. She was glad that the car came up registered, but every time that they received more information, it also felt as though the entire case got more complicated.

Alexandr Bodrov shot by a military-trained sniper…
Has military-level security on his own laptop…
His two sons owe money to the mob, they wind up dead…

For all Alexa knew, the two murders might not even be connected – although she'd discounted that theory almost as soon as she thought of it.

The double-tap shots to the Bodrov siblings. That was military style, too.

But who had hired the killer, and why?

Bang!

There was a muffled bang from across the street, and Alexa looked up as she heard raised voices through her open window.

"That's all you're getting! *You and good-for-nothing Leela!*"

It was Perelli, standing in the doorway hollering at the retreating back of a woman.

A woman dressed in a large overcoat even despite the Miami heat, with a large sun hat and shades, attempting to hide her bob of platinum blonde hair.

Trixi! Alexa saw, fumbling for the door handle and cursing as her tired body struggled to wake up. But she was out, clicking the car locked behind her as she raced after the disappearing blonde woman as she turned, and rushing across the street.

"Trixi!" Alexa shouted to see the woman half turn, their eyes catch, and a look of panic cross her features.

Guilty panic? The thought flashed across Alexa's mind as Trixi turned and dove into the busy, heaving crowds of Miami Beach avenue.

"Damn!" Alexa hissed to herself, lengthening her stride as she ran after her. The Beach was starting to get busy for the coming evening. Revellers and partiers were already out in force, uncomfortably mingling with the last of the middle-aged tourists who were sauntering back to their condos.

I shouldn't have shouted, Alexa thought, cursing herself. For all she knew, Trixi *was* the murderer.

But something told Alexa that wasn't true. Perhaps it was the way that she had been running from Perelli, like she was a scared and frightened animal, not a military killer.

Alexa dashed through the crowds, bobbing and weaving first one way and then the next, skidding to a halt where the road opened out into an intersection, with people streaming either towards the beach or congregating around the nightclubs. It was no use. There easily had to be a couple hundred people here alone.

"Damnit!" Alexa shouted in the air. Trixi could have gone anywhere at all.

But then the thought struck her.

"But I have your home address, Trixi Kiss," she muttered, turning back and running towards the car. Or at least the address that she had given her employer, anyway.

CHAPTER SEVENTEEN

4:45 PM. MIAMI BEACH SOUTH

"Landers, don't you believe in picking up your phone!?" Kage grumbled as he walked back towards the VIV, a good thirty minutes of travel in this traffic to find that his partner had disappeared.

Alexa had gone somewhere, and now it seemed as though she wasn't even answering her phone. *Wonderful.*

Kage picked up his phone, about to call for a replacement Bureau car when he saw the message from Dee.

Florida Speedies, Miami Beach 212.

It took a little bit of googling, but he found that Florida Speedies was a ridiculously small car rental service operating in one of the wealthiest luxury cities in America.

And it was still open, and would remain so until 10pm.

"Ugh," Kage groaned as he considered the time. Speedies was at the other end of the Beach, but the entire island wasn't even that long. He could get there, pull the details on the car and the driver that had met Zholdin…and maybe get a step closer to tying this case together.

"Fine," he groaned again, finding the address on his phone's map before hailing a taxi.

⁂

"Mr. Costa Ortiz, 232 Avenue, Little Haiti," the clerk at *Florida Speedies* read out the sheet as he handed it over to Kage. It seemed that this small firm had absolutely no qualms with complying with the Federal Bureau of Investigations, as all Kage had to do was flash his badge and ask to see the details of this particular car's rental history.

Then again, if I was still a civilian, would I start arguing with Bureau agents? Kage considered not as he thanked the small, younger man who looked vaguely terrified.

The entire Speedies set up was pretty sub-par, Kage thought. He figured they could be making a whole lot more money on the Beach, and he asked why they didn't.

"Everyone wants limousines out here, and we haven't got the time or the money for that. The Beach is so small that most people don't bother driving anyway, but we stick it out. We got our regulars," the young man said, pointing at the lower end of the printout sheet.

"Only one booking that day. The Ortiz guy."

"Do people log their journeys with you?" Kage asked on the off chance.

The young man snorted. "This is still a free country, man! It wouldn't be worth my time asking what our clients are up to, if you get my drift. I'm guessing that there are a lot of married men going on holiday to the Beach who suddenly become weekend bachelors."

"I bet," Kage nodded to himself, looking at the paper.

Costa Ortiz, who are you? he asked, tapping the details into his phone to remind him to ask Dempsey to run a check on the name.

"Say, is this same car still in? Can I take a look?"

The young man looked at Kage for a moment, clearly wondering if this was the point that he should start asking if there was any need for warrants, but he still checked the computer files just the same.

"Nah, out of luck, bro. She's out. D'you want that booking as well??"

Kage shook his head. "Not yet, anyway," he laughed, turning to the door to try Landers again to once again find her line busy.

Argh! It was so frustrating being in the Bureau sometimes. He realized it was past five, coming on 6 pm and he was at the far end of the Beach. It could take ages for the Bureau to get a spare car out to him at this rate, and he couldn't hire an Uber to take him to the secret FBI Miami HQ, could he?

"Say… How much to rent a car for the night?" Kage turned and asked, utilizing his best winning smile.

In all truth, it wasn't out of character for the Bureau to use car rentals, Kage had to remind himself. When in the field, an agent was expected to be resourceful, and sometimes Ubers and rentals provided an extra layer of anonymity that was essential for their job.

But the traffic out of the Beach was still hell as Kage pulled out of *Speedies* and headed down towards the McArthur Causeway, the main trunk line on and off the Island.

He was starting to wonder quite seriously where his partner had got to, when suddenly, he lost control of the car.

What-!?

He felt the impact a split second later, although in truth it must have happened at the same time. There was a cataclysmic noise like someone had dropped a bomb on his car, and Kage was screeching and skidding to one side.

What happened!? What happened!?

The Buick in front of him was suddenly *very* in front of him as he skidded across the road straight towards it. Kage twisted the wheel, the rental car suddenly skidding wildly to one side.

One wheel's gone!

Kage hit the accelerator, throwing himself forward down the thin gap in the middle of the roadway between the cars before slamming on the brakes and screeching to a halt.

One of my tires went. A sound like an explosion.

His brain was trying to register something with him, but there was too much happening all at once for Kage to hear it.

Alarms were blaring from all sides as cars were sliding to a halt around his own stalled car, and from the sounds of it there were even a few fender-benders happening, too.

"Damnit, sorry!" Kage gasped for air, turning to open the door and bail out to see what had happened to him-

BANG!

Just as the back window of the rental exploded in a shower of glass. Suddenly, everything that Kage's brain had been trying to say rushed in at him at once.

Sound came second. The strike was too powerful for a burst tire. The wheel had been shot out.

Kage dove to the floor, just as there was another of those nasty, waspish noises and this time a patch of the empty roadway sparked and burst as a bullet ricocheted off of it.

Someone is shooting at me. Using something powerful. Pretty powerful.

The special agent already had his gun in his hand as he ducked, working his way to the front bumper of the car and once again crouching. He saw people getting out of cars around him, and some of them starting to scream as they quickly realized just what was going on.

"Get down! Stay down!" Kage shouted before diving to the far side of the car and raising his gun to sight backwards…

He saw the long Miami Beach avenue behind them, and there was the entrance to *Florida Speedies*. But no tell-tale gunman. There were a series of low buildings on either side, and the shot could have come from anywhere.

Back! Kage ducked back behind the car, and it was just in time, too, as the rear-view light suddenly exploded.

Other side. This time, Kage rolled back as people started screaming and running past, heading for the buildings and beach itself in any effort to get away from the threat that they couldn't even see.

But there was a line of flight, wasn't there? Kage realized. People were running away from the small warehouse-like building that sat adjacent to *Speedies*, some sort of boat repair place. Kage ducked around to the other side, his gun already raised as he sighted along the warehouse.

There. A glint of light by the side of the building. That could be a gun sight…

But then there were people running between Kage and the building, obscuring his vision.

"Get down! Down, FBI!" Kage shouted, breaking cover as he ran, vaulting the small barrier in the middle of the road to where there was the next car stopped, with the people inside cowering. Kage didn't stop. He couldn't use real people as cover; he kept his head down as he sprinted around the back of the vehicle, almost stumbling into a fleeing mom before he got to the pedestrian side of the road. The shooting had stopped, but Kage was now on the same side as the shooter, and an eerie silence had fallen over the scene, split only by muffled sobbing.

You won't get away with this! Kage thought, rushing to the side of the nearest McDonald's, edging to the side and spinning around, gun up.

Nothing. No shots coming for him. Ahead were the bushes that separated the McDonald's and the boat repair place. Kage sprinted, diving through the bushes with a leap as he hit the floor and rolled-

To find the alley where he had seen the glint of light empty. There was nothing here save for a small pile of old wooden boards and a half plastic panelling of some yacht.

Kage realized that wherever the shooter had been, they were definitely gone now. He crouched on his knees, as he heard the sound of approaching police sirens.

CHAPTER EIGHTEEN

5:55 PM. MIAMI SOUTHSIDE, DOWNTOWN, TRIXI & LEELA'S APARTMENT.

Alexa reached Trixi's address on the other side of Miami to find that it was a tenement, or as close to one as this city got.

The dancer lived in one of those small blocks that had been packed into place around business and industrial units. The rest of the city had gentrified around it, but this little quarter of blocks had remained stubbornly the same.

"Come on, Trixi, don't let me down..." Alexa whispered as she parked the car in the alleyway behind the block, and saw that

THE **FLORIDA GIRL**

there were metal stairs going up the side of the building to the various units. She counted until she thought she had found the right floor and then took the stairs, two at a time.

Trixi had vanished into the crowd ahead of her back on the Beach, but the traffic had been hell getting off the Island for some reason, and Alexa was later than she had hoped getting to the address. There was a chance that Trixi had made it home already…

"Floor five, floor five…" Alexa mumbled to herself as she climbed, finally reaching the single door at the turn of the stairs– to see that the door was already ajar.

Crap. Alexa froze at the door, and her hand slid her gun from her under-arm holster. This Trixi Kiss hadn't *looked* like the sort of woman who was capable of orchestrating a murder of two men, but then again, *who knows?* Alexa furrowed her eyes and brought her sights up, staring down the line of the gun as she turned it slightly to one side in her two-handed grip.

Trixi had been in the brothers' apartment at the time of the killings. If anything, she and her partner could be working with the killer…

There was a sound from further inside, a muffled bang, a muttered curse…

And now she could be on the run… Alexa's body reacted. She moved forwards galvanically, nudging the door open with the side of her foot as she stepped forward, seeing a short hallway beyond, opening out into what must be a living room.

A trashed living room, the FBI agent saw immediately. There were clothes on the floor, one of the small tables had been overturned…

"Trixi?" Alexa called, just as the door beside her burst open, and a shape jumped out.

Alexa spun just as the shape barged right in front of her. Her finger flexed towards the trigger, almost pulled it…

Blonde hair. Dyed blonde hair.

But she didn't. Instead, as the figure barged into her, Alexa dropped her gun arm and grabbed with the other, snatching at the dancer's shoulder as they both slammed into the hallway wall.

"Get OFF me!" Trixi Kiss was struggling and shouting but Alexa wouldn't let go. She stuffed her gun back into her jacket pocket and grabbed Trixi's other shoulder, as the dancer clutched a large duffel bag to her chest.

"Trixi, goddammit! I'm not here to hurt you!"

"Who sent you – *who!?*" Trixi struggled again, but Alexa was the stronger. She turned her grab into a forced hug, clutching the dancer to her.

"I'm here to help you, goddamn! I'm Special Agent Alexa Landers, FBI!"

Almost instantaneously, the thin, nearly emaciated woman in her hands suddenly released her fight. She sagged in Alexa's arms, then trembled as a sob tore itself from her frail chest. Alexa found herself comforting the woman with small, almost nonsense murmurings.

She's terrified, Alexa knew, and she was babbling.

"I don't know… I don't know where Leela's gone. She said she was going to stay in – but we didn't have the money. We needed the money from Perelli…"

Alexa could see how devastated she was. Trixi 'Kiss' was a young woman, barely a year or two younger than herself, Alexa thought. But her skin was pale, and underneath the smeared mascara it was blotchy and malnourished. She had clearly been attempting to clear out, with a large cream canvas coat despite the oppressive Florida heat outside, and a duffel bag still unzipped and with clothes spilling out the top.

"Leela. She's gone. But she left without the money Perelli owed us," Trixi uttered through hitches of sobs, as Alexa tried to piece it together.

"Leela was your friend who was with you last night, wasn't she?" she asked, for Trixi's eyes to suddenly widen in fear.

"It's okay. We're trying to catch the person who killed Dimitre and Vadim, and we think that you and Leela were there the night it happened. I think you saw something, didn't you, Trixi?" Alexa asked, and the dancer's eyes remained just as wide, the nervous panic subsiding just a little. She nodded again, and Alexa could tell that she was battling with herself over how much she could say. She was measuring her chances of survival here, with the FBI agent, or out there and alone.

"They're professional, Trixi," Alexa said quickly. "I believe they took out Dimitre and Vadim's father, and I've never seen the likes of it…"

(She didn't point out that she had never seen a murder like this because this was technically her first job; that probably wouldn't help right now, Alexa figured.)

"Make no mistake, Trixi. The killer is very, *very* good at what they do, and they have a plan, that much is obvious. If you're with me, I can keep you safe. The FBI will protect you," Alexa said, then hesitated, before she pushed on, "I promise."

There was another second of that wide-eyed look of terror from the dancer, another desperate look out to the open door, and then Trixi let her duffel bag fall to the floor.

"I told Leela to wait here for me to come back with Perelli's money. We were going to catch the Greyhound as far from Florida as we could…"

Probably not a bad plan, Alexa didn't say. She wondered what she would have done in her position. Probably the same.

"Last night, what happened last night?" Alexa pressed, as her phone started to vibrate in her pocket.

Damnit, not now! she thought. She needed to organize witness protection, proper questioning. This woman had directly seen the killer!

"We went to the Bodrov brothers', just like every other time we do. Everything was going normal – well – normal for them, but then there was a knock on the door. A guy was talking, saying Henderson had sent him-"

"Max Henderson? From Little Haiti?" Alexa asked as her phone rang out, and then immediately started ringing once again. Whoever it was, it was important.

Trix blinked. "Yeah, I think so. I'm not sure where Max lived…"

"This man last night, did you see his face?" Alexa pushed as she pulled her phone out of her pocket. She didn't want to take her eyes off of Trixi's face.

The dancer nodded. "I saw him."

Yes!

But Trixi was still stammering, shaking her head. "I peeked through the bedroom door. I guess I wanted the drugs. He walked right past, and then, he – he shot them both!"

And the killer must never have even seen them, at first, Alexa mused. Maybe the killer had figured out that there were others there later, afterwards...?

Which meant that the other dancer, Leela, was also in danger.

"Do you think she ran before you?" Alexa asked as she gestured for Trixi to go ahead of them into the living room, still clearly shaken.

It looked like there had been a struggle in there, the table smashed, the small, threadbare sofa pushed to one side.

And there was blood on the corner table.

"It was him. He was here, wasn't he? He was looking for us..." Trixi breathed.

Oh crap. Her phone had finally stopped ringing, and she raised it to put a call in for a CSI Team. Where was Murphy, anyway?

It was then that she read the first message on her screen.

Active fire event involving Agent Murphy. Miami Beach South. Agent unhurt. Miami PD attending scene.

"What the actual ever-loving..." Alexa burst out.

CHAPTER NINETEEN

9:15 PM. MIAMI PD HEADQUARTERS

"He was well-trained and professional, for sure," Murphy described with a look of cold fury on his face.

They stood in one of the small corner offices in the large, white, modernist megaplex that was the headquarters of the Miami Police. On the outside it was built with tall, curving white stone walls made to look like pillars that, at night, were lit up with floodlights, giving it an imposing, threatening air. Inside, of course, Alexa found it to be another confusing, noisy, labyrinth of a building filled with uniformed Miami police hurrying about their tasks. The agents had been given a corner office to debrief, while Trixi was being brought through processing downstairs.

"The police have secured the scene, but I don't think they'll find much of anything," Murphy shook his head dispiritedly, squeezing his hands into fists.

"I should have been quicker! I could have got him!" the large agent snarled.

(It was a him, Alexa now knew. Trixi had seen a man enter the Bodrov Brothers' residence.)

Murphy had informed Alexa about the events of that afternoon, including the stationary boat at the Yacht Rentals club, and the rather thunderous events on Miami Beach South later, but despite his professionalism, Alexa hadn't seen Murphy like this before, she realized. Up until this point, the agent had been all cheer and optimism, but now it looked as though the events of this afternoon had shaken him, *no, not shaken;* angered him.

"There was nothing you could have done," Alexa said, remembering her urban policing training at the Academy, where they had a series of warehouses and pre-fab box buildings set up to simulate town shooter scenarios. *That* was always tricky.

"You didn't even know he was coming for you, and the cover and chaos in an urban environment..." she explained before Kage cut her off passionately.

"But I should have known! I heard the first bang and I thought it was a tire, but it clearly wasn't. If I had reacted quicker, I could have found his location sooner! People died!"

Which was true, Alexa thought. Two civilians had been hit by bullets intended for Kage, with one person injured from a ricochet, and one person dead. A further two more civilians were not seriously injured when their cars skidded to a crash.

On the whole, most had gotten off lightly, Alexa thought.

Kage hadn't managed to find the killer, but instead, all that her partner and the police team had found had been a series of old boat parts that could have been used as a sniper's nest, and a few shell casings. They were waiting on the bullet forensics, but even a cursory glance from Alexa could tell that they weren't small.

"They looked like 7.62 rifle shells, the same type as used in the father's murder, I'd be certain of it," Alexa murmured to which Kage dully agreed.

He can't handle losing, Alexa thought for a moment as she looked at the internal war continuing on inside her partner, but no – that wasn't quite right.

He can't handle other people endangered on his watch, Alexa realized, remembering how twitchy he had been about Alexa going on stakeout the first time. This little fact bothered her, not because it showed a vaguely knight-in-shining-armor syndrome, but because it showed a vulnerability in their partnership. They were FBI. Getting into danger, with or without your partner, was always going to be a part of the job.

"It must have been the car," Murphy went on. "I was coming back from *Speedies* with the identity of the man in the car that met with Mikhail Zholdin when the killer decided to take pot-shots at me…"

Pot-shots at a moving car, a pretty hard target, Alexa thought.

Kage grabbed the pieces of paper from the small desk beside them and brandished it in the air as if it were a shield.

"The killer *really* didn't want me to find this identity, which is…" He stopped and flicked through the papers. "Costa Ortiz, living right here in Miami Beach. And would you look at that…"

"What?"

"Little Haiti," Kage said through narrowed eyes.

"The same neighborhood as Henderson," Alexa said, as her mind raced, trying to trace the connections between all the names just like the whiteboard back in the FBI war room.

"Trixi knew Henderson. Henderson is a regular at Perelli's – probably a go-man for them. Next up, Bodrov Sr. is dead and Mikhail Zholdin, Aleksandr's long-lost friend is making some secret meeting with someone from Henderson's hood?" Alexa murmured.

Maybe it's not the Russian super-agent at all. Maybe it's the drug angle? Perelli gets Bodrov's sons mixed up in some drug thing, and it all goes south somehow…

"But how is Zholdin connected to the drugs?" Alexa followed her line of thought.

"Maybe Zholdin put them all up to it. Masterminded it? Maybe he wanted to take down Aleksandr for some reason. Aleksandr Bodrov was a billionaire, must have been a big player in business and manufacturing. I'm thinking Zholdin wanted less competition and decided to take out the family..." Kage nodded. "I think we're close, really close. This Costa Ortiz could *be* the killer."

"He could be," Alexa agreed, "if we're leaning on the Zholdin angle, then this killer is probably a mafia hitman, hired by Zholdin through his Henderson/Perelli connections..."

Kage made an agreeing noise. "Well, the *familia* certainly know how to get this done. They have the contacts."

"And it makes it all the more important to find out what business Bodrov and Zholdin were *really* doing," Alexa said, swiping through her phone until she found Dee's number at FBI Headquarters.

Alexa Landers:
Hi Dee. Can we talk about Bodrov's laptop? Whenever you get the chance.

She was just finishing when the door banged open, and in blustered the rounded shape of Detective Dempsey.

"We got your girl in one of the witness rooms below, ran through her events of the night and took details of the missing person," he said, apparently none too happy with the workload, or working to FBI requests, perhaps.

"Leela LaBelle," Alexa confirmed.

"Leela Mishan, in actual fact," Dempsey corrected with a gruff voice. "That's her real name on the tenancy agreement at the apartment she shared with Trixi Walters, aka Trixi Kiss."

Dempsey scowled for a moment. "The problem is, ladies and gentlemen of the Bureau, that they are both known felons. Both have been arrested for soliciting and drug possession charges, and our investigation of their place turned up yet more Class As, and that, unfortunately, isn't all..."

"Trixi Walters has testified that she delivered drugs multiple times to the Bodrov brothers, and that Max Henderson was a known supplier. She believes that the killer claimed to be bearing more Class As to the residence to gain entry, a mixture of cocaine and MDMA was the regular buy," Dempsey stated matter-of-factly.

"And the blood in their apartment? On the table?" Alexa asked.

The police detective shook his head. "It's way too soon for blood analysis to get back to us, but we already have Leela's DNA on file thanks to the previous charges, so when we have it, I'm sure you'll be the first to know."

"But it's consistent with an intruder; a possible kidnapping?" Alexa pressed.

"Yeah, sure thing, Landers – but excuse me if we have something a bit more important on our plate right now. We had an active shooter incident right on Miami Beach! All our available units are combing the area for witnesses and evidence, and probably will be doing the same thing tomorrow, too." Dempsey glared at everyone in the room – even at Kage, which Alexa thought was pretty unfair, considering all her partner did was have the audacity of getting shot on Dempsey's beat.

"But we do have this, it's not much, and to be honest I think it looks like every other northern schmo we get down here…" Dempsey waved a sheath of papers, laying them on the table to show an artist's reconstruction of the man that Trixi had seen through the crack in the door.

Strong jawbone, a little stubble. Alexa looked at the pictures, saw that the man was wearing a baseball cap but had the edges of tawny or blondish short hair underneath. A sharp nose, and that was about it for defining features.

"The witness reckons blue eyes, but says they could have been hazel or grey. We're looking at a man in his mid-to-late thirties, athletic-type, lean, about six foot," Dempsey sighed. "What we here call a Regular Joe," he added with a hint of resignation.

Kage groaned similarly, and Alexa understood their frustration. The man they were looking at could be almost anyone, any fairly athletic average-American Caucasian white male. Could be the sports coach at your child's little league, or the guy who comes and does your lawns every other Saturday.

"Tan?" Kage said, which, given the fact that his skin was slightly warmer than white, Alexa thought was a little inconsequential.

"Urmm, not that Trixi appeared to remember," the detective said, checking his notes, "regular white complexion."

"Then he's probably a visitor, as you say," Kage nodded. "Even you, Dempsey, have got a bit of a blush going on there, while I have been blessed by my God-given good Irish and Japanese looks."

Alexa looked and realized it was true. The detective was probably more Double Scotch complexion than Miami Beach with his ruddy cheeks, but there was certainly a golden bake around the edges, with pronounced crow's feet around his eyes.

All that fierce Florida sun, Alexa thought, and wondered if she was going to get the same treatment if her posting down here went on for longer.

"Right. Zholdin, Perelli." Alexa shook her head from her cosmetic misgivings. "That's the play. And the missing Leela."

"We've got this Leela Mishan's picture and I'll forward it to the patrol cars, but," Dempsey shrugged a little. "Miami is a busy place, and like I say, most of my officers are on high alert for a public shooter right now."

"Anything you can do, that would be great," Alexa said, although internally she could've shouted. Kage was right, they *were* getting closer to the killer. Close enough that he was rattled; enough to start taking pot-shots at FBI agents, anyway.

And a rattled killer makes mistakes, she thought with grim satisfaction. *But they were also very, very dangerous.*

"Actually, there *is* something you can do for us, Detective," Kage said, offering his own sheets of paper in return for the artist's mock-ups.

"Costa Ortiz. He's the guy who rented the car and met with Zholdin, and the killer seemed to get pretty damn tetchy when I went to find his name. I need everything you have on him."

Dempsey promised that he would do as much.

"We got his license registration and his address. I say we don't waste any time, what do you say?" Kage summarized, already standing up.

"Wait a minute," Alexa interrupted, holding out her hand to her partner. "We've just come off a long day which included a couple bodies and you getting shot at. If we're going to do a take on Ortiz's residence, then we need to be sharp."

"He's out there. He killed innocent civilians," Kage said, his eyes flashing.

"That as may be, but if this Ortiz guy really is the killer, then we know how good he is. We're going to need to be rested and prepared. How long does it take for a SWAT team to be deployed in this part of the world?"

Dempsey pulled a face, as did Murphy, but it was Murphy who answered her.

"Once Chief Williams has authorized it, we can have one in under six hours, I'd say."

Alexa nodded. "Good. That gives us enough time to rest up, eat. We can knock on his door just before dawn, how does that sound?"

"Ortiz could be getting away!" Murphy once again bunched his fists.

"And we have just given his name and driver ID to the police, who are putting all their resources into finding him, aren't you, Detective?" Alexa said.

"Listen to the lady, Agent. She's speaking a lot of sense. I know that there are plenty of cops on my detail who will want to be in on taking down this killer, and by morning we can have his whole neighborhood locked down tighter than a fish's ass."

Colorful, Alexa thought, but she appreciated the sentiment.

"Do it," she nodded. "Have patrol cars keep on eye on Little Haiti, without being too obvious if you can. While we-" she gave Murphy a meaningful look, "are going to get some rest. Got it?"

Murphy wasn't happy about it. He wasn't happy about it *at all*, but she could see that he saw sense in what she was saying.

"Okay, boss," he muttered as he gathered his things.

CHAPTER TWENTY

12:35 PM, FBI SAFE HOUSE, 5 HOURS BEFORE RAID

Despite her previously strong words to her partner a little while ago, Alexa found herself filled with an electric energy and unable to sleep inside the small, one-bed motel room and safe house she had been appointed.

"Ugh!" She threw off the coverlet once more, stifling in the Miami heat that was still omnipresent despite the A/C and the ceiling fan that she had left buzzing on all night.

It was the case. It was the raid tomorrow. It was Florida, she thought as she swung her legs from her bed, got up, and began to pace her room.

THE **FLORIDA GIRL**

She moved under the flickering light, dressed only in her t-shirt and shorts as the buzz and hum of the room accompanied her thoughts. On the bedside table sat the heavy accusation of her gun inside its holster, and somehow her eyes kept returning to it.

Tomorrow morning was going to be a big day. A raid on Costa Ortiz, the man who met Zholdin and the possible killer. Or at least one step closer to the killer.

Who had shown themselves VERY capable of using both long- and short-range firearms, and had probably done military service.

Damn, I should have put in a request to the National Service records on him last night, Alexa thought before realizing that it was too late now. For all she knew Ortiz could be an assumed name anyway; it didn't particularly *sound* regular blonde-hair and blue-eyed American, but then again, how was she to know?

Alexa felt like the events of the last few days had been coming at her too fast, without even a chance to rise for air.

Zholdin...Perelli...Trixi...Henderson...

The names swirled around and around in her head, but she still felt no clearer about the connections between them. This bothered her. It bothered her greatly.

"You always gotta be right, kiddo?" she remembered her father asking her one day when she came home crying how she'd 'flunked' a math test at school, having only scored a measly 70%.

"Not right. But know where I'm wrong," she muttered what she'd said back then to earn a chuckle from her dad and even an affectionate pat on the shoulder.

"That's about all any of us can ask for sometimes, I guess..." he'd said.

But now, Alexa felt like she had no idea where she was wrong. Was it a Russian super-spy? Scratch that. Why the connection between Ortiz, Little Haiti, and Zholdin? Was it a mafia drugs thing? Maybe. The sons were knee-deep in every vice this city could generously put on offer, apparently...

But still, something didn't add up. It didn't feel right.

The killer had must've been tracking Kage and watching us, maybe the whole time, she suddenly thought. He had killed the

Bodrov sons, then found time to keep an eye on the investigation running against him.

Who does that? Who was even capable of doing that?

"Think it through, Kiddo. I know that brain of yours can work it out..."

She heard her father's voice, not husky and breathless yet, as if it were right there beside her.

"If he were a professional, he'd even have an enhanced viewing scope," she reasoned. The man, our Mr. Blonde, could have driven the boat away from the marina and returned to get eyes on what was happening, who turned up. If he had his rifle with him then he could have taken her or Kage's head off without any of them knowing they were in the slightest danger.

And therefore...

He'd been keeping an eye on them since then. Maybe taking their numberplates. Maybe following them.

"He was contracted to do the sons as well, and he had a jammer to knock out the Miami Heights cameras," she reasoned, building a timeline picture in her head of the killer's actions. Maybe Perelli, if he was in on it, even warned the killer of the mouthy FBI agents who had turned up threatening to turn his business over.

The killer, perhaps this Cortiz, might even know they had his name and address now, and would be coming for him...

Alexa moved to her phone, unplugging it from where it was charging to check for updates. There were two.

Det. Dempsey.
Costa Ortiz residence confirmed 1-28 Little Haiti. Previous gang offences inc. firearms. Team ready at 5:30 am.

Dee (work hours only)
Hi Alexa, no problems. Been working 'round the clock and I never sleep anyway...
Kage asked me to chase up 'the pink boat' pictures @ Yacht Rental, South Marina. It's not a rental with the company. I've pinged the DMV + Coastal Authority for the registration, but they're taking time to get back to me...

And on Alexsandr Bodrov's laptop: we've managed to break into the BIOS fairly easily, and have performed a ghost-copy of data before parsing sniffers on it-

(Alexa had no idea what any of this meant)

The bad news is the entire laptop is encrypted, and pretty heavily. But I've managed to trace the TYPE of encryption based on the bit-scatter rate. It's a military-spec level program operated by SYSTEMTECH LABS. Private company, supplies military and private clients. Costs A LOT!!
Good luck and stay safe out there – heard about Kage.

Alexa permitted herself a small smile at that gesture of friendliness. She thought she probably shared some of the same obsessive work ethic with Dee, and admired the cyber-geek's intelligence.

But still, this encryption business was going to prove almost disastrous. She'd had several lectures at the Academy on how it was almost impossible to get a data company to hand over their data, and this SYSTEMTECH sounded like they were top-notch.

It would require a judge, maybe even a senatorial hearing to overturn a dead victim's personal passwords, if the security company held them, that was. Breaking into a user's private data, even a dead user, was still breaking several very important constitutional rights, and could only be done if it was shown that the user was a severe and present threat to 'the people, or way of life of the nation.'

"Dammit!" Alexa grumbled to herself. IF she could get into that laptop, she might be able to find out *why* Zholdin had hired this mafia killer to bump off the Bodrov family.

There was a sudden flare of light from the blinds as a car must have pulled into the motel parking lot, and Alexa froze reflexively. She knew that they couldn't see her, not behind the blinds, but there was something about being caught in the headlights that had her spooked.

The killer had been watching them the whole time. Following them.

You had better be careful, Agent Landers; that was what the note had said, wasn't it?

The car headlights stayed on, glaring at her window for a fraction longer, and Alexa, perhaps through nerves or lack of sleep, gave in to her anxieties. She moved to the side of the window blinds, putting her side to the door as she gingerly teased the blinds apart for a moment…

But the car headlights flared once more and pulling away. Maybe it was someone picking someone up, or dropping off, from the motel; or maybe it was just someone taking a wrong turn…

Or maybe it wasn't.

The car was gone, disappearing back along the main road and getting lost in the traffic, but Alexa stood there for a long time. Eventually, she moved back to bed, pausing to slide her gun from its holster, and place it under her pillow.

CHAPTER TWENTY-ONE

DAY 4.

5:45 AM. COSTA ORTIZ'S RESIDENCE. 1-28 LITTLE HAITI

"All units in place?" Alexa heard Kage whisper over the small radio headsets they were all wearing, supplied courtesy of the FBI Special Weapons and Tactics (SWAT) team, who were right now pulling up in a large van at the end of the street adjacent to theirs.

The Ortiz residence was like any other in this part of Little Haiti, Alexa thought. Perhaps a little bigger. A large, single-floor bungalow that sat at the back of a small street, next to a series of garages. Alexa reckoned that this part of the town must have been designed by urban planners to create a community feel, with everyone allowed to park at one end of the street – but it looked to her from where she sat in the blacked-out SUV at the top of the street like a trap.

Too many windows. Too many alleyways between the houses.

Alexa sat next to Kage in the front of the SUV, while Detective Dempsey and four more Miami PD patrol cars were a block away, waiting to swoop in and close this street and the ones behind it to stop any potential escape.

"No word on Ortiz himself?" Alexa asked, and Kage shook his head. Even though he must have gotten as little sleep as she had, arriving at her motel at 4:30 in the morning to pick her up for this, Kage appeared focussed and intense as he kept his eyes on the house at the end of the street.

"You see the three cars out front? The blue Toyota is registered to Ortiz, and it hasn't moved all last night, but on-foot undercover say that plenty of people have come and gone from the residence."

"Numbers?" Alexa said, sparing a glance down at her phone to look at the downloaded notes that Dempsey had sent through (really just a set of PDFs held in the Miami PD criminal database).

Link to gang activities.

Suspected gun trafficking.

Suspected drug trafficking.

Suspected HQ for 34-27 Crew; Latino gang; suspected Mexican cartel off-shoot…

"Well, Zholdin sure does pick his friends, doesn't he?" Alexa whistled, especially when she got to the write-up of the 34-27 crew.

"A mostly Latinx gang, mixed Cuban, Puerto Rican and Mexican American members. Known to operate throughout Florida state, and has ties to Mexican drug cartels in Mexico City, as study on the flow of narcotics indicates. Highly violent."

Which really didn't sound like a mafia game at all. Alexa furrowed her brows.

"SWAT is good to go. You ready?" Kage said, sparing her a look before he put on the helmet and goggles waiting for them.

Alexa was similarly kitted out in a heavy vest and padded, armored greaves, making her feel like a football or hockey player, but the worst part was the feeling of having her head enclosed in the metal helmet. Oh sure, she didn't want to get shot, but she resisted the way that it closed her vision, making her concentrate on only what was in front of her, not to either side at all.

In her hands was her service pistol, and she had two extra magazines on her belt.

"Weapons live and secure. I'm ready. We're on lead?" Alexa confirmed, and Kage pressed the call button on the side of his helmet, where the radio headset was located.

"Agent Murphy and Agent Landers on point. Go in 10, 9, 8 and-"

Kage opened his door early, jumping out as Alexa did the same, both heading quickly down the street at a slow jog, straight towards the house at the end.

The key was surprise. The key was shock and overwhelming force before anyone could pick their gun from their ass... all of this Alexa knew, but she still felt her heart racing. She felt the adrenaline kicking through her system and knew it for what it was. She could taste metal in the back of her mouth, everything was sharper, brighter as her endorphins kicked in.

Before they even got to the door they heard the sudden rev of the SWAT engine as the van carrying the most deadly FBI officers hurtled down the street.

Steps up to the main porch. No one on guard, but Alexa was sure she saw a flicker of movement from the window.

"Go!" she called, skidding to a halt and kneeling as she took aim, as Murphy bounded up to the main door and banged on it with his free fist.

"FBI! Open up or we're coming in!" he hollered in his 'agent voice.'

"FBI!" Alexa found herself shouting at the same time, but whomever might have been at the window didn't return. The SWAT van was skidding to a halt and the doors were already opening, disgorging a unit of five even more heavily armored men with short, nasty looking automatic rifles already jumping out of the vehicles and running to back up Kage, the first two of whom were carrying one of the black, cylindrical battering rams.

Alexa heard the screech of tires and the approaching sounds of the Miami PD cops who'd been told to just block the streets, not engage.

"OPEN UP! FBI!" Kage hollered one more time as Alexa turned to the alley at the side of the house, as planned.

"Going for the back!" she shouted, leaping past a spray of bushes as the first battering thud landed.

She was halfway down the alleyway to the back of the house when she heard the muffled sound of the next ram hit, and the sudden splintering of the front door. Ahead of her was the back yard of the Ortiz residence, opening out onto the street beyond where there were yet more parked cars.

No knowledge of how many are inside.

The squad cars were taking their time in getting to the back street, Alexa saw in the next moment as she rounded the corner of the house. *They should have had the back yard blocked off by now!*

"Oof!"

There was a grunt as the back door sprang open, and two males burst out of it.

"FREEZE! FBI!" Alexa yelled, but the first didn't even stop as the second barrelled into her. Alexa grunted, hitting the ground and rolling, remembering only to take her finger off the trigger. No misfires here.

"I said freeze!" she yelled, continuing her roll as she kicked a leg out, catching one of the men as he scrambled to his feet, and bringing him down to the ground with a heavy thud.

"Ortiz! Costa Ortiz!" she snarled as she threw her weight against him, knee first into the small of his back.

Whap. Whap.

Then came the unmistakeable sound of bullet fire, only Alexa wasn't sure where from.

"Active fire!"

Someone was shouting from inside her headset. A screech of tires and more shouting in front of her as the delayed police cars arrived, with one of them immediately spilling officers after the running man in the hoodie; the first to leave the Ortiz residence.

"*Peuta!* Get off me, lady! Get off me!" The man underneath her was struggling, or attempting to as Alexa grabbed one arm with one hand and held it behind his back, at the same time as holding her gun.

"Stop moving! FBI! Special Agent Landers, and I'm armed, you idiot. You want to get booked for assaulting a federal officer?"

The man grunted, shrugging another time before relaxing.

"Easy, easy!" he was shouting, as more cops were already racing towards her past the cars.

Whap!

Another sound of gunfire, this time from inside the house as Alexa swore. Kage was in there. The 34-27s were gun runners. How many of them would decide to try and shoot their way out and ditch for Mexico or Cuba instead of life in max security?

"Officers, grab him!" she yelled as the first officer skidded to a halt beside the offender, already roughly grabbing his wrists to cuff him.

"Ortiz. We want Costa Ortiz – where is he?" Alexa was breathing hard, her limbs felt electric.

"Fuck you, lady. Give me my lawyer!" the man barked back just as there was a sudden, unmistakable rat-tat-tat of automatic weapons, and the rear windows of the house burst out in a splinter of glass.

Alexa swore, grabbing at the police officer and ducking his head lower.

"Get out of here. Get back behind the cars!" she ordered as she turned back to the open back door.

You have to wait for SWAT to clear. You have to wait.

The words were ringing in her ears as she crouched, gun up, on the dirty cracked earth of the 34-27 back yard. Everything in her training knew how this had to go. *Had* to go. Too many surprised people in a small space only leads to one thing, and that was happening right now.

But Kage was in there.

"Kage! What's happening? Do you need back up?" Alexa bobbed and ducked her head, trying to get a sense of what was going on without presenting herself as a visible target.

Radio silence.

There was a roar of voices and static over her headset before Kage's garbled voice returned.

"-heavy fire. Heading your direction. Clear out!"

There were more loud thumps and sounds of shouting voices from inside the house as Alexa threw a look around her. There were the parked cars, then the street, then the barricading police cars. Too far to get to the police vehicles, she threw herself to the side of one of the parked cars, sprawling, and then turning in place to pop back up as the sound of shouting got closer and nearer.

A shape appeared at the back door. A man, somewhere north of his thirties, half-turning as he raised his arm back into the building.

"Freeze! FBI!" Alexa shouted.

The man spun towards her, holding something in his hand.

Something dark and blocky.

A gun!

"Drop it!" Alexa managed to shout before the hood of the car she was hiding behind suddenly pranged with one, then two bullets.

Shit!

Alexa swivelled behind the side of the car as more men came barrelling through the back door, shouting.

"I said *FREEZE!*" Alexa popped back up as she heard the police shouting behind her to see a trio of men already racing towards the cars. The one with the wild black hair was in the lead, and he was scowling as he raised his gun towards her…

Whap!

Alexa pulled the trigger, the bullet catching the man in the thigh, spinning him to the ground. He cried out in agony, but the effect it had on the other two was dramatic, as they jumped to either side on the dirt, skidding to the ground.

"Don't shoot!" one of them yelled desperately as Alexa covered them.

"No one move! On the floor! Drop your weapons!" She held her position as there was a pound of heavy footsteps, and the first of the SWAT team appeared, covering the downed men with his own semi-automatic.

"Special Agent Landers!" Alexa called out, identifying herself as early as possible as the square-built FBI agent held his ground, covering the men as the one that Alexa had shot groaned and cursed loudly.

"Clear, all clear. One agent injured. Two shooters down-" Kage's voice returned as the sounds of shouting abruptly stopped, descending them all into an eerie silence.

All of a sudden, it was over, and Alexa felt her body shiver and tremble with all the accumulated adrenaline. But she kept her guns trained on the three men on the ground until she got the official sign from the SWAT member.

"You have the scene?" she asked.

"I have the scene. Safe to proceed," he intoned, as more of his squad arrived behind him. Within minutes, the backup police were called in behind Alexa to surround the men and cuff them, as Alexa moved quickly to the wounded man.

"Ambulance!" she shouted, stripping off her helmet and goggles so she could get a better look of the man on the ground.

It was a clean shot, a through-and-through to the outer thigh, with a possible connection to the bone, she reckoned as she pulled at her belt to unravel the wadding of bandages and apply pressure to his upper thigh. She hadn't hit the artery and he wasn't bleeding profusely. He would live.

"Aaargh!" the man yelled in pain as Alexa signalled for the nearest officers to take over.

"Get this man to the hospital first. No questioning," she said before moving onto the next man trussed on the ground with his hands cuffed behind his back.

"Ortiz? Which one is Costa Ortiz?" she called as neither man said anything.

"*Fine,*" Alexa hissed. "Let's do this the hard way, shall we?" She went through their pockets, finding a steel pipe, a knife, and a few hundred dollars on the silent first perp, and much the same on the second, as well as a wallet.

"Bingo," she said, flipping it to see, rather disappointingly, that this second man was named Costa Ortiz.

Alexa looked at his close-shaven black hair. *Well, you certainly aren't blonde and blue-eyed, are you?* She huffed in frustration, checking the driver's license once again to see if there had been any tampering with the photo. None that she could make out, anyway.

"Damnit!" she snapped, as Kage arrived at the end of the hallway, already with his own helmet off and looking wide-eyed.

"We got firearms, drugs, and at least two attempted murders of federal agents. The DA is going to love this," he said before he saw Alexa's face.

"What is it?"

"He's not our guy. Ortiz. He's not the one," she said, gesturing with her chin down at the man below her and throwing Kage the wallet.

Kage looked at it for a moment, then at the man on the ground. He had to be about five-foot-nine, ten, not six. And once again, certainly not Caucasian.

"He doesn't even look like the man who met Zholdin," Kage muttered, as he waited for the other suspects to be hauled away by the police, and the SWAT to return to the house for a final sweep, leaving two Miami PD and Kage and Alexa with Ortiz, their guy who wasn't their guy.

"Am I under arrest!? What the hell is this?" Costa growled into the ground.

"You certainly will be under arrest, Mr. Ortiz," Kage replied and kneeled down beside him. "But first you can help yourself out a *whole lot* if you answer me why your ID rented a car out of *Speedies Miami Beach* to travel over to Hollywood, Florida…?"

"You can kiss my ass, Bureau-boy, I know my rights," Ortiz sneered.

"Okey-doke," Kage sighed, looking up at Alexa – who had a sudden idea.

"Mr. Ortiz. Your ID has been implicated in an attack on a federal agent. And right in your gang house I bet there are going to be *masses* of your fingerprints on all sorts of things there shouldn't be. Guns. Class As. Weapons. Who knows?"

Costa suddenly went very quiet, and very still.

"That alone will get you plenty of jail time, I'm sure. And as we know this is a 34-27 hideout, then we can charge for criminal conspiracy, wouldn't you say, Agent Murphy?" Alexa nodded to Kage, who took her understanding.

"Any members of the organization can be complicit in the crimes of the organization by federal law. Not only that, but I saw *you*, Costa, with a gun in your hand before you ditched it and fled. That's conspiracy to kill a federal officer."

"Wait – I didn't even shoot anyone!" Costa snarled, as Alexa leaned down and hissed in his ear.

"You don't have to for conspiracy, nitwit. The Bureau is going to throw the book at you, and your only hope is to help us out with this *one* question: Who was using your ID to rent a car? What for?"

Ortiz was silent for a moment longer, but then when his voice came back, it was whispery and thin.

"He'll have me killed. I can't."

"Who will?" Alexa said quickly. *The shooter? Mr. Blonde?*

Ortiz had gone from the strong gangbanger to a scared ageing man in a heartbeat.

"You don't get it. You have no idea who you're messing with. He can reach out and kill me!" Ortiz blubbered.

"Then tell us *who*, Ortiz. The Bureau can protect you!" Alexa said, when Kage cleared his throat.

"And if you don't, one of these men will. That's the beauty of conspiracy charges, Mr. Ortiz. One of those guys won't want to bite an attempted murder charge. Not in Florida. Do you know which one it will be? Because this offer is time-limited."

"What offer?" Costa asked.

Alexa looked at Kage, not knowing what they should promise the man in this jurisdiction. As it happened, Kage did.

"You turn informant on the 34-27s. At least reduced sentencing, no conspiracy."

"*No* charges. I want no charges at all!" Costa howled.

Kage chuckled coldly. "That depends on the quality of your information."

Alexa was certain that the gang member wasn't going to take the deal. She was sure that he was going to refuse – and so she was surprised when he coughed and spluttered into the ground a name.

"*El Tigre*. It was *El Tigre* who used my ID!"

CHAPTER TWENTY-TWO

11:30 AM. FBI HQ [UNDISCLOSED LOCATION]

"E*L TIGRE*, OR ONE CARLOS ZARBOS, IS ONE OF THE up-and-coming Mexican cartel bosses said to now control up to 35% all of the cartel cocaine trade coming into the United States," said the heavy and gruff tones of Chief Williams in front of them as they stood in the Bodrov war room.

On one of the walls were the rather disturbing pictures of the bodies of the father and the two sons already killed. Alexa's eyes slid away from those images, even though she knew that it reminded her of who they were dealing with.

Even if we have NO IDEA who we are dealing with! she inwardly raged.

On the other side of the room was the current whiteboard, with its list of names and connections and possible theories.

RUSSIAN STATE
PERELLI / DRUGS?

Now of course, Alexa realized that she would have to put ZHOLDIN on that list as well as this 'El Tigre' guy, too.

"Your asset, Costa Ortiz, is a member of the 34-27 gang, which although operates on American ground, is *highly* connected to the Zarbos network. If we can prove actual connection, as apparently your witness statement does, then you're opening up a whole load of resources and interest from ATF and DEA…" Williams said, apparently pleased.

"But, sir?" Alexa raised her hand. There was only the chief, Kage, and herself in the room.

"Mexican cartels *isn't* our case, sir, or at least, I didn't think it was."

Williams' brow furrowed just a little for a moment. "Well, seeing as though you haven't got a solid case against anyone yet, Special Agent Landers, then I'd say the *Tigre* option is wide open, wouldn't you?"

Ouch, Alexa thought.

"Yes, sir," she nodded. But it still didn't make any sense to her.

"As I was saying. Your Mr. Ortiz is turning state evidence, and I thoroughly expect that he will be granted leniency, probably witness protection in return for as much information about Carlos Zorbas as possible."

"Like, what he is doing meeting Zholdin?" Kage jumped in, as Williams turned to click a few times on a laptop, and an image of young middle-aged man to appear on the screen. He was good looking, Alexa thought.

"And here's your photos," Williams said, as a series of images from Kage's stakeout on Mikhail Zholdin appeared. They showed

THE FLORIDA GIRL

the battered sedan car, the man in the wide panama hat getting out of the car, the dark hair…

"It's him," both Kage and Alexa said at once. They could make out the line of the nose, the sharp brow line. It looked to be the same guy, indeed.

"Our new informant Mr. Ortiz states that he has no idea why Zarbos made such a trip to the US, only that he was told by his regional boss to hand over his driver's license, to which, of course, Ortiz agreed," Chief Williams said heavily.

"However, Ortiz did claim that the rumors were that *El Tigre* had business with some big Russian businessman, but he doesn't know who, what, or why," Williams said, clicking off the photos before looking up at the two agents.

"Zholdin," Kage confirmed. "We can bring him in for more questioning on that, but I'm not sure we'll be able to get to the bottom of it unless we have something…the laptop? What about access to Zholdin's personal communications?" He looked over at Alexa, who shook her head.

"It's going to require like, *a lot,*" she groaned. "We'll need to get a court warrant for the security provider he uses to open up their code."

"A subpoena," Chief Williams corrected. "I have a few friendly judges who might be willing to sign off on that, especially now that we have *El Tigre* involved in the case. But we'd have to be VERY careful about what we're asking, and to whom. I think we can ask for Aleksandr Bodrov's laptop and Mikhail Zholdin's personal comms to be accessed because of their direct relationship to a crime. But OGRE's, Zholdin's company? That will put us toe-to-toe with their lawyers." The chief gave them a small grimace before breaking out into a wide grin.

"Luckily, I have no qualms about getting into fights with jumped-up Silicon Valley law firms. I'll talk to Judge Oakland."

Yes! Alexa could have hugged him, not that she thought the chief would ever appreciate it.

"However," the chief began, his smile fading as quickly as a rain cloud evaporates in the Miami sky. "You've got an active shooter taking shots at you, and a total of four dead, three murder suspects, one civilian, and a missing woman; this Leela Mishan character. This is turning into a very serious case, and as yet I still haven't heard a plausible theory as to *just what the hell is going on!*"

The chief ended with exasperation, and Alexa could see his earlier good humor, although genuine, only covered a much deeper frustration.

"Our best theory is that this is a hired killer who has been working either for Zholdin, Perelli, and now this *El Tigre*," Alexa said in irritation. In truth, she shared the chief's frustration. "We know that the Bodrov sons owed Perelli money, but maybe it was more than that. Maybe it was an honor thing."

"The Russian sons were apparently pretty wild," Kage offered. "They could easily have stepped on toes."

A thought struck Alexa. "What if it was the Bodrov sons who were the real targets? And the killer took out the dad because of his obvious power?"

"So, you're axing this," the chief turned around and drew a thick line through one of the theories on the whiteboard.

RUSSIAN STATE?

"I guess we have to put that on the back burner, at least for now," Alexa agreed. She hated the way she felt about it, apologetic that her earlier theory might have been wrong.

I'm better than this.

"I know that brain of yours can work it out, kiddo…"

"What, *all* of them?" the chief turned back to them. "You are suggesting some sort of criminal mega-conspiracy between the mafia and the Mexican cartels?"

The question hung in the air, and it was a heavy one. Alexa knew that if she answered 'yes' at this point then it would have ramifications. It wouldn't just be the work of this small war room and this small FBI field office anymore. They really *would* need to bring in cross-agency, cross-jurisdictional support. ATF. DEA. Marshals…

But at the center of it all is a dead billionaire, Alexa thought. *Get to the facts. Just the facts.*

There was a witness – Trixi. And there was a killer.

"The killer is an ex-military professional. That has got to come at a high price. Someone with enough money and motive to hire our Mr. Blonde," she murmured, that brain of hers swirling and coalescing. It all hinged on the killer. That was the root of this, it always would be.

"We need the killer," Alexa said, earning a gripe of annoyance from the chief in front of her. She could almost hear him saying 'well, duh!?' in the back of his mind.

"And what plans do you have to catch him?" the chief asked pointedly.

"We have Trixi. We have an artist's impression. We have multiple crime scenes…" she muttered under the harsh, exacting eye of the chief.

"Then you'd better work them then, huh?" Williams grumbled, collecting his papers, and walking out of the door.

CHAPTER TWENTY-THREE

3:45 PM. MIAMI PD HEADQUARTERS

"U*GH!*" Alexa groaned as she leaned back in her chair and looked at the grey-painted breeze block walls around her. This was impossible.

In front of her was a bare metal desk bolted to the floor, and right across from where she sat was a large black-window screen. A moment later there was a knock on the door and it opened for Kage to walk in, with a similar look of resignation on his face.

"Same result?" he inquired softly as he slapped a sheath of interview papers on the desk in a manilla envelope.

"Yep. Not one of the 34-27 crew know anything about why *El Tigre* was here in the US, either that or they're all brilliant liars," she groaned, picking up the sheets to leaf through the top few papers. A myriad of mugshots and names met her eyes before transcripts that mostly covered a variety of the same thing: *Absolute Bubkiss, as my dad would have said…*

The FBI agents had returned to the Miami Police Department (much to the general dismay of Detective Dempsey, it had to be said) to 'help' with the interviews of the gang suspects. In actual fact, Alexa and Kage just wanted to sit in and see if there was any connection they could find between *El Tigre*, Zholdin, and Perelli.

Anything. Someone they had known in common. Some place they had all gone to at the same time. Anything to prove that their hesitant theory that the Bodrov family had fallen into some criminal turf-war.

"Well, of any of my three, none of them knew anything about Vadim or Dimitre," Kage said. "I showed them the mugshots, and it didn't seem to ring any bells…but they could be lying, as you say."

"Henderson?" Alexa asked, receiving another shake of the head from her partner. The truth was that her interviews had turned up the same zero result. None of the men she had talked to seemed to have any interest in business, or manufacturing, or anything that Aleksandr Bodrov had surrounded himself with.

But that is what they would've been told to say, right? she self-questioned before groaning once more and rubbing her eyes wearily.

"Two of mine admitted to knowing *of* the VIV Lounge but said they could never afford to go there – and, quite frankly, I think I believe them. A group of young Latino gangbangers heading into one of the Beach's premier nightspots?" Alexa shrugged. "What do you think?"

Kage considered for a moment. "I think Perelli would have them thrown out at a drop of a hat."

Alexa murmured desultorily, "Me too," but then she thought about it. "But would Perelli ask *El Tigre* to get the job done *for* the mafia?"

She saw Kage nodding at that. "It feels like the sort of thing he would do. Insulate the mafia from direct involvement. Get another gang to do the hit for him."

"And take the fall for it," Alexa added.

So where did Zholdin fit into this? Was he just a go-between? she thought.

They needed stronger ties between the three: Zholdin, Perelli, and *El Tigre*. They needed evidence of conspiracy, or strong enough presumption that it would convince 12 jurors to indict.

Twelve out of sixteen, Alexa knew. That was the numbers for a grand jury, and given the characters and the multiple murders involved in this case, then that was the sort of jury it would be.

And hell, I'm not sure EVEN I believe this, Alexa grumbled, when there was a knock on the door, and a young, fresh-faced Miami police officer rushed in.

"Agent Landers, Murphy?" she nodded at them both. "Dempsey wants you, asap. A body's been found at Miami Beach North. He said you'll definitely want to know about this. African American woman in her twenties, signs of being strangled."

"What-?" Kage was confused, but Alexa's heart had already sunk.

"Leela. It's Leela Mishan."

CHAPTER TWENTY-FOUR

5:15 PM. MIAMI BEACH NORTH, WATER-SIDE

THE WOMAN'S BODY STILL LAY WHERE THE BEACH-WALKERS had found her, half hidden under one of the small marina piers that jutted out onto the cerulean waters. Above the grisly scene on the Beach roadway there were cars zipping past blaring music, and the near laughs and calls of people enjoying the sights.

Not this sight, though.

Alexa's lip curled in disgust. If she raised her head, she could see the tops of the tall buildings of the Beach, already with their lights starting to flash and entice as they called in the night.

Somewhere there was the smell of a drift of cannabis wafting over the Beach from the revellers.

Alexa returned her attention to the woman dressed in dark, formfitting leggings and a white vest top. Nothing else. No coat, no jewellery, no bags, no earrings, no adornments. Even if those leggings did have pockets (and quite how they would have fitted them in, Alexa had no idea) she didn't think that they would find anything in them at all.

No, because she was taken from her apartment, wasn't she? Alexa thought back to that small, two-room hovel in the center of downtown Miami. Trashed, the obvious scene of a struggle.

That strike of blood against the corner of the table.

He probably followed her home. Or maybe Mr. Blonde was already waiting for her when she got there. She tried not to imagine all the terrible ways that it might have gone; the screams, the shouts, the calls of help or perhaps the quiet terror falling on Leela when a gun was pointed at her face...

But it was her job to walk through the terrible, wasn't it?

The body of the woman was splayed out, one leg half over the other and her arms up, head thrown back, with her top half-riding up her torso, exposing a smooth, muscular belly. Leela Labelle – Leela Mishan – had been beautiful. She still was in many ways, apart from the obvious complications.

Her hair was braided but was in a spray over the sand and rocks of this darkened, grubby place under the marine pilings. Much of it had started to fray out of its tight braids that must've taken hours and hours to get right, the agent thought.

"A walker saw her this afternoon, and we got the call in," the detective commented. "But given how public it is on the beach, we're thinking she was dumped in the water and floated in. Strangulation," Dempsey grunted, pointing at the darker marks around the dancer's clearly exposed neck. Around them, Miami PD had already set up a hasty cordon of police tape, and there was a forensic team moving in to take pictures and catalogue the body in place. Alexa was starting to recognize at least two of the forensic workers and thought that they were starting to look harried.

Don't blame them, she thought. *How many sights across Miami had her investigation called them out on?*

"How many days has it been?" Alexa asked.

One of the forensics specialists looked up and pulled a face before moving to the body and starting to turn and prod at her torso.

"I'd not even say a day. A few hours in the water perhaps, water retention is low…"

No, I meant the investigation itself, Alexa thought. Four days. It had only been four days and now four bodies.

"The water retention proves the dumped in the water theory," Kage explained, turning to look out over the darkening waters, and all the pretty lights of the boats out there, floating on the darkness.

But Alexa was still thinking about days. And the killer. *Bring it back to the killer, the actual heart of it all…*

"He's not going anywhere," something inside of her made her say, although she couldn't quite understand *why* she knew this to be true.

"Alexa?" Kage looked at her with concern.

He's probably wondering if this was all too much for me, the special agent thought, and wondered the same. The killing of the Bodrov family was still in the news cycle, and the murder of the two sons Dimitre and Vadim had leaked to the tabloids and the radio stations somehow. Alexa wondered if she would have to talk to Dempsey about information security.

On the way over they had flicked through the local news channels, and Dempsey had shown them when they arrived the latest headline for 'Russian Playboys Slaughtered in Beach Hit!' It had been full of sordid details about the lives of the Bodrov brothers, including their love for nightclubs, strip bars, and partying.

Well, Perelli, was it worth the spotlight? she wondered. Surely this much attention couldn't be good for business.

There had also been talk of the morning raid in Little Haiti on the radio, but so far, no one had managed to link the two together.

Good, Alexa thought, and then, *Had it really only been this morning that I had been shot at by the 34-27!?*

"It's day four. The killer isn't going anywhere," Alexa announced with a nod to the body.

Dempsey blinked. "How can you figure that? Hires usually come and go. Do the job and disappear, right? Isn't that their M.O.?"

Alexa nodded. But it wasn't the case this time. "He took out Aleksandr, and then almost a day later, while we're all running around Star Island, he takes out the sons. Later that night or the next morning, our Mr. Blonde goes for Leela," Alexa stated, looking at Kage and Dempsey carefully.

"And let's not ignore the fact that he has been tracking *our* movements," she said, feeling a shiver run up through her spine. What if the killer was somewhere near them right now? Looking at them through a long-range sniper scope?

She threw a glance to the constant, omnipresent boats that were always out on the waters of the Florida coast. Any one of them could be harboring a killer – if he were brash enough to reveal his position by such an attack.

"You think we should be wearing armor?" Demspey appeared more fazed than Alexa did, as he sidled to one side of one of the marine stanchions quickly.

"Maybe. But I was more thinking that a hired professional should be doing just what you say, Detective. Get the job done, get paid and go. But it's now four days later and he's still at it."

Kage grunted his agreement. She could see that her words had shaken him a little, as he was moving back and forth on the balls of his feet. But then again, he *had* been the one shot at just yesterday, hadn't he?

"You think he's not done yet," Kage stated flatly.

Alexa shook her head. "No, I don't think he is. He tracked the dancers who could ID him, and now he's coming for them. He's trying to clear up all his loose ends, and *then* we might never see him again," she said tartly.

"Thankfully for us, he's not going to get anywhere with Trixi, as she's safe and secure with you, isn't she, Detective?" Alexa felt a small relief at that. At least there was one life she could save amidst all this chaos.

"Ah..." Detective Dempsey was looking at her awkwardly. "There might be a problem with that. We're holding her for the maximum time we had, which is, uh-" he checked his watch, "twenty-four hours. Which was up right about a half hour ago."

CHAPTER TWENTY-FIVE

6:45 PM. MIAMI SOUTHSIDE, DOWNTOWN, TRIXI'S APARTMENT

"What the hell was he thinking of, letting her go!?" Alexa exploded for what had to be the fourth time as she and Kage swerved through the traffic to get to downtown Miami as fast as possible.

There should have been local PD on the scene already, but given yesterday's active shooter event in Miami Beach North, and then the Little Haiti raid, Dempsey had admitted to them that he had to commit most of the patrol cars to extra circuits – as a show of confidence, if nothing else.

Which might be just as well. Alexa gritted her teeth. If Trixi got one look at a police car she might run, given the way they'd already treated her.

"I told him that she was to be in protective custody! And they kept her in the cells!" Alexa complained.

Kage, very wisely, didn't comment as he smoothly wove them through the traffic before coming to a near screech of a halt at a red light.

"We could run it," Alexa said, feeling her heart hammer with every second that passed. Another second that Trixi, their sole eyewitness, was in danger.

"Not unless in active pursuit of a crime," Kage said in his locked-down, tight voice. Alexa was starting to realize that there were these multiple sides to her partner. For the most part, they were breezy and light, but that hid a very tight, wound-up man who couldn't stand to think that he was doing the wrong thing.

We'll have to work on that, she thought, *but not right now.* More important things now, like trying to stop Trixi from getting murdered.

Alexa couldn't explain how she knew that the killer would be going for Trixi, only that she did. *It was his M.O.,* she thought. *This Mr. Blonde doesn't leave any stone unturned, does he? He doesn't like loose ends. He plans through every action he takes to an incredible level, coming up with a boat and shooting a gun at five hundred yards, or getting a professional jamming system to block wireless security cameras...*

He would be waiting for his opportunity, Alexa could feel it.

The light turned green, and Kage put their SUV into a wheelspin to send them racing ahead of the pack. They had crossed the McArthur Causeway in record time, a bare fraction of the commuting time it generally took in the dense, crazed, overpopulated strip of a city between the swamps and the coast.

Within a few minutes, they were surrounded by the tall high-rise buildings of downtown, as Kage followed Alexa's directions through the tightening maze of streets to the more rundown, ex-industrial area where Trixi lived.

"It's a fifth-floor apartment. Only one way in and out through the metal stairs, as far as I know," Alexa said. She didn't spell it out, but the implication was obvious. If the killer had already been there, or was about to go, then they would meet him head on.

"You ready?" Kage said, nodding at her as he pulled into the small road that fed the back of the apartment block. It wasn't a through road, just a place where delivery drivers and garbagemen could pick up and unload from the local businesses.

Of course I am ready, Alexa thought, but then realized that he was parking and taking out the gun from the glovebox. He'd meant her firearms. They didn't have any protective gear this time around, and Alexa suddenly wondered if she'd gone through the correct procedure when she'd handed in her gun at the end of the raid this morning.

This morning. Thirteen hours ago.

Alexa checked her own heavy pistol. Her magazine was only down by one, where she'd shot the 34-27 guy.

You almost killed someone today, Alexa. And now you're going in hot again, some part of her reminded herself.

"I'm ready," she said, as Kage was the first out, checking that the metal stairs were indeed the only way up, and started. He moved quickly, but his regulation black boots clacked on the external metal stairs, making Alexa wince.

Best to get their quickly than too late, she thought, following right behind him.

First flight. Second. Kage was outpacing her thanks to his bigger size and physique, which Alexa hated.

Third flight.

"Hold back at the door! I'm going to need back up," Kage relayed as he crossed to the next flight of stairs at the fourth flight and kept on going.

"What are you talking about!?" Alexa whispered. It was more of this same stuff once again, wasn't it? Don't let the little woman hurt herself. What was this crap!?

"Kage, there's no way I'm going to-" Alexa began, but Kage had already reached level five as she hit level four.

"Door's open!" he whispered, not even pausing as he threw himself inside.

"Kage! Wait!" Alexa said, following as fast as she could.

Fifth flight. There was the door, and it was wide open.

There was a sudden crash, and a scream, as Alexa saw shapes cross in front of her vision. Two shapes, struggling.

"Freeze! FBI!" Alexa shouted, skidding to a halt at the door and raising her gun as there was another crash as one of the other of the assailants destroyed furniture before someone was flying back across the hallway opening. It was Kage!

"*Kage!*" Alexa shouted, breaking into a run, but she didn't even get two paces before there was another scream as Trixi burst from around the hallway, running straight towards Alexa, straight in her line of sight.

"Trixi, down!" Alexa shouted, as she saw Kage once again throw himself across the room to be met with another angered snarl, another series of smashes.

"It's him! Alexa, it's him!" Trixi had finally got the message and was cowering by the side of the open door as Alexa sighted into the hallway again. No one was there.

"Wait here, goddammit!" Alexa swore as she ran down the hallway, pistol up and head tucked in.

"Kage!?"

The front room, which was already a mess to begin with, had now been completely trashed by the fight, Alexa saw. The sofa was turned on its back, the table that had already been on its side was now smashed, as was the television screen at the bottom of the wall, and the mirror; and Kage Murphy himself was slumped against the small dividing wall that separated the living room from the small kitchenette space.

"Kage, you alright!? Where is he!?" Alexa skidded to Kage's side to see him grumbling as he shook his head. There was blood running from a cut on his brow, but it wasn't deep.

"There!" her partner pointed across the room where there was a wide, billowing window sash.

Not a window, a balcony! Alexa realized, jumping up as she heard the clanking sound of feet on the other side.

There was another set of stairs; an emergency fire escape!

Alexa hissed, jumping to the window and rushing out to the narrow balcony behind, having to stop suddenly as the balcony was barely a few feet wide.

"*Crap!*" She caught a hold of the railing with both hands to stop herself from tumbling. There was a drop-down ladder from the side of the balcony to the level below. She heard a clank and a sudden whoosh as the killer was already using the ladder the flight below hers.

"Freeze!" she shouted, pointing her gun – but the metal grate of the stairs itself was too narrow. She could look down and see the top of his dark blue baseball cap as he swung himself around the next balcony, kicked out the ladder protector and jumped down to floor three – and then paused, threw a glare back up at her.

Alexa looked their killer, the man who had terrorized Miami for four days, full in the face, and a shock of recognition ran through her. She had seen this man before. He had been wearing darker clothes, but she was sure of it. He had that same chiselled, square jaw. The stubble, the light grey-blue eyes.

Henderson's! Max Henderson's!

She had been jumped by someone fleeing Max's house, hadn't she? Someone had run out of the house, knocking her to the floor, kneeing her in the process and jumping the fence of the house opposite…

It had been him. This guy, she was sure of it.

The moment must have lasted not even a second because then the man was turning and leaping to the neck ladder protector.

"Damnit!" Alexa took a breath, slid to the side of the opening that led to the first ladder and dangled herself over it before letting herself drop to the fourth-floor balcony with a heavy clang.

"Urk!" It was a shock to her knees as she stumbled against the window of the next apartment, but it was faster than climbing down a ladder. She could hear a grouse of annoyance as Mr. Blonde below her decided to do the same.

Alexa threw herself down the next ladder flight in the same way, but Mr. Blonde was keeping pace with her; he was fast and athletic, she knew, as he kept a flight between them.

"FBI! *Freeze!*" she shouted before she hit flight three, throwing herself across the balcony to the next open ladder protector and-

"*Oof!*" There was a grunt from below as the killer must have hit the ground and tumbled. Alexa was on the second flight.

I can do this. I can make this! she was thinking, turning to the balcony railings, just as-

Crack! Crack!

Sparks spit from the balcony and the stairs around her as the killer fired up at her. Alexa swore and dove to the dubious protection of the window opening, before there was another final *crack* against the glass, shattering it above her before the sounds of running feet.

"Alexa!" She heard Murphy's voice shouting from above, but Alexa was only thinking about her catch.

"No way. Oh no you don't!" Alexa hissed to herself, tumbling down the next ladder hole to the first-floor balcony and then, instead of using the ladder once more she grabbed the railings, threw her legs over the side and lowered herself down on her arms. A floor was only ten, twelve feet down at most. She'd be fine.

She let go and felt a moment of weightlessness before suddenly she hit the ground hard and rolled.

"Argh!" she winced as pain shot up her legs and across her shoulders as she grazed them, but she had remembered to tuck her head in, and she still had her gun.

"Alexa! Wait for backup!" Murphy shouted, but Alexa ignored him. She spun on her heel and took aim down the alley – just in time to see their killer swerve behind one of the big industrial bins.

Shit! She jumped to her feet, charging down the alleyway after him.

He wasn't going to get away this time.

CHAPTER TWENTY-SIX

7:15 PM. MIAMI SOUTHSIDE, DOWNTOWN

She didn't have a radio. Why didn't she have an emergency radio!? The thought flashed through her head at the same time as she sped around the side of the large industrial bin to hear the sudden clang and shout of outraged voices.

"*-che de palle!*"

"Hey!"

Steam hit Alexa from the burst open door, and she heard the crash of metal as she realized the killer had flung himself through the back of a kitchen.

They were clearly already deep in the swing of service, as there were people wearing white everywhere, disarrayed around a long, stainless steel table in the center of the room.

"*Cagacazzo!*"

Alexa saw the line of destruction ahead of her, as the swing doors out to the main restaurant were slamming backwards and mitigating more shouts of outrage from behind.

"FBI! Out of the way!" Alexa jumped through the kitchen after the man, swerving to avoid colliding with a man carrying a huge tray of something wet and boiling.

Heck! "Out of the way!" she shouted, ducking to one side and following the sound of shouts to the swing doors, bursting through them.

Into the sounds of fast-paced, string Italian music, and a wide, low-ceilinged restaurant already filled with annoyed-looking customers. There was one waiter on the floor, with red all over his arms and shoulder and spreading across the floor…

No!

But Alexa's worst fears were unfounded. It was bolognese sauce from the bowls he had dropped when he had been sent spinning to the floor by the progress of the man. Mr. Blonde. Who was almost at the front of the restaurant.

"STOP!" Alexa shouted, raising her pistol, which was met with the sudden shouts and screams of everyone in the restaurant around her.

Mr. Blonde had no such qualms, however. He fired his own gun in the air, eliciting more screams and mayhem as people dove from their seats to hide under tables – and get in the way of his pursuit before he ran to the glass double doors to the street outside, and was out.

Damnit! Alexa cursed, leaping over the first hunkered person and then skidding around the next. "Out of the way, damnit! FBI! Out of the way!"

She hit the front doors just a few heartbeats after the man had gotten there, barging out into the still warm Floridian night to find that this section of downtown was busy, but not packed.

There were shops and restaurants still open, their lights streaming onto the street under the tall reaches of palm trees.

And *there*, right up ahead was a disturbance in the crowd, as the killer had pushed some walkers aside as he fled, crossing the street to the roar and bleating horns of traffic…

"FBI! Everybody down!" Alexa shouted as she ran between parked cars after the man, a squeal of tires as another large car avoided hitting her, causing her heart to skip a beat before following the man across the road to the next set of shops and eateries.

She didn't have a clear line of fire. There were too many people out here, and the killer seemed to be heading towards the larger streets.

Heading to where there's cover. Or hostages, Alexa considered as she saw him suddenly change course; instead of running up the pavement he abruptly swerved to his right, disappearing down one of the next smaller alleyways to the sides of the buildings.

He was trying to get to the main boulevard, Alexa thought. The one that led right down to the seafront, which would be teeming with people and cars.

She put on an extra burst of speed as she crossed the street and sprinted after him.

Keep your strength. Lengthen your stride. She remembered her training, timed her breath into short, explosive bursts as she allowed her body to perform to the level that she knew it could, running past the windows of a sushi bar as people suddenly looked up at the disturbance outside; slowing a bit around the side of the alley as she heard sirens dimly somewhere behind her…

The alley was narrow, and the buildings on either side were high. It was also dark and cluttered with more large, plastic wheeled bins and stacks of pallets, ready to be taken by the garbagemen tomorrow.

One thing that Alexa hadn't been expecting, however, was that there was a wall across the end of the alleyway. It didn't connect straight through to the next set of shops and the main downtown Miami boulevard beyond.

A wall. A brick wall.

Where was he? Alexa thought, just as a shape launched itself from the side of one of the bins, swinging its arm in an arc straight towards her head; an arm that ended in a gun-

Alexa reacted, letting her weight fall backwards at the same time as she shot out her own arm reflexively.

CRACK!

The sound of the gun going off right in front of her was deafening. It was so near and so loud that Alexa felt the percussive wave first, and then a sheet of white noise as she swung her own gun around.

"*Urk!*"

She felt a pain in her wrist as it was grabbed by the man, but Alexa's senses were still in shock. She wasn't moving as fast as she would have liked when another blow hit her on the side of the temples, and she spiralled to the floor, with one wrist still held by Mr. Blonde.

His strike had made her drop her gun, but then so had he. She heard the man seethe as suddenly his large form was over her, terribly close, and she could smell the faint mixture of sweat and deodorant as he was twisting her arm, trying to break it.

No.

Alexa's body reacted faster than her mind, calling on the tumbling and ju-jitsu training she was taught in the Academy. She leaned *into* the man's pull, flared her legs to grab the attacker around the knee, and twist with her hip...

"*Oof!*" Suddenly, the man fell to the floor with a grunt, letting go of her hand as he did so. But he was rolling, scrabbling, reaching for one of the dropped guns that had clattered across the alleyway floor.

No you don't! Alexa threw herself on him, one hand grabbing him around the chest, the other reaching for his arm. The killer growled as the sudden weight bore him down, and twisted.

He knew how to use his body in grapple situations. His movements were trained and coordinated as he twisted his hips and slammed an elbow into Alexa's chest. The strike was powerful and excruciating, but Alexa knew she was more winded than injured. She snatched at him as she fell backwards, grabbing a handful of his shirt and tearing it from his neck and shoulder.

"Back *off!*" the man spat as he stamp-kicked her back from him. Now *this* blow was much more painful, grazing off her head as Alexa saw stars for a moment...

And the killer was suddenly free. He was clambering away from her, snatching up her gun as he jumped to his feet, and Alexa tried to do the same.

"I wouldn't," a deep, gravelly American voice said as Alexa looked straight up to see the line of the man's arm and the gun it held. It was the side that his shirt had been torn from, and she could clearly see a large tattoo on his shoulder. It looked like some sort of lightning bolt and a cloud, with two words written underneath it...

"You'd be killing a federal officer," Alexa gasped up at the man as she stared at him, full in the face. Trixi's identification and the artist's impression had been bang on; she was looking at an athletic, muscular, slightly scruffy all-American Joe. Stubble and clear, almost piercing grey-blue eyes. A square jaw but with high cheekbones, too. He could fit in anywhere in America...

There was the rising howl of sirens from the road behind them as Alexa glared at the man above her.

"I've done worse," the man countered quickly, and Alexa saw it. She saw the coldness in his face, the emotional insulation that came with training. A part of her wondered if her own face expressed exactly the same look.

"I'm afraid that you've already seen too much, Agent Landers," the man said.

She saw his eyes settle, the moment before he would pull a trigger...

Buy some time! More time! Alexa demanded of herself.

"Who do you work for!?" she snapped, saying almost anything to break his concentration.

In response, the man broke his stoicism for a smile to quirk the corner of his mouth. He didn't say anything. He was too well trained. The smile flickered back into that stone cold, glassy look once more.

"*Hey!* FBI! Drop your weapon!" There was a shout from the end of the tunnel as tires screeched to a halt, and the police sirens were deafening.

Kage. Alexa recognized that voice immediately. She saw the man's eyes flicker upwards, and she moved, throwing herself forwards into a roll that smacked into the killer's legs as a gun went off.

CRACK!

"Ugh!" the killer grunted as he hit the floor on a roll, and sirens and blue and white flashing lights began filling the alleyway darkness, but Alexa was confused in the scramble. Someone had fired – but who?

She heard a snarl of anger as the killer was struggling to his feet. *Where is my gun!?* She saw it just a couple of feet away and dove for it, but by the time she had grabbed the handle, the man was already leaping and disappearing over the wall.

"FREEZE! Police! Weapons down!"

There were booted feet running into the alleyway and the man was gone.

"FBI!" Alexa shouted, frozen in place as the police managed to surround her. "I'm FBI. Special Agent Landers, and my partner Special Agent Murphy!"

But the voice of the first policeman to arrive at her side filled her with a sudden horror.

"FBI? You mean the wounded man at the other end of the alley?"

It wasn't Kage who had fired the last bullet. Kage had been shot.

CHAPTER TWENTY-SEVEN

DAY 5.

2:35 AM. UNIVERSITY OF MIAMI HOSPITAL

A LEXA HATED THE BLEEP, BLEEP, BLEEP OF MONITORING machines. In fact, she hated hospitals as a general rule. It had been the last place her mom had disappeared into, and in the last couple of years she had been making ever increasing visits there with her dad.

It was hard not to think of the hours of waiting and tests that she had gone through with him, even when Kage was lying in front of her, hooked up to the same damn bleeping machines.

Her partner looked like crap, she had to admit. He lay in a small, private room in the central, University of Miami Hospital inside a private wing. Apparently law enforcement agencies had a special dispensation with the UoMH, and Alexa had to wonder if that meant that Miami was a more dangerous place even than she had thought it was.

It certainly felt that way, anyway.

The room was nice, actually. There was a bedside cabinet where someone had even put a jug of flowers, and the room was large enough for a scatter of chairs and a television screen on the opposite wall. Kage lay on the bed, under a thin white sheet, with multiple tubes and sensors and all sorts of things snaking in and out from the machines arrayed around his bed to disappear discretely under the white.

There was a soft snore that broke the otherwise clinical beep, but it didn't come from Kage. Alexa could hardly hear him breathing at all. The snore in fact came from the other side of the room, where Trixi Kiss was curled up as best she could on one of the chairs, with a UoMH blanket wrapped around her body.

"I couldn't just leave her out there, not after the police dropped the ball so spectacularly," Alexa murmured somewhat apologetically to the unconscious Kage, not that he appeared to mind. He hadn't even flickered an eyelid since coming out of surgery at some time just before midnight last night, and even though Kage didn't look about to wake up any time soon, Alexa couldn't bring herself to leave him just yet.

For the umpteenth time, she ran through the checklist that she thought she was supposed to do.

Called in the incident to Field Office. Check.
Registered Kage's injury. Check.
Filled in my witness brief with Miami PD. Check.
Witness Protection Request form filed with Field Office. Check.

It all felt so cold and useless, compared to the fact that her partner was lying here, possibly fighting for his life.

"Agent Landers?" There was a soft knock on the door as a thin man in blue shirt and formal trousers poked his head through the door. He had with him a clipboard, and balanced on top of that a tray with a couple bottles of water and a couple of packed sandwiches.

"I'm not sure that'll do him any good," Alexa muttered before instantly feeling guilty for her rattiness. "I'm sorry, I didn't mean that, I'm tired..." she started to say.

"Don't apologize, I understand," the man said, easing himself into the room to put the tray on the bedside table.

"The sandwiches are for you and your friend, actually. I'm Dr. Ibrahim, I'm on call tonight and wanted to let you know..." he looked down at his board and flipped through the pieces of paper. "Mr. Murphy sustained a gunshot to the side of his abdomen. Luckily for us, it quite miraculously didn't hit any major organs," the doctor said with a warming smile.

"The biggest danger was internal bleeding, and system shock, both of which we have managed to arrest. But his condition will remain critical for the next twenty-four hours, I think. No single body can go through that much trauma easily..."

The doctor must have seen the look on Alexa's face because he hurriedly put the clipboard down and instead looked her in the eyes, he paused, and spoke softly.

"But Agent Murphy is a very strong man. His blood pressure, vital signs, heart rate are all good. Better than good, in fact. I fully expect him to be able to pull through this, just so long as we keep on taking care of him for the next day or more. He won't be coming back to active duty any time soon, however. Not in the next month at least, I should think."

Out and to the benches, Alexa thought. Another favorite phrase of her dad's.

"It'll probably only slow him down anyway," Alexa replied, offering a thin smile. "Which would be a good thing, I think."

The doctor made agreeing noises, but there seemed to be something on his mind. Or maybe these ghostly hours of the night brought out the philosopher in everyone.

"Of course it's the nature of the job, but this young man has had a rough few years," the doctor offered a wan smile. "I can't help feeling for my patients sometimes, especially when I know them..."

"You know him?" Alexa blinked, surprised.

"Oh yes, only because I treated his fiancée, some three years ago," the doctor winced. "I remember because we get a special notification when it's law enforcement. You lot come through more direct protocols, and I was the trauma surgeon on hand that day."

"Trauma surgeon?" Alexa whispered, once again looking at Kage. She hadn't realized he had been engaged. He hadn't mentioned it.

"Yes. Truck accident. Although, of course, any accident with connection to your uh, the Bureau, had an awful lot of reports attached to it. In the end…" The doctor shook his head sadly.

"There was nothing we could do. Her car had been hit by a 26k pounder… I remember the poor man being destroyed by it. I am amazed that he returned to work at all."

So that explains it, Alexa thought as she looked at Kage. His bright and breezy attitude, his always-eager, almost light approach.

It was all an act. An act to cover up for a terrible, terrible hurt.

In that moment, Alexa felt something shift in her. A deep wave of grief and emotion for the young man – until the doctor made a small cough, and Alexa could see from the way he was looking at her and Trixi that he had probably just come in here to check on them, as much as Kage.

"Thank you for the understanding, Doctor. We'll be moving out of here just as soon…" Alexa fumbled for the right words. *Just as soon as he's safe? Just as soon as anyone is safe?*

She shot a look at Trixi and a frown crossed her features just briefly. She was almost as worried for Trixi as she was for Kage, truth be told. The killer had just about told her that he was out to kill anyone who had 'seen too much.' Right now, that meant Trixi, their star witness. She was one person who could make a positive ID on him, and the crimes he had committed at the Miami Heights.

"We still don't have him tied to the boat yet, though," she muttered out loud, for the doctor to look at her oddly.

"I'm sorry?"

"It's nothing. Just...tired thoughts, you know?" Alexa thanked him, and, after another careful appraising look at her, the doctor urged her to get some food and some rest at least, before leaving her to her thoughts.

I have to get Trixi to the FBI. The Miami PD witness protection process was too slow and required too many forms. Surely the FBI had a safe room inside the field office they could use?

The thought crossed her mind that maybe she could even bring her back to her FBI-approved motel, but then shook her head vigorously against it.

'You had better be careful, Agent Landers'
The killer had been watching them this whole time.

What if the killer knew they were at the hospital right now, and was waiting for them in some darkened car outside, knowing that Trixi would have to come out of the building sooner or later...?

No. Get her to the field office, Alexa decided. She'd already put in a request for FBI Witness Protection but decided that her only choice was to 'anticipate the approval' so to speak. Even if the killer followed them to the field office, there was no way he was going to burst in there, guns blazing. Even if he was well trained.

Her thoughts flickered to the tattoo she had seen on his shoulder, and cursed herself why she hadn't thought of it sooner. Grabbing her notebook, she tried to sketch it out, coming up with a broadly circular design with a small cloud, a thunderbolt, and two words underneath it...

It looks familiar. She looked at her hastily scribbled image and tried to work out just what was so familiar about it.

"And what were those words? *Few? Father?"*

Alexa's mind jumped from 'father' to her own father, the US Navy officer who was right now far, far away. He often didn't sleep at night, thanks to his breathing and his life of service. Looking over at the sleeping Trixi, and seeing her deep in a moment of peace she grabbed her phone and got up soundlessly from her chair, exiting the room to walk through the ward to where there was a small lounge area at the end of the corridor. She thumbed her dad's number at the same time as she got another coffee from one of those awful vending machines.

To her surprise, he answered.

"Kiddo," her father's voice was raspy and imperfect. But it was there. *"Why am I not surprised you are phoning me in the middle of the night?"*

"Dad, it's great to hear you," Alexa said, and meant it. She hadn't thought that she was shaken about what had happened to her today, to having a gun pointed straight at her face, but maybe she was. Suddenly she felt the distance between them intensely and would have given anything in the world to be just a little kid again, running into his arms.

"I know, you can't talk about it. I signed those papers, too, remember?" the voice of her dad came back after a moment, as if he had guessed her reticence. Instead, he burbled slowly and hesitantly about his day, about how the roses outside were getting straggly again, and how he was worried about the Abernickles next door. Alexa let him ramble and knew that she needed that conversation, too. She needed to talk about something that wasn't about the case.

But the case was still there, as was her wounded partner and her terrified witness, just at the end of the hall.

"Dad, I do have a question for you, actually. Do you remember a military tag or motif, like a cloud and a lightning bolt...?" She described the tattoo she had seen.

"Although I'm not a hundred percent, I think the two words were *Few* and something, but I can't be sure..."

"Cloud? Damned if I know any unit that has a cloud in its insignia," her father said, pausing to take a few long, measured breaths for a moment. *"But bobbly? Rounded? Could it have been an open parachute?"*

Alexa blinked. "Yes. Yes, that was it. A parachute and a thunderbolt."

"That's easy then, sport. Parachute and lightning, and First There underneath."

"You got it!" Alexa could suddenly see the tattooed words clearly.

"I don't know what pop quiz you lot play down there, but that's the Combat Controllers. Real 'I spit bullets' type. Check them out.

I've only seen them in action once, but most of the time they were sent ahead of any marine troops we deployed."

Alexa swiped with her phone to pull up some info on the 'Combat Controllers,' and then whistled.

"Oh crap," she said.

"Indeed, kiddo. You don't want to tussle with those guys. What do I win?"

Alexa barely heard her father as she read about the unit. US Air Force, deployed ahead of everyone else in a combat zone to set up the landing zones and insertion points for the rest of the forces. They were the ones who parachuted into enemy cities to blow up anti-aircraft guns, or dropped into the sea, or neutralized enemy locations to make it safe for the rest.

"I'll get you that bottle of Jameson's for Thanksgiving, Dad. I promised I would anyway," Alexa said, earning a pleased, wheezing chuckle from the other end, and then another pause.

"Anything else an old fart like me can help you with, kiddo? You sure you're alright down there?"

No, Dad, no I'm not alright. My partner has been shot and I have to stop a highly trained, ex-special forces Combat Controller from killing my witness, Alexa thought. But of course she didn't say any of that.

"I'm good, Dad, I promise. I'll wrap this up and get some leave, come and see you," she promised.

"Sure thing, kiddo, sure thing," her father said, but Alexa still felt guilty when the phone clicked off.

"Oh, I wouldn't have that stuff, it's as weak as ditch water," a voice said from behind her, surprising her as she suddenly looked up to see that one of the doctors in blue scrubs, a middle-aged, thin man had entered the lounge, and was pointing at the coffee vending machine. Instead, in his hands he had a cardboard cup of coffee, which he set on the table.

"The real stuff. It might help," the nurse or doctor said as he turned and walked back out of the lounge, and through the swing doors to the side.

"Oh, thanks…" Alexa said, mostly surprised as she looked between one cup of coffee and the next.

To see that the cup that the doctor had set down had something written on it in black ink.

"What the-?"

Alexa leaned closer and mumbled the lines out loud to herself.

"Why did Aleksandr have military grade security?" she whispered, and underneath it was a number.

What? Wait.

Alexa jumped up and ran to the swing door at the end to find that they opened into access stairs down to the next level, and then the level beyond that, too. The University of Miami Hospital was a big place. She went down the first flight of stairs but couldn't hear anything, the mysterious man could have disappeared anywhere.

"Damnit!" Alexa swore, racing back up the stairs, pausing only to pick up the coffee and rush to Kage and Trixi's room; only to find them both still soundly asleep, as peacefully as when she had left them.

"What the hell?" she whispered to herself, tapping in her phone the number written on the cup for it to just ring out and not get answered.

CHAPTER TWENTY-EIGHT

9:45 AM. FBI HQ [UNDISCLOSED LOCATION]

YOU SHOULD BE VERY CAREFUL, AGENT LANDERS.
Why did Aleksandr have military grade security?
Someone was trying to tell her something, Alexa was thinking as she moved through the FBI field offices. It was busy everywhere, as agents were working in their offices on their own cases or working through the reports and files that her and Kage's investigation had generated. Which was a lot.
Somehow, despite all the busyness going on, the agents had found time to put a card in their war room, filled with well wishes for Murphy. Alexa hadn't even seen them come in and do that last

night, as she had once again taken to her sleeping bag and coat on the fold-out camp bed in the war room instead of heading back to her motel.

It wasn't that she was scared of running into the killer again – although the thought had crossed her mind when she had ghosted Trixi through the main doors of the University of Miami Hospital to the parking lot, to the car, and then here in the twilight hours of the morning.

Here was safer than the motel for Trixi. Here was safer for everyone.

Alexa nodded at Elijah, the guard at the door as she used her pass to access the elevators.

"Awful sorry to hear about Kage, me and a few of the others were thinking of going to go visit him after our shift," Elijah said in low, consoling tones.

"Do that," Alexa nodded, offering a wan, tired smile in response before the elevator doors closed and she selected the last level but one to get to her target.

The doors opened to a level like any other, painted white and blue walls, cold, and electric lighting. Hopefully it wouldn't freak Trixi out as much as a cell would, she hoped as she stopped at the first door and looked through the wire-reinforced window to see what was in respects a bedroom: a single bed, a desk, a lamp and chair, and even a scrap of carpet on the floor.

And there was Trixi, still curled up inside the middle of the bed, asleep to the world. Elijah had said that he had word of her Witness Protection request, but until Chief Williams signed off on it, there were spare agent rooms below that he had put Trixi in; they were designed for agents who, like herself, chose to sleep at the field offices rather than go home.

There was an intercom buzzer by her bed which Elijah told her would come through to him, and he would see that she got whatever takeout she wanted.

Right. Next, Alexa thought as she moved back to the elevator, this time going down to the last floor. Her mind was still ringing with the events of last night, and not just the killer.

1. Who was ex-military. In fact, one of the toughest military units there was.

2. He didn't like loose ends. He didn't like leaving anyone alive who had seen his face.

But then there was the mysterious message that she had received, starting with the note in her pocket, and now the coffee cup that was still in the pocket of her blazer. She knew that she should hand both into evidence to see if she could get a print off of them, but something told her that they wouldn't find anything. The 'doctor' had been wearing scrub gloves, hadn't he?

If he was a doctor at all, Alexa seriously doubted.

The door opened into a very short corridor and a heavy security door at the end which Alexa *didn't* have the access to; she thumbed the door buzzer instead for the camera above her head to flicker a green light, and a woman's voice to come back a moment later.

"I see you, Alexa, wait up!"

A moment later and there was the sound of electronic locks sliding back into place, and the door was yanked open by the black-haired Dee Hopkins, who beamed at her, before her face collapsed into worry.

"God, I'm sorry to hear about last night, are you-?"

"Fine," Alexa waved her off. She was getting tired of these questions, even from people that she respected. "A question about the case," she said, as Dee waved her into her 'lair,' which was actually too well-lit to be described as such even if it did manage to have a claustrophobic air.

Miami's Department for Digital Analysis, Investigation & Security must occupy the entire floor space of the building, Alexa saw, not that she could see that far as there were multiple walls of servers and blinking computing equipment creating small cubicles and work spaces stretching off under the day-light bulbs overhead. Alexa saw a few others working at their own units, mostly clacking away on laptops, but a few with the guts of machines already opened up as they poked, prodded, and soldered their way through the innards of the equipment.

"Excuse the racket. We're doing manual data recovery for another investigation, which is an absolute pain in the tutu, I'd say!" Dee said, gesturing her forwards past the first series of desks to where there was a large office space with glass walls and a series of computers and blinking equipment in there, too. As soon as they walked inside, all sound from the rest of the cyber department outside vanished, and Alexa realized that the temperature in here was a couple degrees lower, as well.

"Ah, we're isolated from the rest of the facility here, but don't worry – it has its own oxygen system. It's a bit colder, but you don't notice it after a while. Or maybe I just don't notice it!" Dee said, swinging a couple of chairs around past a long series of desks where there appeared to be a variety of technical objects sitting inside plastic tubs.

When Dee saw her looking, she explained, "either evidence-sensitive items, or else so delicate that we keep them in temperature- and moisture-controlled environment. We've even got a deep cold unit at the back for some of the physical hard drives we want to keep for as long as possible."

"Impressive," Alexa mumbled because she could hardly think of anything else to say. This was all alien to her, who had always preferred physical police work to digital intelligence gathering.

"Right, Agent Landers, how can I help you?" Dee asked.

Tell me how to find an ex-military sniper, the thought flashed through Alexa's mind at first.

Or why am I getting messages from mysterious men, then she shook them both aside.

"The laptop," she said. "Aleksandr Bodrov's laptop. Do you still have it?"

Dee blinked as if this was a stupid question.

"Of course! In fact, you're in luck, as I'm working on it right now..."

She rolled her chair over to the other side of the room, where a screen showed what looked to be a very boring and very imminently-about-to-lose game of space invaders. Lines of red blocks marched endlessly across the screen, while a small, shaded area in green fluctuated slightly, sometimes gaining a few millimetres, sometimes losing. Lines of code ran along the bottom in a flicker-fast, nonstop jibber.

"This is a drive map of Bodrov's device," Dee explained, gesturing at the screen, but also at the wires that snaked out of it to a small, silver square unit barely bigger than a coaster, held on a small black plastic cradle.

"And that's the hard drive?" Dee figured.

"No, actually that is a clone of the hard drive. We have kept the original inside...*here*," Dee gestured next to the computer screen, where there was another large plastic tub with a silver laptop inside. Alexa recognized it.

"We try to clone where possible to preserve the original chain of evidence as much as possible, and every time you mess with hard data, investigating, scanning, prodding, there is always the risk of either viral contamination or data loss. So we clone-"

"Make a copy," Alexa clarified.

"Indeed, make a copy of the original and work from there. If it works, we can repeat the procedure on the original if we need to," Dee said, moving her hands back and forth from one to the other, and then back to the losing space invaders game.

"As you can see, all of this red space is the encrypted data," Dee explained with another swoosh of her hand.

"The SystemTech Laboratory stuff?" Alexa asked.

"Quite. All of that data has been encrypted by the SystemTech security software, which basically runs interference between the main accessing system and the data packets, offering ridiculously complex keys which no human has a hope of figuring out."

"Oh," Alexa's shoulder slumped. "I was rather hoping that you wouldn't tell me that."

Dee winced. "I know. It's a nightmare. I think you have to be a professional masochist to do my job. But luckily we have Big Bettie, here," she said as she slapped the sides of one of the stacks of computer boxes that looked to Dee more like a stack of old-time music players. Each one was oblong, and a little over six or seven inches high.

"She's not quite a super-computer, although I wouldn't tell that to her face; and god knows the amount of times I've asked for funding for one from Requisitions!" Dee explained.

"But she is smart. Very smart. Probably has one of the fastest processors and largest available memories this side of Tampa," Dee said proudly, before looking suddenly puzzled.

"Although that might not be true. NASA's at Cape Canaveral, and I would love to get an hour in their data room!" Dee said.

"I thought I heard somewhere that a modern phone has more processing power than it took to put people on the moon," Dee said, as an errant fact ran through her tired brain. It was something that Dad had said, probably.

"Yes, but they're talking about Mars now. And the secret alien technology," Dee said.

Alexa looked at her for a moment – just before Dee burst out laughing.

"Only kidding. Or am I? Anyway, as you can see there is this green sector at the bottom? It's basically like a lobby room in a computer, where a lot of general infrastructure that *enables* the rest of the infrastructure to work takes place. Your basic explorer exe, for example, general partitioning rules, NET frameworks."

"I have no idea what you just said," Alexa pointed out.

Another wince from Dee. "I get that a lot. This is like the waiting room of a hotel, which has all the emergency exits listed in it when you arrive. It should direct you to where you need to go, but then the rest of this-" another wave at the encryption, "stops you from going there. What I am doing is trying to find back doors from that waiting lobby into the rest of the data. A registry entry that wasn't encrypted, or a higher-order command that might be crackable by Big Bettie, you see?"

"Oh," Alexa kind of saw. But it still didn't help her at all right now.

Why was Aleksandr running military grade security?

"Why would someone do this?" Alexa said. "I mean, I know Bodrov was rich, but did he really need that level of encryption?"

"Not at all," Dee laughed. "There is such a thing as industrial hacking out there, where companies steal each other's secrets, or top-level hackers encrypt your data from afar for a ransom, but generally what everyone forgets is that all of those things fail when you get to the *human interface.*"

Alexa blinked. "What do you mean?"

"Well, the thing with cybersecurity is this: I hate to say it, but you are NEVER safe, not entirely. Everything you do online is recorded somewhere, by someone. If I was a hacker-" the tiniest pause here, "-then I wouldn't need to break into Aleksandr Bodrov's personal computers to steal his money. I would instal a trojan or a listening app on his phone, watch where he goes online, map his activities, and then use one of those things to blackmail him, or scoop his bank details from some third-party auction site or whatever. It's easy, and it happens all the time. In fact, I probably wouldn't even have to do that, and certainly wouldn't need to try and break into ports to get to his data when I could trick him into putting in his card details on some other site, right?"

Alexa nodded. This, at least, was something that she had heard about. Fake sites that masqueraded as PayPal, or Wallet, or Amazon Pay or whatever.

"All of this," Dee waved at the hard drive, "is really just for show, in the end. Whatever Aleksandr thought he was securing; his business, his bank accounts, his personal porn or whatever; I'd say you do this because you want *everyone else* to know that you are tighter than Fort Knox. Or, I guess, you have some pretty heavy trust issues."

Alexa nodded. "Well, seeing Aleksandr had turned state evidence on Russia, as the CIA told us, then I wouldn't be surprised if he *was* a pretty worried man..."

No, wait, that wasn't true, was it? Alexa thought of his Star Island residence, his vast opulent mansion. If anything, Aleksandr had been as much of a playboy as his two deceased sons, but in a more sedate, King-of-the-Hill kind of a way.

Which led her to thinking about the sons, and why they were now lying in deep freeze in the city morgue. The killer, Mr. Blonde, had been paid to take them out, and was now going to extreme lengths to take out the witnesses.

And all they had done was owe Perelli money, Alexa thought.

THE **FLORIDA GIRL**

"How about the sons?" Alexa asked. "Have you taken a look through their digital effects?"

"Ha!" Dee laughed, nodding to the rest of the room outside. "You mean their phones and iPads? None of them had anything worth a damn on them, apart from incriminating photos and a very questionable taste in adult entertainment." Dee shook herself all over.

Hm. Odd, Alexa thought. "So the father has all this high-end security, but the sons don't."

"Maybe they weren't privy to their father's private business," Dee pointed out. "Or, as I say, maybe they knew that their father had paid for this level of security, and so knew that they were shut out of the circle of trust?"

"Not if they had the password," Alexa offered. But something was still bothering her.

"SystemTech Laboratories. The people who made this stuff. How many clients do you think they have for this sort of product?"

Dee shook her head. "Impossible to say, but, given the cost of this product I'd say that it would be very few. If you go to the SystemTech website they don't even offer a consumer security package, you have to directly phone them up."

"Which means you have to know that they offer it. Someone will have to have told you," Alexa reasoned. She could feel something here, a thread of something, but she wasn't sure what would be at the other end when she pulled.

Dee made another disagreeing face. "Yes, but it's not exactly a secret. If you pay half an eye of attention to cybersecurity you know that SystemTech creates custom security systems for companies. Not only that, but you would probably be aware that most of their product is sold to military industrial networks."

"Military industrial?" Alexa's ears pricked up. "Wasn't that how Bodrov claimed asylum here in the first place?" The special agent struggled to remember, and then she got it.

"Yes, Officer Voorn, the CIA woman said that Bodrov offered us intelligence on Russian-Soviet infrastructure, and that was how he was allowed to remain an asset," she said, knowing that Dee had been in the same room at the time of the call.

"Okay...?" Dee didn't see the connection, and, quite frankly, neither could Alexa.

Suddenly, Alexa felt maddened at this gap in their knowledge. She could feel that there was something here, something that the big, brash, showy Aleksandr Bodrov wanted to prove to the world by building his billionaire playground mansion and having his top-notch security.

Truly random crimes are exceptionally rare, her training told her. *There is always a connection, and that comes from understanding the victims...*

Aleksandr Bodrov. A cat who thought he had gotten away with the cream. Lived in luxury. Tolerated his wild sons. Was flashy with his life as well as his security...

He didn't tolerate Max Henderson, though, did he? Alexa's mind ran back to the start of the case. The Perelli stooge who supplied the Bodrov sons with cocaine.

Suddenly, Alexa's mind made that small connecting feeling that it did. She had missed that feeling.

I saw the killer at Henderson's, he had been escaping that time when me and Kage went to bring Henderson in...

But the Bodrov sons hadn't known the killer, had they? Trixi had said that Mr. Blonde pretended to be a runner for Henderson to get into the apartment...

...and the secure key card to the Miami Heights complex! Alexa remembered. That was what the killer had been doing at Henderson's, wasn't it? He had been stealing his key card to smuggle himself into Miami Heights, to kill the sons!

Suddenly, Alexa was sitting in a world all of her own as her mind whirled and whirred like one of Dee's CPU processors.

If Perelli wanted the Bodrovs dead because of a debt, then why didn't he just order Henderson to hand over his Miami Heights pass card to the hired Mr. Blonde?

Henderson had complained about a break-in when they had got there – and Alexa had stumbled right into the killer!

So therefore, the killer wanted the Bodrov sons dead, not Perelli, who could get it done in a much easier way – and besides which, why would Perelli send two of his girls to the Bodrov sons the

THE FLORIDA GIRL

very night that they were to be hit? It would just be a pain in the ass to cover up.

Therefore: Perelli out. Henderson out.

Zholdin and El Tigre are back in the game...

"Yeah, well, it would be SO much easier if he had written the password down on a sticky note and kept it in his drawer, just like everyone else!" Dee commented as Alexa blinked and came back to reality.

The special agent thought that something had shifted, but she couldn't exactly say what. She felt that her thinking had gotten a little clearer, and she wondered if it was having the pressure of her partner in a near-death experience so close that it gave her this laser-guided insight.

"Yeah, if only," Alexa almost laughed. After all, Aleksandr had kept that tray of gold chips right there in his office desk, hadn't he? Along with the photo of his wife-

And that treehouse.

Wait.

Alexa's mind slammed in full stop. She felt her breath quicken. Her entire body quivered, as she saw what it was. She saw the connection.

"Maybe he did keep his password right on his desk," Alexa said, already gesturing to the original laptop still in its sealed plastic crate.

"What? You want it?" Dee looked at her oddly.

Alexa nodded as her mind still whirred. "It was something Zholdin said, actually..." Alexa spoke quickly as Dee presented gloves for them both to wear before plugging the laptop in and handing it over. Alexa hit the keys for a serene blue screen to appear with *ALEKSANDR* written on the front and a blank password space. Alexa grabbed her phone.

"Okay to use this down here?" she asked.

Dee shook her head violently and instead directed her to an old fashioned, internal hard-line system on the edge of the desk. "Takes you to switchboard, I'm sorry, but we're really tight on radio frequency variance down here..."

"I still have no idea what you just said," Alexa said, but it didn't matter. She found that the line led to the field office switchboard.

"Cecil Pinkerton, please," Alexa said quickly, as she was routed to the Chief Science Officer on site, as well as for his department of CSI and Evidence Analysis. Within a few moments she was listening to the much-harried tones of the older gentleman, as somewhere behind him there was clanging and banging. She asked for a clarification, and Dee saw her write down a phrase on a scrap of paper, before thanking him and signing off.

"What is that?" The cyber technician looked at her in confusion.

"Mansion of the Woods," Alexa said, as she started typing into the password box.

"Or osobnyak v lesu, 1963 – it was the name of his beloved treehouse, according to Zholdin," Alexa said, hitting the return button.

The password box suddenly shook in error.

"Damnit! I was sure that would work!" Alexa grumbled, returning to the keyboard and instead just typed in 'osobnyak.'

Another error shake.

"Be careful, you'll only get one more try before the system shuts you out completely, and then it'll be hell as I'll have to go into the BIOS system and restart from there," Dee said carefully.

Wow. Way to put the pressure on, Alexa thought.

But she knew that she had to be right. She could feel it. What was it that Zholdin had said about the dead Aleksandr? *'One day I will build a real mansion, you will see, Mikhail!'*

Aleksandr Bodrov had been a man who had an ax to grind. He had something to prove to everyone, to the entire world. That was why he came here to the US after all, and why he had bought one of the most expensive properties in all of America. Both he and Mikhail had played the game, and they had successfully escaped the shackles of their poorer past and stuck a middle finger at everyone when they did it.

Dig deep. Get to know the victim. Get into their life. Alexa remembered those snippets from her training. The clues were always with the victim, weren't they? That was what they had been doing wrong all this time, concentrating on the possible motives of the killer, instead of concentrating on the victim.

On an impulse, because Alexa knew that most people would probably add numbers to a password in the belief that it made it more secure, she instead typed osobnyakvlesu1963

Hello, Aleksandr!

A moment later the screen faded away to be replaced with a desktop image of the same treehouse, this time seen from a much closer angle, along with a string of folders and apps and documents.

"Yes!" Alexa punched the air, as Dee hastily retrieved the laptop from her.

"Like I said, the human factor is the always the most important thing in cybersecurity," Dee commented as she started to click through the folders.

"This was his business laptop, clearly, so there is very little actual personal details here… But there are a lot of invoices, a lot of transcripts…" Dee went on as Alexa was forced to her feet, her body filled with electric power.

"Why did Aleksandr have military grade security?" Alexa asked out loud, before coming to hover over Dee's shoulder. There had to be something there. An explanation. Something.

"I'll start working through the files, starting with the most recent transactions and business reports…" Dee responded, idly clicking through the navigation system.

"He seemed to be working on something. This is a new company's register. Something called 'Cenodyne.' He was building a new company?" Dee said, frowning a little as she opened and closed multiple large PDF files, one after another in succession.

"Legal forms. Insurances. Approvals. All the sorts of things you need to create a company. Mr. Bodrov was doing this absolutely by the book, it looks like…" Dee explained, when they were both startled by the landline wringing. Dee frowned at it for a moment.

"In truth, not many people actually phone us down here in the basement," she said, picking it up, making a few 'uh-huh' noises, and then handing it to Alexa.

"It's the chief. He wants you," Dee said.

"Chief Williams, I think we're onto something-" Alexa started to say before being rudely interrupted.

"No time for that now. State police have returned a positive ID on a car attached to the 34-27 crew you raided yesterday morning. A gangbanger's sister, or should be. But our eyes have it's not her driving it. It's our man Zarbos. We're going for the intercept right now, Agent."

Zarbos. *El Tigre,* Alexa thought as her heart hammered. She was already turning for the door, remembering to grab her badge and phone on the way out.

"Landers?" Dee called after her.

"Just do what you can, Dee! Find out what was so important about Cenodyne!" Alexa said, already racing for the door.

CHAPTER TWENTY-NINE

12:15 PM. US ROUTE 41, EVERGLADES NATIONAL PARK, MIAMI, FLORIDA

"I really wish Kage was driving…" Alexa muttered under her breath as their unmarked dark grey SUV went way past cruising speed on the long, broad stretch of US Highway 41.

This particular road was nothing but a dead-arrow highway stretching right across the Florida peninsula, cutting into the everglades and then making a sharp detour upwards towards Fort Meyers, Sarasota, and eventually Tampa.

Which was a smart move on Zarbos's account, Alexa thought. While the larger cities of Miami central, Orlando and Jacksonville were all on the East Coast of Florida, the West Coast was a lot sparser populated, given over as it was to the omnipresent, humid green of the Everglade swamps and waterways. As Miami stretched a good ways along the Apalachee Bay and mainland US, it meant that if you stuck to the smaller Highway Routes, and kept heading as westwards as possible, you could follow the Gulf of Mexico clear to skip across the toes of Alabama and Mississippi, and then you were into Louisiana and Texas.

"Next stop, Mexico." Alexa felt her stomach start to lurch as their driver added another five-to-ten miles to the hour as they raced along that straight, no-way-out Highway 41.

Taking these smaller highways rather than the interstates would mean less eyes on him, of course, Alexa thought as she ran through the things that she was sure Kage would be asking her.

Protective gear?

She thumped the bulletproof vest over her shirt, which was making her sweat, and secured the straps a little tighter at her sides. Her helmet was by her side, ready to be donned when needed.

Equipment?

She had her earbud in and was half-listening to the chatter from the agents and PD officers in the other cars as they raced along behind. A lot of tense, macho kind of talk as usual. The stuff guys say when they're anxious and want to put some spit and fire in their bones before-

"We got eyes, ma'am," said the FBI driver, whom Alexa was sure was probably a good driver in any other circumstance, but a high-speed get-to-the-perp-before-they-got-away wasn't one of them.

"Show me," she said, leaning as far forward as her seatbelt would allow at where there was a blue car ahead of them, still small in the distance and then, just beyond that, a tiny blip of a silver car.

"I can pull pole with his position in 3, I'm thinking," the man said, with his hand already moving towards the gear stick.

"No. Wait. There's an awful lot of road and a lot of not very much going on," Alexa said, nodding to either side of their window where endless green stretched in every direction. They were cutting across the top of the Everglades. It was just palm and shrub and sudden water out there for leagues and leagues and leagues, Alexa knew.

There was nowhere for Zarbos to go to, but that wasn't a good thing. Bad people with bad options did bad things.

"We're unmarked. We pass them at the bend, then slow down, then pull them. Flash our lights, pull him over. I'm betting he will want to bluff his way out at first because he's still a long way from home. While we're pulling in, the Miami PD cruise to the front, box his car in. Understood?" she said, before relaying the plan to Field Chief Williams, and Dempsey.

"Good," came Williams' call over the phone from where the field chief supervisor was currently very securely seated.

"You want the FBI to take all the glory for catching this Tiger guy, right?" was Detective Dempsey's contrasting opinion.

"No, Detective, that is not right," Alexa said. She had zero tolerance for his bad mood today. Not at all.

"This is an FBI case, or so everyone keeps telling me. You're taking the investigative lead and we're offering support, right?" Dempsey, who sounded about as happy with the fast-driving experience as Landers was.

"Well, I think it's about time maybe the Miami PD got a commendation or two. You've got zero traffic experience, we're the experts here!"

Alexa muttered a very unpleasant word under her breath before sighing. *Whatever. Maybe this was actually better, anyway. Maybe the sight of the police cars would make Zarbos slow down, certain that he could fool them.*

"Fine. I'll support, come on in at the first sign of trouble," Alexa grumbled, clicking off the connection with her ear bud and instead focussing on that small dot of silver far up ahead.

"How far to the turn?" Alexa asked.

"Tamaimi Ranger Station, ma'am?" her rather blocky-looking driver said gruffly. "Only a few. But he won't want to be taking the bend fast. On the other side of that there green is the Miccosukee Indian Village. Some traffic coming right out onto the 41 right there. He'll be slowing up, for sure," the man said in a broad Floridian accent; all sun-drenched, barbecue, and twang.

"Okay. Dempsey will take him at the bend then before he can accelerate," Alexa said before an idea struck her.

"Does this thing even have a, you know, light?" Alexa completely forgot the name of the thing, as the driver laughed.

"Sure. Glove compartment."

Unfortunately, Alexa realized that her vest had the large 'FBI' emblazoned across it. There was no way that she could pretend to be an undercover highway cop, making a routine speeding stop. As soon as they pulled around after the PD, and she got out, Zarbos would know that it was an official sting. *That* was when things would get interesting, as a drug cartel boss would be looking at the rest of his life on max security for certain, Alexa thought.

Well, kiddo, sometimes the breaks are just bad, she thought she could hear her dad say with a growl as she reached for the glove compartment to find the magnet-attached blue light, ready to go.

"All units at the ready," Alexa whispered at her ear buds. "PD? You are good to go..."

"*Damn right we are!*" Dempsey growled, as suddenly there was a squeal of tires behind them, and the sudden long, accusing wail of a police siren as the first squad car pulled out and raced ahead.

Dear God, Alexa thought with a groan, as she kept her eyes fixed on the silver car of *El Tigre*.

This was it. This man right here could well be the one who orchestrated the killing of not only Aleksandr Bodrov but his two sons, as well. He was connected to Zholdin, somehow, and he was clearly powerful. A Mexican drug lord, with tentacles into the Latino gang network spreading as far as Miami, Florida.

"Why did you do it, Carlos?" Alexa growled at the suspect's car. "What did it have to do with Cenodyne?"

Dempsey's squad car was approaching the turn off to Tamaimi Ranger Station; she watched it pull up behind Zarbos's silver car, sirens wailing as it flashed its lights.

For a giddying moment, she wondered if Carlos was going to tear off into the distance. But the bend was right there. He had to slow down to take it, he had to…

She saw Carlos's car slowing as it approached the bend. Her hand went unconsciously to the gun at her belt, even though she knew it would do her no good from back here…

And then the *Tigre's* car was slowing to pull over, just past the bend, and the cop car was pulling just behind it.

"Slow, slowly does it," she whispered to her driver, wishing that it was Kage in the driving seat, not this man. Kage would know how to play this. Kage, for all of his seeming recklessness, was solid.

They slowed down to a cruise, then even slower still as she saw Dempsey get out of one side, and the driver of the squad car get out the other and start sauntering towards the driver's side.

There was only one driver sighted in the car, wasn't there? Alexa suddenly thought. She hadn't noticed any other in the report, but now she wished that she had checked a second time.

They were moving too fast. They were already approaching the bend and pulling out from the stopped cars, ready to pull over in front of them. Alexa looked out of the tinted windows to see the cop tapping on the driver's window, while Dempsey approached from the passenger side. Maybe this was going to be too easy. Maybe this was going to be textbook.

"Okay, forget it," Alexa said as they were already pulling in front of Zarbos's car, for her to pull out the light and stick it to the top of car roof through one window.

He'll see we're FBI as soon as we pull out, Alexa thought, along with the fact that 'the Tiger' was a Mexican drug lord. He had probably seen plenty people killed, executed, or tortured; he wouldn't even cast an eye at…

Stop it. Nothing will change it now, Alexa told herself. She just had to roll the dice, as they say. She opened the car door and turned to step out as quickly as possible – just as there was the unmistakeable, unforgettable, loud bang of a gun.

"Shit!" She twisted in place, already bring up her gun as she sighted down the length of the car just in time to see the squad officer who had been at the driver's side hitting the dirt, and Carlos's car suddenly roar forwards.

"FREEZE! FBI!" Alexa shouted, her eyes reflexively tracking where to put the bullets. Two in the driver's side-

WHAP! WHAP! WHAP!

Someone – a second person in the car! – had popped from the window to fire three shots at her. They were wild, no hope of hitting Alexa thought as one pinged off of the top of their service SUV.

Alexa plugged another bullet into the driver's window, but Carlos's car was already pulling out and roaring ahead, arcing across the Tamaimi bend and heading straight up the middle of the highway.

"Damnit! Get going!" Alexa shouted as she leapt, rolling over the tarmac and asphalt to come up smoothly in a crouch, raising her gun to sight at the fast-retreating vehicle.

Twenty yards away. Thirty. Forty.

There.

She focussed on the right rear wheel and started firing. One shot. Two as *El Tigre's* car did everything it could to speed up. It swerved across the roadway as a truck was coming down the other side, and-

Bingo. The tire burst with a sound like a clap of thunder, and Carlos's car was skidding, turning, hitting the dirt on one side of the verge and continuing as sparks sprayed back from its ruined hub.

Alexa broke into a run, starting to race forward over the tarmac towards the gangster's car as it slowed into a skid amongst palms and overgrown spindle bushes.

"Landers!" the FBI driver was shouting as their SUV pulled out around her, racing ahead as the driver's door popped open, and a man slumped out, at first attempting to stagger to his feet, but falling on the ground instead. Even from this distance, Alexa could see that one of her first shots had hit, and the driver was bleeding heavily from a wound to the shoulder.

But it wasn't Zarbos.

The second squad car was behind her, the police already with Dempsey and the downed squad officer as Alexa orientated her run, heading to the far side of the stalled car instead.

Zarbos was still inside there somewhere. He hadn't been the driver, and there had been two other people in the car.

"HANDS UP! FBI!" Alexa's FBI driver was shouting as he screeched their car into a halt.

The passenger door was open. Alexa saw Carlos hunkering beside it as he took a shot at their SUV. She saw the windscreen radiate into a fractal spiderweb shatter.

"Gun down!" Alexa shouted, raising her gun as Carlos flinched, turning around.

His gun was up. Too up. He hadn't dropped it.

With a flick of her wrist, she twitched her hand downwards and pulled the trigger, seeing Carlos grunt in pain as he flung himself towards the green, suddenly off balance by the burst of red at his calf.

"*Puerta!*" the man yelled and hit the floor with a grunt of pain as Alexa closed the distance between them. He still had his gun in his hands. His only hope was to shoot his way out of this mess...

Alexa got to his wrist before he could raise it, and she kicked savagely at Zarbos's hand to send the gun spinning as she fell on him, one knee forward to crunch into his belly as she held her gun in two hands.

"Don't move! Don't move – you're under arrest!" she hissed with cold fury as Zarbos attempted to struggle, but the man was wounded and Alexa was on top of him. She grabbed one arm and pushed it down as the other threatened to flail at her...but then the FBI driver was there, sliding across the dirt as he landed heavily on Zarbos's legs.

"You're done, Zarbos, you're done!" Alexa shouted, and, after one more snarl of frustration, the man went limp, but he still spoke a string of cursing Spanish at her.

Alexa kept her gun on him as the FBI driver cuffed him, and then came the wash of shivering, trembling adrenaline as it was all over.

"Check the other guy," Alexa said, allowing herself back to her feet to step a few feet backwards, once more kicking the drug dealer's gun even further away before checking the rest of the car. No more passengers. No one waiting with a loaded gun to take anyone out.

Cars were starting to slow down around them, and Alexa cursed herself, keeping an eye on them just in case *El Tigre* had the foresight to request back-up from 34-27 on his runaway out of town.

He hadn't, and the other cars were just rubberneckers, daytrippers, and families trying to get a look at the action. Alexa ignored them, turning back to the scene.

"One dead," her driver relayed as he stood by the body of his opposite number. Alexa really would have to get her driver's name, but right now her mind was too wired to bring it up.

"Some sharp shooting. You got him through the wind shield. He must have thrown the vehicle into acceleration as he was bleeding out," her unknown FBI driver commented, as Alexa checked what was happening with Dempsey.

"Officer injured, requesting immediate medical assistance… Tamaimi Ranger base, yes, Indian Village. No active shooters…" she could overhear Dempsey saying as Alexa realized it was done. It was over.

"I need medical over here, too," Alexa barked, as she eyed the injured Carlos, before turning back to hunker down beside him.

"I want my lawyer. He's good. This is entrapment," were the first words out of Zarbos's mouth.

"Fine. You can call it whatever you want, Zarbos, but I see one injured police officer, and an attempt to kill several federal agents. That and the multiple homicide of the Bodrov family we've got on you, and you won't be seeing your side of the border for a very long time yet…" Alexa smiled thinly.

"What!?" Zarbos blinked at her in confusion.

"Am I not making myself clear? We've got you for conspiracy to kill three people-" *four, if you count Leela*, "and attempted murder on a further three, maybe four," Alexa permitted herself a dry chuckle. "What's the penalty in Florida state for that? I can't remember…"

"What? You're mad! I know nothing about any of this!" Zarbos responded as Alexa suddenly felt a rush of hot hatred run through her body.

Kage was currently lying in a hospital bed thanks to this jerk. He'd come within an inch or more from dying. He still might die, in all honesty.

"Cut your crap," Alexa said, hunkering down next to him as behind her the chatter of police radios and shouting voices faded to a low-level, criminal static hum behind her.

"All I want to know is *why*," Alexa asked, leaning closer in, her voice a low growl. "Why kill Aleksandr, and his sons? Believe me, if you tell me now this will go a whole lot easier for you…"

"I didn't kill them!" Zarbos hissed back with outrage in his eyes. "Why on earth would I?"

"We know you met with Mikhail Zholdin." Alexa once again almost purred with satisfaction. It was going to feel good to put this guy behind bars. Finally.

"I never-" Zarbos tried to argue, but Alexa cut him off at once.

"We've got evidence, photos, eyewitnesses," she said in grim satisfaction. "Even if you're a few steps removed, you'll go down. What juror is ever going to believe you?"

At the mention of Zholdin's name and the evidence stacking up against him, Alexa saw the man open and close his mouth briefly, and then his face spasm as another wave of pain came up from his calf. Alexa thought that she should probably take a look at it to see if he was okay. It was a grazing shot, taking out a line of his white denim jeans and grazing the side of his calf muscles. An awful lot of blood, though.

"Look, *it wasn't me!*" Zarbos blubbered desperately, muttering low. "I never killed Bodrov. Or his damn sons. I was trying to do a deal with him!"

What? It was Alexa's turn to blink in surprise.

"Talk," she almost growled at him. "And I'll know if you're lying," she lied. "We have *a lot* of evidence stacking up."

Carlos groaned, whether in pain or frustration or both, Alexa had no idea. Either way, he licked his lips as there was the sound of approaching, distant sirens.

"Talk now because once you're in the system..." Alexa once again threatened, although she really didn't know what would happen once he was inside the system. But being partially responsible (or deemed to be) responsible for shooting an FBI officer wasn't going to turn out well for him, she was sure.

"Zholdin was an outside broker. Bodrov had some manufacturing deal, high-end microprocessor chips. He was offering them to me, and I would sell them on the black market. All three of us would make billions," Carlos said quickly.

"You remember the name of the companies?" Alexa insisted, and Zarbos glared at her, and then accepted defeat.

"Of course. It was to be Bodrov's first manufacture. Cenodyne."

Oh crapsticks, Alexa thought, as outwardly she merely nodded and leaned back where she crouched.

So that was what Aleksandr Bodrov was up to with Cenodyne, was it? Manufacturing high-end microprocessors?

It was a very, very small win in the sea of information, Alexa thought as she got herself up, waving to the approaching squad cars that they had one to take in behind her.

Who else was left who could have killed the billionaire and his sons?

So that leaves Zholdin, maybe, Alexa mused as she glared at the endless, hot and humid green of the Florida swamps.

CHAPTER THIRTY

7:28 PM. UNIVERSITY OF MIAMI HOSPITAL

Processing the scene out by Muccosokee took a long time, several hours' worth of crime scene photographing and analyzing and medical attention to the injured officer (who was whisked off back to Miami Hospital) and then crime scene reports before Alexa was finally allowed to leave.

Several hours' worth of paperwork for only several minutes' worth of action, Alexa thought with a heavy groan as she pulled into the UofM Hospital, there to once again check on Kage.

Trixi was fine, Alexa reminded herself. She was still at the FBI HQ and had made friends with Elijah the door guard. The poor woman had apparently spent most of the day asleep, and then had been quite happy to have whatever takeout she wanted delivered straight to her.

She was safe, Alexa repeated. That was all that mattered. It was a small victory compared to the fact that the killer had taken so many – but it felt significant.

One life you haven't managed to get, the woman smiled to herself under the bright, antiseptic gleam of the hospital lights above.

The hospital itself was quieter tonight, Alexa thought. Well, in so far as hospitals were ever quieter. There were still bleepers going off and nurses rushing back and forth, but Alexa felt that there was something different in the air. A lull. Maybe it was just her, she considered. The take down of a major crime boss like Zarbos – even if he wasn't the one behind the killing – surely merited some sort of applause, didn't it?

Kage had been moved to a rehab ward on a different wing, now that he was safely out of the critical care component of his stay.

He still looked like shit, however, Alexa thought as she peeked into his room to find him sleeping soundly in a private room. There was an overabundance of flowers and cards left on his bedside table from the field office, and some joker had even put one of the mealy-mouthed public information flyers *'Have you or someone you know been the victim of gun violence?'* by them.

Ha-ha. Police humor, she thought.

Her eyes flickered to the Asian-Irish American sleeping deeply in his bed. His black hair was ruffled and all over the place, and his skin was a deathly pale, but he appeared to be sleeping soundly. He looked five years younger, Alexa thought, as once again she felt that tug of empathy run through her heart.

This was one of the inevitable consequences of doing the work we do, she thought, and wasn't sure if that was a piece of advice given to her by her father or by the Academy.

It was tough, but this was the job.

"It wasn't Zarbos," Alexa muttered to his sleeping form, knowing somehow that the very act of talking to her sleeping partner would make her thinking clearer, somehow.

Kage, of course, said nothing.

"He was involved in some deal with Bodrov, if you believe that. So, we're back to square one. It wasn't Henderson, it might have been Perelli, or Zholdin maybe wanted to betray his oldest friend; but then he wouldn't get the money from the deal with Cenodyne, right? How does that make any sense?" She was thinking and sighing.

A part of her wondered if she had come here just in case that mysterious non-doctor showed up again. She had kept an eye out, but the strange, thin, almost-balding man who had written on her coffee cup hadn't showed. As it was, she was sure that if she tried to shake down the hospital staff then she would find out that he didn't even work there at all.

I have a friend. Or someone trying to lead me astray, she thought, as her mind suddenly turned to the clicks and whirrs on her phone, the headlights at her supposedly safe motel.

The killer was watching us.

Someone is watching us.

And someone is giving us tips.

"But you were shot at when you went for the car details, Zarbos, and the 34-27 car details..." Alexa thought aloud as she looked at her sleeping partner, wondering just what dreams he was currently immersed in right now.

So, how did that make sense? The killer had been watching them, following them. She thought back to the events of that day. Two days ago, when Kage had been pinned down with fire from the killer in Miami Beach South and had managed to get away without injury.

(No such luck a second time around, of course.)

Somehow it felt like a lifetime ago to Alexa, as she picked up her notebook and scrolled through the various entries.

"We had been at Miami Heights that morning for the murder of the Bodrov sons," Alexa noted. It made sense that the killer (Mr. I-spit-bullets Combat Controller man) had been watching their investigation then. There had been two witnesses, Trixi and Leela, and he had probably wanted to know where they were.

The next set of notes for Alexa had been VIV, when she had gone to talk to Perelli about the two 'dancers.' Surely the killer would have followed her there?

But no, apparently not. For some reason the killer had followed *Kage,* not her.

"Huh," Alexa stopped. That was odd. It seemed...out of character.

Instead, the killer had followed Kage as he had gone to check out the *Speedies* car rental place, hadn't he? The car that Zarbos had hired to talk to Zholdin...

But that hadn't been all that he had been doing that day, had it? Alexa suddenly remembered in a flash of insight.

"The rental car had been an extra. We hadn't even discussed it that morning!" Alexa remembered.

Instead, Kage had been down at the south marina, hadn't he? Where he had successfully identified the killer's boat-

"-and given those details to the DSMV and Port Authority!" Alexa realized.

This wasn't about the car and Zarbos at all, was it? The reason why Kage had been followed, had been targeted that day, was because he had come close to finding out the boat which had been the killer's route of attack.

Alexa knew that she was onto something. It felt right. It made too much sense. If the killer had successfully killed Kage, then all of his work that day might have died with him. Any small details he remembered about the boat footage, or whom he had spoken to, might not have gotten filed.

It was only sheer good diligence on Kage's part, after all, that he had phoned in the boat details before going for the car rental. If he hadn't, and if Mr I-spit-bullets guy had been an inch or two luckier...

Alexa shivered. It didn't bear thinking about, but what did was the fact that the killer had tried to stop Kage from getting access to the boat information.

Because he must have slipped up. He must have thought we'd never work out the shot came from a boat at all! Alexa thought, already grabbing her phone and flinging a message at Dee.

Hi Dee. Are you still working? God, I hope you are. That DSMV Port Authority thing. The 'pink boat' Kage was chasing up. Did they ever get back to you with a registration? Urgent.

Just a few seconds later, Alexa's phone chimed.

Dee (work hours only):
Ugh. Of course I'm still working. Despite the name. Been working on the laptop. Interesting stuff! Military contracts, looks like. Computer parts. Will check boat reg.

Alexa felt a little sorry for disturbing her, but not that sorry. She felt as though the case was starting to pull itself together, the threads were starting to pull in a net, and the killer was going to be at the center of it…

The boat could be the key link to the killer, it had to be – otherwise why did the killer go for Kage as soon as he could?

That left Cenodyne.

"Military contracts huh? Computer parts meaning…" Alexa whispered. *Microprocessors.* What Zarbos had said that he was going to buy off of Aleksandr for a heavy, heavy price.

Alexa turned to the door to open the shutters just a little to check the corridor outside. No one but a blue-suited nurse walking into the nurse stations. Satisfied, she turned her attention back to the phone.

In her pocket she had a scrap of paper with the copied number that had been written on her coffee cup.

'Why did Aleksandr have military grade security?' her strange informant had asked. And now Alexa knew the answer. She raised the phone to tap in the informant's number but paused. She needed more. She hit Dee's number, to be met by a rather grumpy Cyber Officer.

"Seriously, Landers. I said I was on it. The Port Authority didn't even send an email. They made a phone call. That someone else took, and I'm trying to track who took it and what it was..." Dee said. In the background, Alexa could hear the distinct whirr and beeps of digital machines.

"Thanks. That is really, really a great help. Could be key to the whole case, in fact," Alexa tried to reassure her quickly. "But what I wanted to talk to you about, apart from that, was Cenodyne. These microprocessors. Zarbos said Aleksandr was going to sell him some to put on the black market..."

"Well, that would have been HIGHLY bad news!" Dee sounded a whole lot more animated on this topic than she had on running up a number.

"From what I found out today, Cenodyne had been awarded a contract to produce these new type of microprocessors. They're like low-AI level designs that integrate into systems to work on threat analysis, deep data research. Really, the applications could be anything... Have you heard of Game Theory?"

Dee's mind appeared to take a sudden tangent that Alexa hadn't been prepared for at all.

"Ugh...no?"

"Nevermind. We can't all have had an MIT background. Game Theory came along decades ago, but really ran to the races in the Cold War. It's all mathematics and psychology, threat-analysis. In Chess, what do you do if your opponent has taken out your Queen and your Bishop; can you still win, kind of thing?"

"I have no idea what relevance that has," Alexa said honestly. Neither Aleksandr and definitely not his children appeared to be playing at that level of genius intellect.

"Very relevant. Very, very relevant indeed. Game Theory looks at any simulation between opposing parties, and asks what the conditions for a win, a stalemate, a defeat or mutual annihilation might mean. It was the big thing behind why we never nuked Cuba during the missile crisis. What do you do when your opponent had seven thousand tactical warheads pointing at you and you have a few thousand more, right?"

"Are you telling me this is nuclear? National Security?" Alexa breathed. They had been briefed by the CIA. But that had been about possible Russian involvement (which was all completely false now, by the way, she thought).

"No. Maybe. Anyway, Game Theory is mostly military strategy, but it means a hell of a lot to flight simulations, air traffic control, et cetera. It's a way at looking at a situation and working out how to win, with what you got. Well – these AI microprocessors were that. They would plug into your defence plan, your strategy computer or even your personal soldiers' weapons and guidance systems, and give the best solutions. THAT is why they were so important, and why any military in the world would kill to-"

"Oh," Alexa said at the same time as Dee. That was precisely what had happened to Aleksandr, after all. He had died.

"Aleksandr's company was working on these things? Did he have state approval?"

"And more! That was what all that new company set-up business was. He had just been awarded the contract to manufacture these new AI microprocessors, and from what little research I've done, it must have put a whole lot of noses out..."

"You think?" Alexa asked, but to her it already made sense after all, anyway. Cenodyne was a nobody company, a start-up really, and it was muscling into some of the biggest US military contracts yet to be seen, probably. The fact that Cenodyne's CEO was an actual recovering Soviet himself was probably pretty shocking.

"Maybe we need to find out just whose noses," Alexa murmured, before Dee kept on talking.

"Ah. There's Kevin. I'm sure he was the one who took the Port Authority call. Let me collar him, and I'm sure I'll have the results – good or bad – for you on the pink boat. Maybe they got its registration, maybe not."

"Here's hoping," Alexa whispered, as her attention swirled yet again. She clicked off the call and was now thinking about microprocessors and upstart companies.

Anyone annoyed at the decision had been right. As soon as Cenodyne was awarded the contract, Aleksandr had contacted his old friend Zholdin to broker a deal for them on the black market.

Surely someone was going to be REALLY pissed at that.

The agent's hand once again went to her pocket, feeling the scrunch of paper that she pulled out.

Why did Aleksandr have military grade security?

She knew the answer now. She thumbed the number, and this time dial tone turned to pick up. Silence at the other end. Alexa said one word.

"Cenodyne."

CHAPTER THIRTY-ONE

7:55 PM.

"So... I see you got there in the end, Agent Landers." The man's voice on the other end of the line had an accent, but Alexa couldn't place what it was, or where it came from. It had a thick guttural element and choked at the ends. It made Alexa think of Eastern Europe perhaps, not Mediterranean. Not African or Asian...

"Who are you?" Alexa asked immediately, earning a small chuckle at the far end of the line. Again that accent that wasn't exactly American.

Not the killer himself then, Alexa thought. As the man that she had seen had sounded as American home-boy as they had come.

"An interested party. Or let's just say I represent an interested party," the man said, and Alexa could hear the amusement in his voice. He was enjoying this game of cat and mouse.

"Do you make it a habit of leaving notes in people's pockets?" Alexa said, feeling a sudden wave of dislike for all this cloak and dagger stuff. She was an FBI agent, she liked a puzzle, but she didn't like obfuscation. It was one of the things that had set her on this path, after all.

"How long have you been following us? What is Aleksandr Bodrov to you!?" she pressed, immediately hearing an almost angered hiss on the other end of the line.

"Enough, Agent, I have been following you enough. There is a limit to what I will answer and what I won't. Please be very clear on this, Agent Landers, that I am not here to help YOU. I am here to help those I represent and, at the moment, that means that I am here, at the end of the line, listening to an FBI agent demand the world revolve around them!"

"Fine. Cenodyne," Alexa repeated. "I know that Aleksandr was tied to a new manufacturing process, and that he was killed for it."

"A military manufacturing process, I am sure you know by now. A lot of people were very wary of our Aleksandr suddenly turning up and offering to make AI-assisted microprocessors…"

"You got a name?" Alexa asked. "A name for a company that had the biggest beef with Cenodyne?"

This time, there was a more full-throated laugh from the other end of the line. The mysterious man appeared to find her suggestion hilarious.

"Biggest Beef. Such a mid-west term. Positively parochial. And as for competitors, why not take your pick? Boeing, Blackwater, Lockhead & Mears… Any and all of them were rightfully angered at this multi-billion contract being awarded to a Soviet."

Russian, Alexa thought. It was a small but important distinction.

"But still. If that is what you are suggesting…" Alexa urged, for the man to make another sigh at the end of the line once again.

"Really. You were floundering if I hadn't stepped in to help you. Why not see what competing firms are, as you so delightfully put it, 'home grown.'"

"Homegrown, what the hell does that mean?" Alexa asked. All of the manufacturing companies that the man had mentioned were US companies after all, weren't they? And was he really suggesting that another military company, one that worked for the defence and stability of the United States was really about to also go around killing people?

Duh. Aleksandr was a CIA intelligence asset, or had been, once a long time ago. What if he decided to change? What if word that he was about to defraud the United States government of some however-many billions of dollars, and potentially endangering the country itself when he sold these new AI microprocessors, got out?

Then Aleksandr would be a traitor two times over, Alexa thought. She wondered for a moment what her dad, a celebrated veteran, would say. She could almost hear him saying *'maybe he got what he deserved...'*

Her father wasn't a bloodthirsty man by any stretch of the imagination. But he was a patriot, through and through. Alexa wondered, fleetingly, if she was *right* to start pointing the fingers at US companies, taking action to defend their country...

"Ah. I can assume from your silence that you are wary of taking this matter further. Perhaps your sense of patriotic loyalty clouds your judgement. Well. So be it. I had thought that perhaps you were a person interested in justice above all things. Perhaps I was mistaken. Good night, Agent Landers."

There was a click, and the man's voice was gone as the line suddenly went dead.

"Wait," Alexa whispered, but he was gone. She half thought of phoning the number back again but decided against it. Her mysterious Deep Throat was clearly a man of dedication. He wouldn't waste time picking up the phone if he wasn't already dismantling it and destroying it as quickly as the thought came to her.

But the thing was, his words had stung.

This wasn't the way that problems should be resolved in America, she swore to herself. Whatever games the killer or their employers were playing – even if Mr. Deep Throat was someone she could trust or not – she knew this one thing: She believed in the rule of law.

The law was a thin thread that kept society in place. That held civilization together in the absence of any other virtue, when it came to it.

But it was more than that. The reason why she had become an FBI agent wasn't just about the law, not in that way. It had been about helping people. About stopping the bad guys.

Well, wasn't Aleksandr one of the bad guys in this? her devil's advocate asked.

Yes. Of course he was. But his sons, as venal and as corrupt and stupid as they were, probably weren't. Neither was Leela, or Trixi, or Kage. The civilians injured in the shoot-out on Miami Beach.

The killer was the bad guy, and whomever sanctioned the deaths of all those people, Alexa knew with a certainty that lent strength to her steps as she opened the door back to the ward outside, already moving for the corridor. She would go back to the motel tonight, just for tonight. It had felt like days since she had actually slept in a bed, rather than the office floor at the field office. If she wasn't too wired to sleep at all, that was...

She googled 'Defence Companies, Florida' just on the off chance that she might find a name that might be considered 'homegrown.'

To her surprise, a name popped up straight away, and it was based right here in Miami.

Vanguard Systems.

A moment later she was on the phone.

"Dee? This is Landers-"

"*Oh, dear lord. Do you ever let a woman do her work? And maybe even go home for the night? Wait. Who am I kidding? I'm going to be working this case 'til 4 am, I'm sure of it…*"

"I'm sorry, Dee, it's just I've got something that I really need your help with. Details on Vanguard Systems."

"Vanguard? Hell, I can help you with that right now. I went to a couple Future of Security conferences that they run. They make bits for fighter planes, but I can't remember which bit... What, you think they're connected to all this? Another company in competition with Cenodyne?" Dee asked.

"Could be. Just working an angle at the moment," Alexa said, feeling that fire in her belly. It was a long angle, to be honest. Some mysterious man tells her that a homegrown defence contractor is involved? She needed proof. Hard evidence.

"Excellent. Anything you have on Vanguard, anyway. CEO's, Headquarters, that kind of thing."

"Got it. Most of it will be online anyway, a few things might need a public records search, which means it will happen tomorrow."

Fine, Alexa thought as she moved down the hallway. She wondered if she might even get some sleep tonight. Ridiculous. Like Dee, who was she kidding?

"Same thing goes for the pink boat. Kevin said it was a call back to the Port Authority. They'd found some conflicting registrations for her."

Really? That piqued Alexa's interest.

"You should get a call from the Port Authority guys tomorrow morning about it. Best I can do right now, I'm afraid..."

"It's amazing," Alexa laughed, feeling her teeth jitter with electricity.

She was close. She could feel it.

CHAPTER THIRTY-TWO

DAY 6.

6:58 AM. FBI SAFE HOUSE

ALEXA HAD BEEN ABSOLUTELY RIGHT. SHE COULD BARELY sleep a wink at all through the night, and instead spent many long hours staring at her ceiling, as the occasional light from the passing cars rose and faded across her blinds.

You have to be careful. The killer has been following you.

She couldn't get her mysterious informant out of her head. Who were they? Why were they helping her? Who did they represent?

THE **FLORIDA GIRL**

Worse than that was the undeniable fact of the man's accent. Eastern European. So far Eastern as to perhaps be- Russian?

Russian, not Soviet, she had corrected. But what if the man in question had been speaking the truth? That Aleksandr was in fact a defected Soviet because his tenure as a Russian oligarch had been going for a long, long time. Aleksandr had grown up when the Cold War had been in full swing...

At some point Alexa must have fallen asleep because she remembered dreaming of crazed bunkers full of people playing games in order to work out precisely how many times a sniper could shoot in order to kill everyone else. The dream shifted, showing her sniper pulling the trigger, and when the bullet fired, it lanced through the air like an intercontinental ballistic missile-

"Huh!" Alexa awoke with a start to find her cell busy ringing.

Unrecognized Number.

"Hello?" she asked, a moment of anxiety mixed with excitement in her belly. Was this going to be her informant again? Or what if it was someone else...

Be careful, Agent Landers...

"Am I speaking to Special Agent Landers, of the FBI?" asked a gruff male voice on the other end of the line.

"Yes?" Alexa thought this would be a great way to ascertain her whereabouts if the speaker already had her phone location. She slid from the bed, one hand reaching for the gun by the side of the pillow...

"Richmond Jones, Port Authority. *I'm giving you a call back on a request put in at some really inhospitable hour last night...* "

Alexa checked the times. Barely past seven. "You guys work early, don't you?"

"*Tide waits for no man, and certainly not my sleep cycle, ma'am,*" Richmond said.

"*Someone in the office ran the request last night, but it came up conflicted so I thought I'd phone you as soon as I had some clarity; and it was a sensible hour to do so...* "

Alexa figured he could have passed on the 'sensible hour' thing, but there we go. Like Dee, and like poor Richmond Jones here, it appeared that sleep was a commodity when you had the jobs they did.

"Go on," she said, dropping the holster for her gun and instead reaching for her notepad.

"Well, the pink yacht you mentioned turned up a couple of times, but it had been scrubbed, too."

"Scrubbed?"

"Change of ownership, and the previous owner didn't want their details kept on file. It happens, not very often, but it does. Some people are pretty conscious about their data protection, so they ask that their previous details be redacted."

"Any way of finding out who they were?"

"Not from my end, ma'am. You'd have to put a court order request for that. Even I don't get to see the data."

Damn, Alexa thought.

"Anyway. The yacht itself, color scheme and more importantly, current registration, matches up to an eight-footer we have registered to Mr. Theo Wilson, right here in Miami."

Alexa felt a cold shiver run through her body, even though it was always warm in Florida.

Was Theo Wilson her killer? Was he the man she had looked in the eye and waited for him to pull the trigger?

"You got an address with that?" she started noting.

"Well, that's the interesting thing, ma'am. I've got an owner address, but it's a bit unexpected."

Great, Alexa could have groaned.

"It's a doozie. Humbolt Cole, Everglades National Park."

"Where's that?" Alexa asked, having no idea. Weren't the Everglades on the other side of Florida? With Miami on the east, and the Everglades to the west?

"Your guess was as good as mine until about a half hour ago, and I found it on some old land registration. It's a spit of swamp from what I can tell, old Army land that was decommed and put up to auction. Out southwest of Miami-Dade County. Nothing down there but swamp and gators."

"Okay..." Alexa opened her phone, tapped through to Google. "But that's gotta be only about, what, two hours away tops? Can you get to it by water? Can you moor a yacht there?"

"*Technically, I suppose, but it's an awful long commute. You'd pass Biscayne Bay, come up Florida Keys probably, and after that I'd have no idea. There are so many old waterways running up through the South Everglades, and they change every year, everything from sea inflow to old irrigation ditches that you'd never know your way back around again in my book... The problem is, ma'am, that deep in the swamps you can't bring sea vessels in easily. The water is too shallow and clogged up with mosses, weeds, roots, rocks, more gators... A yacht's hull is too sharp, and it would clog your engine. That's why we use airboats out there.*"

Maybe you could find a way if you were trained, Alexa thought. Like, if your job as a Combat Controller was all about being in hostile environments for periods of time, navigating terrain that no one else thought you could navigate...

"But it might be technically possible for a yacht to navigate, if some of the water channels were deep enough?" Alexa asked once more.

"*Technically. But the channels overgrow every year. You'd have to really know which route you were taking, and, as I say, it's a labyrinth down there...*"

"Okay. Humbolt Cole. I'm guessing it doesn't show up on GPS?"

"*You would be correct there, Special Agent. I have grid references for ya.*"

Grid references. Alexa shook her head. It really was out in the sticks. She thanked the man and tried to find it on Google Maps. It didn't show, and instead she put in the co-ordinates Richmond had sent.

Humbolt Cole was only an hour south of the city, but it looked a long way out from where Alexa was sitting. It looked as though it was surrounded by miles and miles of nothing but green.

Alexa put in a request with the field office for details on Theo Wilson before getting washed and dressed and raiding the mini fridge for any remnants of a breakfast. The results were poor, but the phone rang once again by the time she had jumped out of the shower.

"Landers? It's Williams," her field chief said over the phone. "Good to see you're starting early."

Alexa checked her watch to see that the time was barely eight o'clock. Back in any normal climate (north of Virginia, for sure) she'd have been up at six for a run, so the time was nothing.

And besides, this might be the day she catches a killer.

"Your request, Theo Wilson. It pinged off my desk because he's the nephew of Miami-Dade Senator Gunderson. He counts as a high-profile person."

"A nephew of a senator counts as high-profile?" Alexa asked dimly, then shook her head. Well, well, well, Theo Wilson. Looks like you have been engaging in some extracurricular activities... like killing Russian billionaires.

"Yes. Although he's not close, apparently. But he's on the registered family list that every senator has to provide," the field chief stated. "Care to explain what's going on?"

"Does this Theo have military experience, sir?" Alexa asked as innocently as possible. Maybe her Deep Throat informant was starting to make sense now after all. Maybe the killer couldn't be accessed through normal channels...

"Absolutely not. If anything, the guy seems a bit of a deadbeat. Flunked out of junior high. Tried to do some mail order start-up thing, which failed. Then a botanical hot house. Got busted a few times for growing marijuana," the field chief sighed.

"I'm guessing he's never worked at a company called Vanguard Systems then?" Alexa asked on the off chance.

"Nope. Why would you ask that?" Williams asked, and Alexa paused. She was drawing a blank with this, clearly.

"Well, Theo Wilson's boat was the one that the killer used to shoot Aleksandr Bodrov, sir. And Theo lives out in Who Knows Cole, Middle of Nowhere, Everglades," Alexa pointed out.

"Then it looks to me a simple case of a stolen vessel, clearly. I'd get Mr. Wilson's details and phone him, ask if he has reported his boat stolen over the last few months," Williams directed, but something was pulling at Alexa's mind.

She didn't like it. She felt close to the killer. Very close. The killer had gone to extreme lengths to try and stop Kage from tracking down his boat, after all – and Williams just wants her to phone up this Wilson guy?

"I'd rather have eyes on him, sir. I was going to put in a request for PD backup-"

"Not for a general inquiry, Agent Landers. Not with a senator's nephew, no matter how disgraced he is. You know as well as I that FBI and PD showing up will turn into news. Given the week we've had, I'd rather avoid that."

"Sir-" Alexa tried, but there was no point in arguing with him. The field chief was adamant. Question, get a lost or stolen report from him, but don't show up flying the colors.

She thought once again about what her mysterious informant had said. That sometimes patriotism might cloud judgement.

Well, not me, Alexa was thinking as she got dressed, and clipped her gun into her underarm shoulder holster.

She'd drive all the way to Humbolt Who-Where-Now and get the answers she needed. Even if she had to do it alone.

CHAPTER THIRTY-THREE

10:15 AM. HUMBOLT COLE, SOUTH WEST EVERGLADES, MIAMI-DADE COUNTY

O*KAY, SO THIS REALLY IS THE MIDDLE OF NOWHERE,* Alexa thought as she saw the rusted, ancient sign signalling Humbolt Cole and the turn off.

She had been driving along what appeared to be a little more than a raised access road southwest out of the conurbation, shallow, muddy ditches on either side of her before a blanket of green swamp vegetation. She didn't know the name for the trees out here, but she recognized some of the green as palms, some as rhododendrons, and plenty more spike- and soft-leafed things that she had no name for whatsoever.

Just woke up! Williams filled me in, and says I'm still not allowed to return to duty. See if the Mary-Belle has a personal GPS.

A message from Kage arrived almost an hour into her journey, and Alexa felt a rush of relief, and then a pang of guilt for somehow not telling him what she was doing herself. The text was followed by a lot of angry emojis, so Alexa figured that a man like Kage was already tearing himself up about not being here.

Don't worry, I got this. Rest. This is just a questioning.

The route had been fairly straightforward until she hit the Southern Glades, as Alexa had taken one of the Bureau's black SUVs down through the city, through the long, built-up and industrial areas of Pinecrest and Homestead, as the roads grew ever quieter, and the sun ever hotter outside. Soon enough, she had been cruising along the wide, open access roads looking at a whole lot of blue skies and green around her, as she tried to keep half an eye on the map coordinates she had typed into her custom GPS app.

No actual location marker, of course, Alexa groaned as she pulled off the road into what looked little more than a raised dirt track, rutted on two sides with broken ditch embankments keeping out the worst of the encroaching swamp.

Still, the road was more than wide enough for her SUV, and a few miles out, she was beginning to wonder if she was looking at an old industrial road, especially when it opened out to access an abandoned, chain-linked concrete lot, slap-bang in the middle of the swamps, with its cracked flooring slowly giving way to young trees and vines.

Old Army land, she remembered the Port Authority guy saying. She knew there had had been at some point a lot of military action down here in the swamps, even with tell of some missile base secreted somewhere.

She wondered if Mr. I Spit Bullets Combat-Controller chose this spot because he knew the area? Maybe trained here?

Whatever. Useless to guess, she knew. "And besides…" she muttered to herself. Mr. Theo Wilson, senator Gunderson's wayward nephew, looked to be about as murderous as a wet potato.

Although everyone had their breaking point, Alexa knew. It was her job to know where those breaking points were.

Whether Theo was capable of murder wasn't the question; everyone was, Alexa already knew; the real question was whether Theo had colluded with Mr. I Spit Bullets.

Find the weak link in the chain, as the Academy had taught her. She had figured at first that had been Vadim and Dimitre, or even Henderson – people who could have been blackmailed and leaned on in order for the killer to make his move. She had been right about that in some ways of course (Dimitre and Vadim and Henderson were all compromised by Perelli) but that wasn't the connection.

Theo was the Senator's son.

Theo had the boat that the killer had used.

Could the Senator be involved in this in some way? Or maybe the killer had just seen an opportunity in Theo's boat and taken it?

Either way, what she found out today would lead her one step closer to the killer. Theo would know when he last saw the boat, when it had gone missing – or Alexa would be able to shake the truth out of him why he had handed it over…

Her eyes flickered to her gun in the passenger seat, along with an armored vest she had packed at the last minute. She won't need the vest for a questioning, but still…

"Shoot!" Alexa slammed on the breaks as she raised her eyes just in time to see the largest alligator she had so far witnessed cross the dirt road ahead of her. The damn thing had to be longer than she was tall, she was sure. It got most of the way across the road and stopped, turning it's prehistoric head to look at her, and grin in a toothy threat – before continuing it's slow, confident walk across the roadway, and into the swamps.

Alexa shivered, pausing for a moment before she started up the car again. For some reason, her brief meeting had felt like a premonition.

THE FLORIDA GIRL

The road turned and branched, with the signs for Humbolt Cole appearing in ever smaller and ever more need for repair. These weren't US Highways signs; the last one was a hand-painted sheet of metal nailed to a post that was leaning over to one side, with the paint flecking off as it succumbed to the hot and humid environment.

"What the crap is a Senator's nephew, a guy who is on a special persons list, doing all the way out here!?" Alexa said as she saw that the road only went a little way ahead before it appeared to rise a bit, and for the green to clear out of the way. She saw the edge of a peaked cabin. Dark, treated wood timbers and corrugate plastic for the roof. It was actually far more expensive-looking that she had been expecting out here, in fact.

She pulled her car at the fork, turned it so it was as much off the road as possible, and out of sight from the shack beyond.

Her eyes flickered to the vest at her side, but she dismissed the notion as silly – she didn't want to scare the poor schmuck of a guy, and Chief Williams had said to go in light, hadn't he? Still, she strapped her piece under her arm and put on her smart, form-fitting black jacket loosely over it. No giant blue FBI weather proofer, either.

"We're just going to have a chat, aren't we, Theo?" Alexa said with the slightest of growls as she stepped out of the car and pulled her cap down to keep the sun's glare out of her eyes.

Still, she wished that Kage was here for backup, all the same.

"Hello?" Alexa called as she entered the cleared area that marked the property compound, seeing the well-built cabin on its wooden platform standing proud of a smaller shed, and what looked to be a smaller hydroponics arch out back.

Bingo for the weed cultivation, Alexa thought. That explained why the Senator's black sheep of a nephew lived all the way out here, after all.

The cabin itself seemed to have two entrances. She could see a satellite dish and an aerial on the roof, but she couldn't hear any noise...but one of the windows was open, with a mosquito curtain half billowing out.

You would have to be really reckless to leave that open out here, Alexa thought. Either dumb or Theo was inside.

"Hello? Mr. Wilson!?" Alexa's hand strayed across the middle of her open jacket as she mounted the porch stairs to knock on the door. She didn't like surprises, and the constant hum and buzz of the insects around here was starting to get on her nerves. From somewhere out in the swamps there was the long, hooting call of some bird or otherwise prehistoric creature baying for blood.

"Mr. Wilson, I'm a government official, I'm coming in…" she called, choosing 'government' instead of 'federal' as that was still technically true, but also might not spook him as much as shouting *FBI* through the windows.

The outer wooden door wasn't even locked, leaving the insect door on the inside, which she grabbed the handle to and-

"Hey! Who the hell are you!?" There was a sudden movement from the side of the porch as a young man appeared in a hoody and grey shirt and pants. She recognized his whiskery features at once as the senator's disgraced nephew.

Theo was sweating, and his eyes flickered quickly. *He was nervous,* Alexa could see.

"Mr. Wilson, my name is Special Agent Alexa Landers, I'm with the FBI," she said with a nod of her head. "I just want to have a little chat with you about something…"

"FBI!?" Theo gulped, and she saw the paling look cross his face. He recovered quickly, however.

"Badge. I want to see a badge."

Alexa murmured that it would be no problem, as she smoothly took out her black passport-style ID badge and flipped it open for him to look at it carefully, wince a little, look back at her, and then nod.

"Okay. What's this about? Is it, uh…my uncle?" Theo said at once, as his eyes darted to the cabin door and back to Alexa.

Got something to hide, Theo? Alexa wondered, then realized yeah, of course he did. This whole place stank of marijuana.

"It's not about your uncle, Theo," Alexa used his first name. Always use the first names, it created familiarity, even when the suspect doesn't trust you.

THE **FLORIDA GIRL**

"I just want to ask you a few questions, that's all. It's about missing property, in fact… Shall we go inside?" Alexa suggested with a thin smile.

"You've come an awful long way for missing property." Theo looked nervously back up the road she had come, as if he were expecting an entire team to suddenly emerge from the green, shouting and yelling. Alexa knew that this wasn't his first tussle with the authorities.

"And I haven't got anything missing. Nothing lost, nothing stolen, so, uh, I don't know if this is just my uncle checking on me…"

"Does that a lot, does he?" Alexa asked lightly, not really sure where it would lead, but interested nonetheless. He was a *really* particular victim to pick if the killer had indeed stolen his boat…

Only Theo had just said it wasn't stolen at all, hadn't he?

Theo opened his mouth as if to agree, but then shook his head suddenly as a fresh wave of sweat broke out across his features. He looked ill with worry.

"Look lady, uh, Agent, I mean, I can't help you. And I've got work to do-" Theo started to say, fluttering ineffectually as if to shoo her away before he half turned to head back around the cabin.

"Mr. Wilson," Alexa put a note of steel in her voice that stopped him in his tracks. "It's about the boat. Your boat. The *Mary-Belle,* I believe it is called?"

Alexa saw Theo flinch. Just a little, but he flinched, and in that moment she knew precisely that Theo knew as well. He knew that his boat had been stolen. In some way, he was involved…

"What about it?" Theo said casually, still not turning entirely around as he fiddled with the zipper of his hoodie.

"Mr. Wilson, we have reason to believe-" Alexa began, when Theo suddenly flung himself around the corner of the cabin, vaulting the old wooden railing and onto the green to race desperately towards the back of the property.

"*Theo!* Damnit!" Alexa snarled, bursting into action herself as she launched herself after him, whirling around the corner to see him skidding across the gravel at the back of the cabin and plunging into the open plastic tunnel of his amateur growing set-up.

"Theo! Freeze!" Alexa shouted as she ran after him, feeling her muscles warm and lengthen as she forced more reach and speed into her run…

She was in better shape than he was. She crossed to the end of the porch at the back of the cabin, leapt onto the patch of gravel and in through the open archway into the plastic tunnel, to be immediately surrounded by tall green plants on either side, exuding a heavy scent. Theo was already at the end of the tunnel to where there was another open archway leading out onto a wooden-planked walkway outside…

The boat? Alexa thought as one hand reached for her gun as she tore down the central line between the plants.

"*Ekh!*" Theo grunted as he half-tripped over a stack of plant pots at the back of the greenhouse, slipped into the side of the arch and righted himself…

As Alexa closed the distance, grabbing onto the back of his clothes and bringing him slamming to the floor, falling out of the plastic grow tunnel and onto the rotted boards beyond with a heavy thump.

"Agh! Get off me, lady! I didn't do anything!" Theo was clearly not a very competent criminal. He struggled as if he were in a frat house brawl, and Alexa levelled her forearm across his back and thumped him down onto the wooden boards to hear them creak.

Okay, so maybe that wasn't a particularly friendly move of hers, but it got the point across.

"Stop struggling, Theo. Or if you want I can cuff you. How about that?" Alexa growled at him.

Theo was scared, terrified in fact.

"Look, I didn't do anything, honest to God, I didn't do *anything!*" he blubbered, as Alexa checked him for concealed weapons, nothing but a lighter and a pouch of loose, hand-rolling tobacco, and a wallet with his ID in it.

"Then why run?" Alexa said, finally standing up and letting him turn over. In front of them was a wooden boardwalk that crossed over murky, swampy ground that was crowded with more tall, reaching greenery, making a turn a little way out and plunging into the green.

"Where's the boat, Theo? Is it this way?" Alexa said with a snap, turning to look up and down the boardwalk but could see no sign of it.

"I – I thought you were coming for my weed, that's why I ran," Theo said quickly, in what Alexa thought was a quickly considered cover story.

"Of course. But I think you know that I'm not here for your weed. The *Mary-Belle*. Are you telling me you have it? Is it docked right here?" Alexa said, watching him intently.

Theo's head half turned, back towards the grow tunnel, the cabin beyond. Was he still thinking of running? Surely a senator's son would know that was pretty impossible.

He was nervous. Very nervous.

"It's up there. Moored and safe. I don't know what you're talking about…"

"You're saying that with certainty," Alexa pointed out. "I haven't even told you *why* I want the boat…"

Again, there was another nervous look around him, and Alexa wondered if now was the time to put him in handcuffs. He knew more than he was letting on, so it was clearly the time for official questioning.

"Okay, let's do this," Alexa said with a heavy sigh, putting her gun back in its holster as she hunkered down across from him to look him dead in the eye.

"Listen up. We have reason to believe that your boat was used in the murder of one Aleksandr Bodrov, of Star Island, Miami. Do you have anything to say about that, Theo Wilson – and I would choose your next words very carefully because it will mean all the difference as to what I say next…"

Theo opened and closed his mouth, looked down at his hands, then up at her. It was a pleading, desperate look – but he said nothing.

"Theo, if you are in trouble of any kind, now is the time to tell me. I can help. The Bureau can help," Alexa said in a lower voice.

Theo looked about to say something, and then, "The boat is that way. I never use it at all, and I'm only here half the time. If it was used for anything, like, stolen, then I wouldn't even know about it..."

So he was going to try and hard-ball? Alexa thought. *Deny everything?* Maybe the kid had learned something from his uncle about how to deal with the law.

"Okay, Mr. Wilson," Alexa said and straightened back up. "Looks like you're going to have to come with me. I won't be cuffing you because I am a friendly kind of a person, but you are *not* free to go, and you *will* be coming back with me to Miami. And please do not forget that you are in the custody of an agent of the Federal Bureau of Investigations," she instructed, gesturing to the wooden boards and letting her jacket swing open as she stood, so that Theo had a good look at the butt of her pistol.

"Show me," she said, for Theo to get up slowly, once again flashing that nervous look back to his plants before he trudged very slowly past her along the boards.

Alexa kept pace with him, one hand at her side, and the other on the butt of her gun. Theo was young, late twenties maybe, and he was clearly erratic. He might get a stupid idea in his head, but Alexa rather thought that he wouldn't.

Maybe the killer forced him to give up the boat. Gave him a whack load of money. Alexa was mentally noting all this as they made the turn to see that the boards meandered from slightly solid patch of ground to the next slightly solid patch of ground, past stakes driven into the dirt on either side, and dense, overcrowding vines and greenery.

It was only a short walk, but then the greenery opened up on either side to reveal a wider water course, edges with reeds and more densely packed trees, with a narrow patch of sky above. The wind was starting to pick up, and the sky was starting to cloud over, but there by the side of the wooden boardings was moored a short and squat pink yacht, its sides looking like they needed a fresh lick of paint, with a small pilot's cab in the center and the fading words *The Mary-Belle* written across its side.

"I have no idea if it's been there, I haven't used it since last year-" Theo began before a sharp glance from Alexa told him that it was better for him not to bother.

"You keep a key?" she said.

Theo blinked and shook his head. "Not on me. It's usually on the driving desk, behind the wheel. Anyone could have access to it…"

"Save it, Mr. Wilson," Alexa said grimly, nodding for him to move forward to the boat as she took out her gun. There was hardly any place for anyone to hide, but if she discovered a high-powered military rifle just sitting there, then she would have to move things up a notch. Like secure Theo and call for back up.

"On the boat please, Mr. Wilson, and don't touch anything. I need to take that key. Does the boat come equipped with a GPS?" Alexa said as Theo slowly got over the side, with Alexa waiting a moment before following him. The younger man stood in the middle of the deck and looked fairly awkward about him, as if the boat were as dangerous as the alligators that called this place their home.

"The boathouse," Theo whispered as Alexa scanned the deck to see nothing out of the ordinary as far as she could tell. Then again, she wasn't really much of a sailor, either.

Alexa nodded, motioning for Theo to wait to one side as she moved to the side of the small central pilot's cabin, quickly sliding out across the open doorway to see that it was empty before glancing at Theo. He hadn't even dared to move. Instead, he just stood, looking hopeless in the center of the boat, as if everything else was just a matter of time.

Which I guess it might be, now, Alexa considered. Theo Wilson didn't look the radical sort. Or someone to be wound up in professional drug or criminal gangs, either – and certainly nothing to do with military microprocessors. He would crack under questioning, she was sure of it.

"The GPS?" she said, Theo looking warily back the way they had come, and then trudging towards her, flicking a long-fingered hand under the wheel to where there was a black unit with a small screen and a few input buttons on the outer side.

"It's only local. It just tells you where you are," Theo said as he hunkered down to start unbolting it from its housing.

But I bet it keeps a record of where it's been, too, she mused.

"Stop. I got it from here. You go stand over there, and please don't think about doing anything silly," Alexa growled as she bent down to retrieve the unit that was barely bigger than her smartphone but a lot heavier and bulkier. Coil wires moved from its back to the boat itself, which Alexa guessed would attach to an antenna somewhere. She didn't know if she needed that, too, and wished that she'd taken some more engineering classes when she had been in the Academy.

She didn't seriously believe that Theo would try anything. She was a Bureau agent, and her movements were always tracked – or her car was, anyway. If he wanted to stick to his line of not even knowing where the boat was, then he'd have to act cool and pretend like this was no big deal.

Theo's feet shuffled a little on the deck revealing that he was nervous. Trembling nervous.

Alexa's eyes flicked up to him to find that they were locked in horror out of the window past her, over her shoulder.

As if he were staring at something. Or someone.

Oh crap.

CHAPTER THIRTY-FOUR

12:02 PM.

O H CRAP.
Alexa dropped her knee and turned; a move built almost purely out of instinct, nothing else. In that same moment she heard the large crack of splintering glass as the front pilot's window suddenly blew out.

Gunshot. Someone was shooting at her.

"Down!" Alexa shouted at Theo, seeing that he already had the idea in mind, scampering out of the small boat house to the far side as he put the more solid walls between them.

Damnit! "FBI!" Alexa shouted, as another bullet pinged off the metal frame of the door and she dove to the far window, stuffing the GPS in her pocket before popping up.

She saw the figure on the boardwalk right by the boat, hunched forward with two hands holding a heavy pistol, not his trademark sniper's rifle. Baseball cap over blonde hair. Stubble. Mr. I Spit Bullets; and he was already flicking his wrist towards her in a practised, professional move.

Alexa didn't even have time to get off a shot as she threw herself back down, lying on the floor this time as first one bullet went right through the glass, and then the next went through the wooden panelling of the boathouse itself, not eight inches above her head.

He has the upper hand. This flimsy piece of driftwood is no cover at all.

"FBI! Drop your weapon!" Alexa shouted again as she rolled to the far side of the small shack, seeing Theo's cowering form trembling on the far side. He was placing a whole lot more faith in one-inch wood than she was.

Crap. I need to get him out of here. In one piece.

"I know who you are, Agent," the man crowed as she heard his heavy boots step onto the boat, and he fired another steady one, two, three through the wooden panels of the cabin where Alexa had shouted from.

Alexa was pushing Theo in a crouch ahead of her around the far side of the boat shack. She could take him out, but now wasn't the time. She had to get Theo to the car, and then out of here.

"Come out, come out. This will only get messy and horrible…" the man sing-songed as he fired another two shots through the driver's shack, and this time Alexa heard him slide around the side suddenly as he must have attempted to surprise her in there.

"Go!" Alexa hissed, pushing Theo ahead of her towards the end of the boat house, and the railing beyond as she stood up, turned around to bring her gun to bear-

BANG!

The killer was right there. He had crossed the distance back through the boat house faster than she had thought possible. He

was pulling his pistol back after one shot, and Alexa knew where that bullet was going at the same time that she heard a grunt of pain.

"ARGH!"

With a snarl, Alexa crossed the distance with her pistol levelling at him.

As the man turned, almost spinning in place as he darted not out of the way but *towards* her, slapping her arm down with his pistol hand with such force that her hand slammed against the side of the boat wall, and she dropped her gun.

"Theo!" Alexa called, but she had no time to check as the man thumped her in the jaw with his elbow, sending her reeling backwards and slipping over to crash onto the deck.

"This has taken too long already," the killer growled as he advanced on Alexa, keeping his gun on her as he picked up her own, casually tossing it into the waters beyond.

"Get to the car, Theo!" Alexa shouted, as the killer made his mistake. His big mistake. Instead of shooting her, he chose to inflict more damage, kicking her in the stomach, *hard*.

"*Ugh!*" Alexa felt pain explode across her belly as she turned and retched, but then turned back to flail her legs back at the killer, managing to strike him in the knee and drive him to the floor.

I can do this. I can take him…

Alexa threw herself on top of the man, her hands reaching for the man's wrists to try and get the pistol.

The killer didn't say a thing. He didn't swear at her. He grunted as he struggled, bunching his shoulders as Alexa tried to wrangle the pistol from his grasp.

"I won't let you get away, you piece of crap," Alexa hissed, feeling the man kick her in the side but tuning out the pain. All she needed was the gun. Only the gun.

"YAAARGH!" But suddenly, in a move that was worthy of a pro-wrestler, the killer threw himself into a backwards crouch as he slammed Alexa against the side railing of the boat.

Alexa lost her grip on the man's wrists. She felt one leg sliding, her torso overbalancing…

And suddenly she was falling over the edge of the boat, hitting the murky swamp water with a splash as she fell into the deep channel.

Crap! No!

Alexa floundered for a moment, turning in the water as she opened her eyes to see the slightly lighter curve of the *Mary-Belle* right beside her, and the green-grey murk of the waters everywhere else. There was a faint, muffled thump and a sudden whipping line of white bubbles lanced through the waters behind her. And then another.

The killer was shooting at her!

Alexa kicked, trying her best to ignore her need to claw for breath as she grabbed the bottom of the boat and pulled herself underneath it, not even seeing the bottom it was so deep and dark.

And gators. Don't forget the gators.

But Alexa needed to breath more importantly. And she needed to get to Theo. She had lost her gun, but she could still feel the weight of the GPS unit in her jacket pocket.

Whip!

Another silvering line shot through the water behind her as Alexa pulled herself along the hull and up the far side, at first not even noticing where she was. It was dark up there, too dark…

The boards. It was the planks of the boardwalk that she had come up under, and she heard the heavy thump of the killer on the boat just a few yards away.

No!

He was casting around for her, probably scanning the near shore and the overgrown mangrove swamps.

I have to get to Theo, Alexa deduced, pulling herself along the bottom of the boards until she felt her knees scrape against rock and sludge. She kept on going, following the line of the water and not the wooden boards until she couldn't go any further to see that she had moved upriver of the boardwalk. The ground was more solid here, with heavy mangrove-type trees everywhere as she grabbed the branches and pulled herself up.

Which way was the cabin? Alexa thought for a dizzying, terrifying moment. Had she gotten lost? Turned around in the water and the darkening, storm-laden skies?

Whip! Another high-frequency sound as something shot through the undergrowth just a little ways away from her thigh. In a moment of sheer adrenaline, it felt to Alexa as if time itself had slowed down. She was looking at the tattered remains of a waxy leaf as it fluttered back down, heard the splinter of wood as the bullet took it apart...

Bullet. Gun. Shooter!

The killer had seen her and was leaping onto the boardwalk some fifteen-twenty yards away to get a clearer shot.

Damnit!

Alexa couldn't go back towards the cabin. She threw herself through the undergrowth instead, hearing the whip of bullets swim past her shoulder as she grabbed the nearest tree and used it as a swing to turn her direction, fleeing on marshy and reedy ground as the killer attempted to take her out...

Run. Just run, Alexa, run!

But the Florida swamps are dense, deep and dark, and by the time that Alexa had taken seven lunging steps she was already surrounded by a blanket of green, as the bullets kept on flying in her direction.

Keep running, loop back to the car... Alexa told herself as she zigzagged, knowing that the killer could probably hear her, and knowing that he could very well be coming after her.

BANG! BANG!

Another bullet, wider this time, shot through the branches to her left, and Alexa rolled, feeling something sharp and tiny spike into her arms as she slithered to one side, and then tried to orientate herself.

She turned in a crouch, looking back the way she had thought she had come to see nothing but a green wall of vegetation.

Just as the first drops of the storm hit.

CHAPTER THIRTY-FIVE

3:44 PM.

HOW COULD I HAVE GOTTEN SO DAMNED TURNED AROUND!? Alexa asked herself for what must have been the twenty-seventh time.

Unfortunately, the answer was all too clear. Everywhere she turned, there were mangroves and vines and spindly things which had no name whatsoever but awfully sharp leaves. At least, that was how Alexa felt, anyway.

There were strange noises in the canopy, and in the water underfoot. There were things that slithered, things that sang, things that whistled, and things that croaked and clicked.

THE FLORIDA GIRL

Alexa was pretty sure that at least half of the things around her were trying to kill her, and that wasn't even counting the killer. Mr. Blonde. Mr. I Spit Bullets Combat-Controller.

I got so close! Alexa cursed herself for being such a fool as to come here without backup. The answer was clear: Theo had been terrified, and the killer had been using him.

"And we did track you down, you son of a-" Alexa murmured to herself as she once again tried to peer through the green around her. She cursed herself for running away, but knew that it had been the only sensible play.

If I still had my gun, then things would've been very different indeed, she promised herself.

But, even despite her predicament, there was a wild, crazed exultation running through her. She knew that the tables had turned. They were onto him, and by now Chief Williams might even be sending a force to work out what had happened to her, his Academy-star special agent.

(Alexa couldn't call him, of course, because she had worked out pretty early on that her phone must have slipped her jeans pocket when she had been in the river. That was a problem.)

Yeah, you're on the run, Alexa realized grimly. They had the boat, the means of attack, they had at least three people who could positively ID him, and – she still had the GPS, which hadn't fallen in the river. That would place the boat at the scene.

Alexa didn't have much hope that Theo was still alive, as the ghostly words of the killer came back from the alleyway, just two days ago.

'*Too many people have seen my face already...* '

He was a man who didn't like loose ends. That was why he had gone after Leela and Trixi, after all.

But why kill the Bodrov sons!? Who had hired him in the first place? There were still so many maddening questions, but Alexa was fairly sure that she could get those answers out of Theo. If, that was, if...

"ssss-"

There was a noise through the undergrowth that wasn't entirely like a hiss, more like a guttural purr and Alexa froze as something nosed it's way through the low-hanging mangrove leaves towards her, and stopped.

It was the long, dark brown snout of an alligator, and it looked *big*. The snout (jaws) alone must have been the length of Alexa's forearm.

"Oh crap, oh crap, oh-" Alexa tried to remember any advice she might have ever been given about alligators.

Nothing. Apart from her brother jokingly telling her to 'stay away from them.'

Well, I've already blown that one, haven't I?

She started to hold her hands up in front of her…

"ssss…"

That rattling sound came again, and Alexa immediately froze. The hands-up method had been a dumb move. The placating sort of move you might do to a person or other mammal to show that you were unarmed. A reptile with a brain that was plumbed back into however-many-x-million years of evolution didn't care about peaceful gestures.

Alexa took a step backward, and the hissing sound continued at a steady rate for a moment, and then appeared to lower. She hoped that maybe the monster had already eaten something. It was raining pretty hard now, and maybe it didn't fancy a snack in the wet…

It's an alligator, dummy. It lives in the wet.

She took another step away, and then, as soon as the impasse was broken, Alexa took another step, and another, her calves banging into branches on the way back before she treaded awkwardly over them.

The creatures hissing had stopped, but it's beady eyes were still entirely focussed on her movements.

"Good boy. Or girl. I'll just give you indigestion…" Alexa whispered in horror as she kept on walking, for the greenery to slowly close in between them, and she turned and upped her pace. She really hoped that she was going in the right direction, as the rain started to come in harder and-

THE FLORIDA GIRL

A sound, out in the swamps, and for a moment Alexa was sure it was another deep-throated chug of the monster alligator behind her, until her ears corrected themselves.

No, that was a car. There was a car passing her, and not very far away. The agent hunkered down instinctively and saw a pale beam of light cut through the heavy rain and disappear a little way to her right.

"Have I made it to the road?" She thanked her lucky stars as she turned and started climbing through the undergrowth in the direction the car had gone – for her nose to pick up the sudden waft of something familiar.

The unmistakeable scent of marijuana.

Theo's. Humbolt Cole!

Another few climbing, scratching yards proved her suspicions as she was suddenly confronted with the view of the cleared-out parcel of land, the shed, the polytunnel and Theo's cabin, now looking almost homely with its lights gleaming through the windows.

There were two cars parked here now, Alexa saw. Her SUV would still, hopefully, be back at the fork, but now there was a regular blue small economy car, next to a larger, dark metallic blue chunky Chevrolet with tinted windows.

Alexa heard muffled shouts, raised voices from the cabin.

Check on Theo. Get him out if I can... Alexa concluded, wishing that the other cars might belong to the FBI but somehow doubted it. Something here felt wrong. All too wrong indeed.

She crossed to the back of the shack, and then, with her heart in her throat, ran the empty green lot to the side of the porch, sliding down beside a large black plastic water container.

"*-they'll find him and that will be the end of it. They have their man, the boat, and a dead FBI agent.*"

What? Alexa thought for a moment before she realized that they meant her, of course. It was the killer's voice. He was talking about *her.*

And Theo. Theo was already dead, hopefully that shot at the boat had taken him out, Alexa figured grimly.

A moment of silence before a voice returned. "*Still, this is too close. He's my nephew, goddammit! How can you just stand there and-*"

"*Oh, cut the crap and hand over the money, Senator. You set this up. You gave me Theo's boat for the op. You always knew this shitbird of a relative was going to take the heat if it came to it; and now it has-*"

"*Mike, honestly. You have left a trail of bodies behind you-*"

"*WHAT DID I TELL YOU!? DON'T EVER USE MY GODDAMN NAME!*" There was the sudden, unmistakeable sound of a slap ringing through the night.

Alexa listened in hushed tones and desperately wished that she had her gun, at least. And her phone. She could record what was going on, she could…

The next words from above her head chilled her to the bone. It was the killer speaking again.

"*Hand over the money, Gunderson! You owe me. The FBI were on this from day one. I should think that earns me quite a bonus, don't you think? Or do I have to add another body to the one already lying here?*"

"*You – you wouldn't dare!*" the senator replied.

"*You'll get your nice little contract. Your kickback from Vanguard, I'm sure will be very healthy. Enough to fund next year's ticket, am I right? Or have you got bigger things in mind? A run for the Whitehouse, perhaps?*"

Kickbacks? Contracts? Alexa struggled to understand for a moment, as the cold and driving wet was slowing her down.

But then she saw it. Gunderson and the killer (Mike) had just as much confessed to everything already, hadn't they? Senator Gunderson was somehow connected to Vanguard Systems, the rival American company that really didn't like the fact that a Russian (*Soviet*) oligarch was about to muscle in on their multi-billion-dollar microprocessor deal.

And who else had the necessary contacts in the ex-military space to hire a Combat Controller like this Mike?

Alexa felt sick. This hadn't been about personal vendettas or rival gangs. This had always been about money. Dirty, corrupting money.

"You'll get half. I have to clean up this mess after you've gone..." Gunderson explained, then suddenly stopped as something changed in the room.

"You will give me all of the money, Senator. Or I will take matters into my own hands."

"Now you are being ridiculous! Put that thing away. You can't get away with killing a sitting US senator."

"I've got away with worse," the killer said quietly, and then quieter, as if to himself, "too many people know my face as it is. You. The dancer. The FBI man in University Hospital. My job relies on my anonymity, Senator."

"What are you going on about? Here is your half, and that is all-" BANG!

The gun, when it fired, was muted through the building and the storm that was building outside, but it was still loud enough to make Alexa jump.

"No!" she breathed, racing from around the water to the side of the porch, pulling herself up and scanning for a weapon, anything she could use. Nothing. She ran to the back door as there was another double clang of the front doors, and Alexa was suddenly inside a small kitchen. She grabbed a steak knife from the wall side and raced into the main living area just in time to hear the roar of one of the cars outside, and the killer, Mike, was gone.

He'd left two bodies behind him. One was Theo, who lay sprawled on the floor with just a singular bullet wound in his lower back.

The second was a much older gentleman with only a passing resemblance to his nephew. Senator Gunderson had to be in his early sixties, with receding silvered hair, and dressed in a dark grey business suit, ruined by the spreading blood over his heart.

Alexa swore, racing to grab a pillow from the small couches to stem the wound, but it was already too late. Gunderson was gone.

Alexa checked the senator's pockets and thanked several deities that the senator had his emergency satellite buzzer issued to all higher officials. She pressed it and held it down, hoping that it was in range out here, or that Gunderson hadn't found a way to disable it.

He hadn't. A few minutes later, Gunderson's phone rang.

"*Senator? This is Miami-Dade County Security Office-*" started an official voice at the other end.

"FBI. Contact the FBI Field HQ, Miami, immediately!" Alexa almost shouted down the line. "Senator Gunderson has been shot at Humbolt Cole, Southwestern Everglades."

"*You've failed voice recognition software. Who is this!?*"

"Special Agent Alexa Landers of the Federal Bureau of Investigations. And if you don't get Field Chief Williams of the FBI office on right now, then there might be another murder yet tonight. I believe the killer is en route to the University of Miami Hospital to kill a fellow agent and witness!"

CHAPTER THIRTY-SIX

7:45 PM. UNIVERSITY OF MIAMI HOSPITAL

THE UNIVERSITY HOSPITAL WAS BRIEFED, OF COURSE, which lent a tense friction to an atmosphere that was already loaded with antiseptic worry and emergency bells.

Special Agent Alexa Landers could feel it in her still aching muscles, in her teeth as she checked Kage's room once again to see that everything was still, his covers pulled up, and the lights turned low.

Fine. Everything is fine, Alexa thought to herself, even though she knew that it wasn't. How could it be? There was a killer on the loose.

"Agent?" a voice murmured from the doorway, as Alexa turned to see Field Chief Williams himself standing outside in the small hallway. His dark business suit was gone, and instead he wore a bulletproof vest with a mic in his ear, and a heavy service Glock at his waist.

It was at least a little pleasing to know that he mucked in. Alexa had found some more respect for the man. Not that she hadn't had any before, but in his words earlier at her debrief:

'It's all hands on deck. Everyone at the field office is pretty eager to catch one who hurt one of our own…'

Unsurprisingly, Kage was well-liked at the Field HQ, and Alexa hadn't been surprised when many of her fellow colleagues had signed up to take bodyguard shifts at the hospital protecting him.

"All clear?" Alexa asked, and saw Williams' sharp, singular nod before he cast a wary look around the hallway. The nurses were attempting not to hover, but they were scared. Alexa kept on seeing them appear from their station briefly, looking around furtively before rushing to their next task.

It was the doctor who had been the most trouble, actually.

'This is a place of healing! We cannot have armed officers patrolling the corridors!'

Alexa kinda admired the doctor for that, actually. He had his principles. It didn't matter, however, not when it was explained that a very highly trained, highly skilled, and murderous assassin was probably intent on coming here to murder the last witnesses to his crime.

Not that it would do them much good, Alexa considered. The Bureau was here. And Alexa had a plan.

"You sure that you are up for this?" the field chief looked at her sceptically. She still had the cuts and bruises on her face from her ordeal in the Southern Everglades from earlier, and in truth her body still ached. She'd been advised by the very same doctor to rest up and given anti-inflammatories, but Alexa had refused them. She didn't want anything that might fug her senses, even minutely.

I fought that guy a couple times now, I know how fast he is.

Nevertheless, Alexa was washed and wearing clean, smart civilian clothes with a replacement gun hidden under her shoulder. The debrief had been as quick as possible, but it had been awkward. A dead senator kind of made things...awkward.

"I'm sure, sir," Alexa said before casting a quick look back at Kage. "He went into the 34-27 house without a question, sir, and he tried his best to save the civilians on Miami Beach. I owe him," she said a little gruffly, but it was more than that of course.

He's my partner, she thought, feeling a wave of fierce protectiveness.

So this was what it felt like to be a part of a team. A family.

The field chief nodded gravely, and for once he didn't look annoyed.

"I've been hearing back from Dee and our research team; and apart from Dee complaining that she hasn't slept in a week-"

Join the club, Alexa thought a little wryly. If anything, Kage was the only one who was getting any sleep at the moment...

"-she has nonetheless managed to track down something interesting. Our Senator Gunderson, as you know, is one – scratch that – *was* one of our two sitting senators, both from the same party. He was also a board member of Vanguard Systems back in the '80s before his political career really kicked off."

"Bingo," Alexa countered.

"That's right..." Williams continued heavily, as they walked to the small lounge and the coffee machine that served up shady water. There was no one else in here, as the entire private health wing had been cleared as much as it could for tonight's protection detail.

"As you know, there are some pretty extensive anti-corruption laws stopping a political representative from gaining finance from private companies, but there are PACS."

"PACS?" Alexa had heard the term on the news, but never had the enthusiasm to work it out.

"Political Action Committees. lobbying groups, to put it bluntly. Anyone can form one, from a charity to group of citizens... and private companies."

"Ah," Alexa nodded that she understood. They were ways that politicians got funded, weren't they? Someone had to pay for their massive tours of the state or country. Someone had to pay for all those balloons and brunches.

"Exactly. Vanguard Systems was a fairly prominent member of the Floridian Defence Workers PAC. They contributed some $85k to Senator Gunderson's last committee campaign for office, with $60k of that coming from Vanguard itself."

"Sheesh..." Alexa whistled.

"And that, Dee assured me, might not be all. PACS are attractors. The Floridian Defence Workers PAC play a part in the ecosystem of general defence contributions, forming a 'Super-PAC' cross-State," Williams continued, frowning.

"You mean that whoever is tied with Gunderson is likely to get into power elsewhere?" Alexa asked.

"And more. Those officials could – and this is just wild conjecture, mind you, and certainly not something that I would ever testify or comment on, and neither should you, Agent Landers-"

"Understood, sir."

"-But there might be questions about defence contract awards and facilities built," Williams expounded.

"Like the microprocessors," Alexa nodded, suddenly seeing it. The motive. Nearly a hundred-thousand-dollars' worth of motive, and a multi-billion revenue motive if Vanguard got the microprocessor contract!

Williams coughed loudly. "Be wary of conjecture at this point, Agent Landers. This is being forwarded to the Attorney General's office, where it will probably be bogged down in court for another year..."

Alexa hissed in frustration. Did that mean they wouldn't get a conviction?

But then again, who was there to convict now? Senator Gunderson was dead. Theo was dead. Only the killer remained.

Williams gave a sympathetic groan. "Vanguard might get off. But the important thing is that we catch the killer. We're still chasing down his identity with the US Defence Department, who like to play hardball."

"They won't when we have him in custody," Alexa nodded firmly, aware there was still a question of that hanging in the air. They had to catch him first, after all.

"Indeed. So, I guess then…" Williams scanned the lobby once more; it had emptied of nurses and everyone else, leaving just the two of them next to the shady water machine.

"Yes," Alexa nodded. It was time. There was nothing else to do but start the operation.

Without saying another word, Williams and Alexa both walked to the edge of the lobby where the double doors led out to the rest of the hospital. Alexa was certain to see him to the doors and salute him at the door before opening it and shaking his hand.

"You sure this is entirely necessary? You know he's probably long gone by now!" the field chief said loudly, holding the door open. Alexa thought that was gilding the lily a little, but who knew? The hospital didn't have sound on its cameras, but that didn't mean that the killer, Mike I-Spit-Bullets, didn't have a way to eavesdrop.

"I just want to be sure, just for tonight, sir. Go on, one more night's detail is all I ask," Alexa said with a stiff nod. She saw a few nurses from the larger hallway look up at them nervously, once again staying close so they could overhear what the large guy in the bulletproof vest with FBI written across it was doing here.

"Fine. It's your overtime, I guess," Williams sounded gruffly annoyed, before turning smartly and walking away, signalling to the waiting FBI officer to accompany him.

"Come on, Jenkins! I'm not paying your overtime as well!" he said in a very characteristic grunt, as the two lawmen walked out of the outer room and through the doors, and just like that, they were gone.

Leaving Alexa all alone with the open door, suddenly feeling very exposed indeed.

(*A sniper's rifle could impact clear through the opposite glass windows and these doors*, the rather unhelpful image flared in Alexa's mind).

She closed the door quickly behind her, returning to the quiet convalescence ward and to the small waiting lobby where she could see Kage's door.

"Okay, Alexa, this is all on you, now," she murmured, and settled in for a long night.

She knew the killer would come to take out Kage and her. And when he did, she would be ready.

CHAPTER THIRTY-SEVEN

11:53 PM.

"**M**A'AM?" THE CONCERNED VOICE OF ONE OF THE nurses broke Alexa's musings as she suddenly looked up, startled from her seat in the waiting room lobby.

Crap! Had I been asleep!?

No, she hadn't, but she could feel her eyes getting heavy nonetheless, and her brain was starting to fog over with that heavy, cosseting blanket as her body was trying it's best to tell her that everything was fine, nothing was going to happen tonight.

"Hm?" Alexa looked up at the female nurse before her, who had a clipboard in one hand plus a stack of white cardboard boxes.

Alexa knew that she was the last staffer on duty up here, as all general patients in the restricted convalescence ward had been moved elsewhere in the hospital.

"There's been a call down in the emergency room. They need extra bodies, and I'm here doing nothing, so…"

"Go," Alexa nodded, checking the time. It was getting late, but it was still too early for the killer, Alexa was certain. Mike I Spit Bullets would strike at some ungodly hour in the middle of the night. Two, maybe three or four o'clock. The time when your reflexes are slow, especially if you've been working the case almost non-stop for the last week.

"There's no telling how long, but I should be back in the hour, maybe," the nurse said, giving her one abrupt nod and then turning, she hurried towards the secure stairs at the back of the ward. There were only two ways into this restricted ward, and that was through the lobby doors out to the hallway beyond (where there were elevators to the rest of the facility) and the other was the service stairs. It was a ward usually used for clients or patients who needed low-access needs, or where they could monitor their movements.

"I'll lock the outer door on my way out! You got everything in here you need anyway!" the nurse called out as she got to the stair doors, flashing her ID card and disappearing through for Alexa to hear the mechanical clunk as the door auto-locked behind her.

Fine. Okay, wake-up, kiddo! Alexa shook her head, yawning as she got up, glancing at the camera over the hallway. It still had a green light on. It was still working, which was good, before moving to the double doors that fed into the main hallway area outside, and slipping the bolts that she saw there, too.

Locked in. No way in or out. If the killer wanted to make a move, then he'd have to make an awful goddamn racket to do it!

Still feeling a little woozy, and more than a little stiff, Alexa moved to the small bathroom, propping the door open with a bin as she turned to splash her face with water from the sink.

"Come on, wake up, Alexa," she groaned, wondering what had happened to that twenty-something-year-old who could cram for tests till three and then still be up at five-thirty in the morning for the three-mile training run.

But all this was nothing like the Academy, was it? She paused for a moment, looking at herself in the chipped bathroom mirror. Everything was too bright, and there was the heavy glare of lights overhead. Very bright, Alexa blinked, shielding her eyes a little as another yawn escaped her lips.

She looked at herself in the mirror. She was pale as a ghost, wondering when she'd last eaten something…

The lights overhead were *very* bright, she thought, as her eyelids drooped a little more, and her hand slipped on the sink.

"Come on, Landers!" Alexa shook her head to clear the fog as her eyelids threatened to drop once again. At this rate she'd need a second splash of water…

Wait.

Alexa paused. Her breathing was a little heavy. Her body felt sluggish. Very sluggish. In fact, she felt a little light-headed, too, almost like she was coming down with something…

Or had been drugged.

"No!" Alexa half turned, feeling how her body reacted much slower than it should, than she needed it to. But she hadn't had anything at all. Nothing apart from…

The shady not-coffee water from the machine! Alexa turned, feeling her limbs swimming just a little as the lights overhead were altogether too bright. If she was going to call it, she would say that someone had dosed the coffee with Valium, or some sedative or another.

And who would do that? She wondered sarcastically. Someone with plenty of skill, and certainly enough opportunity as the entire hospital was swimming in drugs.

Yeah, he drugged the coffee machine when he got into town. Probably posing as a janitor or something, Alexa thought with a shudder as she emerged from the bathroom to throw a glance upward. The light on the camera was out, and yet the hall lights were still working. Someone had cut the camera's power.

Alexa, you damn idiot! She almost howled with rage at her own stupidity.

Killer Mike had been right here, and probably aborted his mission when he saw the place was crawling with FBI and police. He loaded the coffee machine up and waited for a quiet moment. In her slightly woozy thoughts, Alexa was fairly sure that he'd probably set-up the emergency call downstairs, too.

But the doors were locked… The thought raced through her mind before she shook it away, cursing her slow thinking. For a guy who had walked into the secure penthouse suite of Miami Heights, then stealing an access ID card would be child's play.

Still, she paused at the hallway and took out her gun, looking to the stairs door (still closed) and then to the main doors (still locked).

"Okay then, you heel, let's see what you got," Alexa hissed to herself as she moved as quietly as she could to the stairs door and gave it a gentle push. Still locked. Then, she moved back down the hallway to the outer doors to see that they, too, were still bolted. From the inside.

Fine. Secure. What's your play? She moved slowly back to the front of Kage's door, holding her gun up as she scanned first one way down the hallway and then the other. There were only two ways in, and the killer had to use one of them, didn't he?

Alexa breathed as her thoughts fogged, and her mind felt wrapped in the soft cotton of sedation. She shook her head once more, trying to focus as her hand moved to the earbud to tap it two times.

"Agent Landers?" It was Williams' voice from where he was still sitting along with a fast-response team a few streets away.

"I got cameras out on my level. This could be cat-and-mouse, seeing what we'll do…" Alexa whispered.

"Or it might be his play. I'm sending people in. Two at main doors, two at ambulance access… Over."

Alexa grimaced. She knew that it wouldn't be enough. The hospital was a big place. It had any number of entrances and exits.

"Plain clothes?" Alexa whispered.

"Of course! This isn't my first rodeo, you know! Over," Williams said before clicking off.

THE **FLORIDA GIRL**

It was then that Landers heard the unmistakeable gentle thud of noise from behind her. From inside Kage's hospital room.

CHAPTER THIRTY-EIGHT

12:26 PM.

No! Alexa burst into the room just in time to hear a small whispering sound; a deadly waspish sort of buzz as there was an explosion of feathers bedding from Kage's convalescence bed.

There was Mike, standing almost over Kage's bed, and behind him was a half-open window, completely taken out of its glass and levered into the room. God alone knew how the killer had done that, as the only clear route to there must have been scaling the building from the outside itself.

THE **FLORIDA GIRL**

Mike wore regular fatigues, with what looked like a climbing harness on over his thighs, belt, and shoulders. He was also holding a pistol in one hand with the very long barrel of a suppressor.

He had just shot Kage.

Or Kage's bed, anyway.

Surprise, crapbird! Alexa thought as she pulled the trigger, two shots, but Mike was already diving to one side. One bullet smashed the window behind, the other slammed into the brick wall – and suddenly the killer was right in front her, sliding the distance in the blink of an eye compared to Alexa's drugged responses.

Slam. A forearm smash across her chest, pushing her gun up as it fired again, and punching his own silenced pistol straight towards her unprotected belly.

But Alexa wasn't so intoxicated, not yet. Maybe the drugs didn't have the time to kick in. Maybe she hadn't had enough cups of coffee through the night. It was ditchwater anyway.

Alexa grabbed Mike's wrist with her free arm, and she still had the strength to push the pistol away so that it fired past her hip, a dangerous, buzzing sound.

But the Combat Controller was a killer, and his military training showed as he stamped forward, twisting his hip into Alexa's as he grabbed her under the shoulder and lifted her from her feet in a throw.

Maybe Mike, too, wasn't feeling as sharp as he should be, as he threw her over his shoulder with a roll and straight onto the massacred bed, not the floor. The bed that Kage wasn't in because he had been secretly transferred down the service stairs as soon as Alexa's emergency call had come in.

"*Agent Landers, respond! Over!*" It was Williams' voice in her ear that Alexa heard as she hit the bed and kicked out with her feet, managing to catch the arm holding the silenced gun and kicking it upwards and out of the way before slamming her feet into his chest, sending him skidding back towards the door-

Whap.

Alexa fired, one shot missing Mike's staggering form but the other catching him high in the chest and sending him flinging through the medical door and out into the lobby.

But he had been wearing a vest, hadn't he? Alexa struggled to remember as she pushed herself forwards into a sprawling stagger towards the still swinging door. Had her shot been enough to take him out? Even to a vest, it could have enough force to break his collarbone and put him on his ass at least…

Alexa shoved the closing door back open, just in time to see the killer's scrambling form reach the other end of the hallway, flicking his pistol back at her.

Shit! She ducked back inside as the bullet hit the glass of the window and she heard another shot, this time hitting metal as the killer must surely be shooting out the locked stairwell door.

He was running, Alexa could hear as she threw herself forwards again, through the door and stumbling across the lobby as she ran after him.

"All units. Convalescence access stairwell! He's on the move!" Alexa shouted with one hand to her ear.

He was running. They had him scared.

CHAPTER THIRTY-NINE

12:41 PM.

"A GENT LANDERS? WHAT'S YOUR POSITION!?" Williams' voice was terse in Alexa's ear as she ran through the busted stairwell door, pausing only to sweep her gun across the stairwell and down as she heard the sound of clattering feet.

Mike was below her, and he was leaping down the stairs like all the hounds of hell were after him.

Well, we are, in fact. Sniffing you out. Alexa did the same, leaping the first stairwell and moving to the edge of the bannister-

Just in time to see the man pointing his gun back up at her.

Alexa managed to stumble backwards as two shots seared the air past her head, and they were both running again, leaping the next stairwell, and the next until Alexa was only a flight behind him. She heard the bang of a set of double doors, and a distant scream…

"Two flights down! Don't know – Surgery?" Alexa snapped over her ear bud comms as she heard shouting, staggering the last set of stairs to crash through the door as the sound of sudden sirens and raised voices crashed into her ears.

The hallway was wide and overly bright, and it was also filled with running, screaming people. One white-suited doctor was on the floor, blood pooling from his chest as two blue-suited nurses were at his side, attempting to administer emergency first aid.

"Clear the halls! Where did he go!?" Alexa shouted, seeing people run in and out of rooms ahead of her.

"That way!" One of the nurses pointed down the hall, from where suddenly came more sounds of screaming. Alexa ran after him as people jumped from one side of the hallway to the other, to see a much larger waiting room at this end. People were already diving for their seats.

And there was the killer, Mike, standing in the middle of the room with a blue-suited nurse held tight to his side and his silencer pistol to his head.

"LET HER GO! DROP YOUR WEAPON!" Alexa shouted, wavering where she stood as she levelled her gun straight at him, and tried to aim the sight at his head.

But Mike was good, holding the woman as much across his body as his could, ducking behind her. He was gasping, and Alexa figured that her shot to his bulletproof vest had done more damage than she had figured.

"How about you drop yours, Agent? Or else the nice lady gets it?" Mike gasped back.

Alexa knew that he would do it. He would have absolutely no qualms about pulling the trigger at all, would he?

"You won't make it out of here, Mike," she used his name purposefully, and saw him grimace in shock and anger.

"You're blown. We know your name. We know you worked for Gunderson. We know you were a Combat Controller. Even if you do manage to get out of here, it's only a matter of time before we hunt you down..." Alexa said, hearing that her voice was heavy and a little woozy.

"Other people have made it work," Mike snapped back. "Even with a blown cover. And I've got the gun to the lady's head, so how about you give me safe passage, a private jet, and half a million dollars, too?" he sneered at her.

Alexa couldn't get a bead on the man's head. He was too well trained. He kept on moving, dragging the nurse with him towards the doors.

"That's not going to happen, Mike," Alexa said as calmly as she could. *How long till Williams gets here?*

"We got this place covered. It was a perfect trap. Right now I got people coming right here to take you out..." Alexa hissed as her vision doubled just a little. She didn't dare fire in her current state anyway.

"A private jet, I said! Or else she dies!" Mike barked, and this time he glanced back at the door behind him. Had he heard the sounds of approaching feet?

"That's not going to happen, Mike. But I can offer you this. You take me instead of her. Release the woman, you know FBI snipers will take shots at you even with a civilian hostage. But not with me, they won't," Alexa said, even moving her gun a little lower, as she staggered forward.

Mike was silent for just a moment.

"Drop your weapon," he spat, as Alexa took another stumbling step forward, as if ready to give herself up...

Alexa listed to one side a bit, shaking her head. "The drugs were a clever move, what was it, *Ambien*?" Alexa said in a thick, slurred voice. "It's me you want anyway, right? Me because I keep on whooping your ass?"

Mike was running out of options. The sounds of shouting voices approaching was getting louder.

"*Drop your weapon!*" Mike shouted as Alexa stumbled to one side, now only three yards away from him.

Alexa was drugged. She was an easy target. Mike whipped his gun arm forward, shoving the nurse out of the way to shoot her dead, as Alexa snapped her pistol up in a hip shot. She might have been drugged, but she hadn't been *that* drugged. Her shot took him at the shoulder, past the protective vest and spun him around with a cry of pain as he slammed into the floor. The nurse screamed as she jumped to one side, and Field Chief Williams slammed through the door.

And Alexa skidded to kick Mike's gun away, and held her own over the man.

"Even drugged up, I'm still a better shot that you," Alexa said to the man with a smirk, as the FBI team surged around them and secured the killer.

CHAPTER FORTY

DAY 7.

8:30 AM. UNIVERSITY OF MIAMI HOSPITAL

"Mike Hampton, ex US Special Air Operations, Combat Controller," Field Chief Williams said as he looked over to where Alexa was sitting with her head in her hands, massaging what was the beginnings of an epic headache.

She had managed to get a few hours of rest, but it hadn't been restful at all. Her body had been too full of warring mixtures of adrenaline and whatever Mike had dosed the coffee machine with for that.

Instead, Alexa had taken herself to the small lobby and waited, answering the doctor's questions when they were asked, and doing her best to fill out her report.

"I think you get the day off, Special Agent," Williams frowned as he looked at her. At some point in the night he had changed back into his business suit, and Alexa wondered if he kept a spare one with him at all times.

The University of Miami Hospital was still abuzz with nerves and shock, and the news teams had already arrived outside the building, sending in reporters to try and get what blood they could out of any willing witnesses. It was all over the morning news, and would be national by lunchtime, Alexa figured.

"That was his name, Mike Hampton. Served his country well, until he didn't," Williams said grimly.

"Until he really didn't," said a voice, as in walked Kage, with the help of a walking stick. "A nurse said I'd find you all holed up in here. Everyone still got the bits they were born with?" he threw at them cheerily, for Alexa to groan. But despite how her head felt, she was glad to see him. She shifted a seat over for him to sit down with a hiss of pain.

"Should you be up and walking, Special Agent Murphy?" Alexa said to him seriously.

"Should you, Special Agent Landers?" he returned with a wry smile.

There was a cough from Williams above them, drawing them back to the matter at hand.

"Anyway, it's with the lawyers now. I can't say if Hampton or Gunderson will get mentioned in the press, or admitted to, but I suppose you can say that it's over," he said, although he was clearly not happy about it.

"The sons?" Alexa grumbled. "Why kill the sons?"

Williams nodded, appreciative of the insightful question. "They would inherit the business. Even if their dad died, they would keep the contract that Vanguard so desperately didn't want them to get."

"The contract," Alexa said. "You know who got it in the end?"

A look clouded Williams' eyes for a moment. "Above my pay grade and yours, Special Agent," he said firmly, and Alexa knew that was that. Whatever was going to happen to those AI-assisted microprocessors, whatever game was going to be played now – she was out of it.

Which was a bit of a relief, actually.

"Trixi?" Alexa said.

Williams appeared to be on much more comfortable ground as he spoke louder.

"Witness protection still. She'll get victim compensation, some eight thousand dollars, probably, along with trauma and narcotics counselling."

"Good," Alexa said. That much would be enough to get her out of Perelli's clutches, for sure. Maybe she could start a-new somewhere else. Leave this Florida heat for a while.

"How about you, Special Agent Landers?" Kage asked her, still with that crooked smile on his face. "First job from the Academy, and you bagged a criminal gang, a Mexican druglord, and an international assassin. Not bad for a week's work, huh? You think you're going to stick it out down here?"

Alexa pulled a face. "I hate the heat," she said before glancing around at the movement of FBI agents busy going about their work, mostly quietly, and mostly unasked and un-thanked.

They were a family. A team. Kage hadn't hesitated to put his life on the line for her.

"But I guess I'll see how it goes," she said as she gave a small shrug. "Who knows? Maybe I'll work on my tan."

AUTHOR'S NOTE

First and foremost, thank you for choosing to embark on this thrilling journey with us in the pages of *The Florida Girl*!

I would also like to take a moment to express my deepest appreciation for my incredible co-author, James Holt. Together, we dove headfirst into the world of crime, conspiracies, and dangerous secrets that lie beneath the vibrant surface of Miami, Florida. James's invaluable contribution and collaboration have enriched this story beyond measure.

As you approach the conclusion of this book, I am filled with excitement to share that it represents the dawn of a captivating new series centered around Special Agent Alexa Landers and the captivating backdrop of Florida. Rest assured, the second installment is already well underway, with only the final act left to go. Soon, you will be able to satisfy your craving for more heart-pounding mysteries in Resort to Kill. Prepare yourself for another riveting chapter in Alexa Landers' thrilling adventures!

As independent writers, we rely on your support to continue writing and bringing you more exciting novels. So, if you enjoyed the book, please take a moment to leave a review and recommend it to others who love mystery thrillers. With your help, we can keep writing and delivering pulse-pounding and entertaining reading experiences like this one.

Once again, thank you for joining us on this wild ride through the treacherous swamps and sun-soaked streets of Florida. You are our motivation to keep going and to keep delivering the stories that you love.

By the way, if you find any typos, have suggestions, or just simply want to reach out to us, feel free to email us at egray@ellegraybooks.com

Your truly,
Elle Gray & James Holt

CONNECT WITH ELLE GRAY

Loved the book? Don't miss out on future reads! Join my newsletter and receive updates on my latest releases, insider content, and exclusive promos. Plus, as a thank you for joining, you'll get a FREE copy of my book Deadly Pursuit!

Deadly Pursuit follows the story of Paxton Arrington, a police officer in Seattle who uncovers corruption within his own precinct. With his career and reputation on the line, he enlists the help of his FBI friend Blake Wilder to bring down the corrupt Strike Team. But the stakes are high, and Paxton must decide whether he's willing to risk everything to do the right thing.

Claiming your freebie is easy! Visit
https://dl.bookfunnel.com/513mluk159
and sign up with your email!

Want more ways to stay connected? Follow me on Facebook and Instagram or sign up for text notifications by texting "blake" to 844-552-1368. Thanks for your support and happy reading!

ALSO BY
ELLE GRAY

Blake Wilder FBI Mystery Thrillers

Book One - The 7 She Saw
Book Two - A Perfect Wife
Book Three - Her Perfect Crime
Book Four - The Chosen Girls
Book Five - The Secret She Kept
Book Six - The Lost Girls
Book Seven - The Lost Sister
Book Eight - The Missing Woman
Book Nine - Night at the Asylum
Book Ten - A Time to Die
Book Eleven - The House on the Hill
Book Twelve - The Missing Girls
Book Thirteen - No More Lies
Book Fourteen - The Unlucky Girl
Book Fifteen - The Heist
Book Sixteen - The Hit List
Book Seventeen - The Missing Daughter
Book Eighteen - The Silent Threat

A Pax Arrington Mystery
Free Prequel - Deadly Pursuit
Book One - I See You
Book Two - Her Last Call
Book Three - Woman In The Water
Book Four - A Wife's Secret

Storyville FBI Mystery Thrillers
Book One - The Chosen Girl
Book Two - The Murder in the Mist

A Sweetwater Falls Mystery
Book One - New Girl in the Falls
Book Two - Missing in the Falls
Book Three - The Girls in the Falls

ALSO BY
ELLE GRAY | K.S. GRAY

Olivia Knight FBI Mystery Thrillers
Book One - New Girl in Town
Book Two - The Murders on Beacon Hill
Book Three - The Woman Behind the Door
Book Four - Love, Lies, and Suicide
Book Five - Murder on the Astoria
Book Six - The Locked Box
Book Seven - The Good Daughter
Book Eight - The Perfect Getaway
Book Nine - Behind Closed Doors

ALSO BY
ELLE GRAY | JAMES HOLT

The Florida Girl FBI Mystery Thrillers
Book One - The Florida Girl

Made in the USA
Columbia, SC
18 April 2025